Gerard Louis Breissan

Proverse Hong Kong
2020

A team of six US servicemen escape from a Viet Cong prison-camp and become an easy prey for Satan. They encounter helpful local residents, the Head of Military Intelligence, pirates dealing in contraband and members of a Roman Catholic mission. The story of the escape is punctuated by tales of demonic possession and an account of religious and medical training.

GÉRARD LOUIS BREISSAN is a native of Aix-en-Provence, South of France; and a Canadian citizen. As a boy, he studied classical literature and showed an early gift for writing, winning many school and regional prizes, as sponsored by the publishers, Hachette and the Lycée Mignet.

He wanted to see the world and chose a career in the Hospitality Industry as a means of achieving this ambition. He has worked in Bermuda, Canada, the UK, and the USA, and has spoken at conferences and given consultancy services in India, the Lebanon, and the Philippines. For four years he was a summer lecturer at the prestigious Cornell University Hotel School, teaching Food and Beverage management for the professional development programme. While in Canada, he was frequently invited by large food organizations – such as the Clover group, Halifax, Nova Scotia, The Canadian Federation of Chefs and Cooks and The Canadian National Hotels (Atlantic Provinces) group – to be a Keynote speaker at events such as trade shows and exhibitions, including The Apex Show (Atlantic Provinces), at well-known venues which have included, for example, The National Art Centre, Ottawa.

Since 2005, he has been working and living in China, where he is the Head of Hospitality and Tourism Management at Jilin University-Lambton College in Changchun, China, taking the chance also to travel around the country to learn about Chinese culture and traditions.

Breissan never forgot his passion for writing. While working in London, England, at famous hotels such as the Savoy, Connaught and Hilton Hyde Park Corner, he studied at West London College, subsequently specializing in English writing and poetry. After moving to Canada and rising to executive positions he continued to write and was in due course appointed the National Editor of Essence magazine, the official publication of the Canadian Federation of Chefs and Cooks. In 1995, he received the Sandy Sanderson Journalism award in tribute to his numerous published articles in Trade magazine. Food service operators have often used these materials for educational purposes and motivational tools. These have included – in Canada – Ocean Pointe Resort (Victoria British Columbia) and The Canadian Restaurant and Food Services Association, Toronto, Ontario; and – in India – the Welcomgroup Hotels, Palaces and Resorts.

Breissan's first novel, *The Day They Came*, was published by Proverse in 2012.

"Being a dad is the best job of all;
if everything falls apart and/or collapses I will still be, "Dad".

For Lauren
Gérard Louis Breissan
Lauren's father

# No Boundaries for Lucifer

Gérard Louis Breissan

*Dedicated to my daughter*

*Lauren Ashley*

No Boundaries for Lucifer
by Gérard Louis Breissan

1st edition published in paperback in Hong Kong
by Proverse Hong Kong
ISBN: 978-988-8491-75-9
Also available as an Ebook: ISBN: 978-988-8491-76-6

Distribution (Hong Kong and worldwide):
The Chinese University Press of Hong Kong,
The Chinese University of Hong Kong, Shatin, New Territories,
Hong Kong SAR.
Email: cup-bus@cuhk.edu.hk; Web: www.cup.cuhk.edu.hk

Distribution (United Kingdom): Stephen Inman, Worcester, UK.

Distribution and other enquiries to:
Proverse Hong Kong, P.O. Box 259, Tung Chung Post Office,
Lantau, NT, Hong Kong SAR, China.
Email: proverse@netvigator.com; Web: www.proversepublishing.com



Cover image: Zhang Yixi
Cover design by Artist Hong Kong.



British Library Cataloguing in Publication Data
A catalogue record is available
from the British Library

## Introduction

While working in Bermuda between 1985-1988 as a professor at Bermuda College, department of Hotel Technology, I met the general, a hotel guest at Stoning Beach Hotel, a resort establishment, owned and operated by the college, which gave practical training to our students.

He was a retired US Five Star general who had come to the island on vacation with his wife to get away from the hustle and bustle of the big city.

My students had been working in the hotel's dining-room and in the evenings I came to check on their progress. He noticed the airborne insignia that I wore on my blazer.

"Were you in the Airborne?" he asked.

"Yes Sir, I was with the French Army with a paratroop regiment, I was a sergeant."

"Did you see any action?"

"Yes Sir, I did in Africa."

He nodded and I went back to work with my students.

Later on that evening we talked at great length in the lounge about his five tours of Vietnam, and somehow I could sense that he had a strong desire to open up so I asked him point-blank if he wanted to meet me privately and discuss some of his military experiences; he accepted without hesitation; we then organized a meeting for the next day…

## Preface

War is always ugly and does not bring anything constructive but chaos and misery. Conflicts are games of death created and manipulated by politicians sitting in their ivory towers and who only care about securing votes. Enlisted men and women fight and die for their country; that is the way it usually goes.

In this novel you will meet the general who reminisces about the Vietnam War. While a "colonel," in the airborne, he escaped from the notorious prison-camp #1 with five other élite soldiers. In the jungle he encounters a more lethal enemy than the VC (Vietcong), the "Devil" himself. Can Sister Marie Catherine the Mother Superior of the French Mission save his soul? Subsequently you follow me through a perilous prisoner's extraction in the Republic of the Congo. These amazing exploits reinforced my religious beliefs to this day. Coincidentally we both faced the devil at different times. Did it leave indelible scars in our minds?

Truth or Fiction? You will be the judge…

## TABLE OF CONTENTS

# CHAPTER ONE

# THE GENERAL

On the following days I met with the general in my classroom. He was cordial and relaxed and we talked openly about his military life and experiences. He had risen from humble origins to graduate from West Point with top honours. He had always dreamt of becoming a military officer. He served in Korea followed by five tours in Vietnam. He was wounded twice and promoted to higher ranks for his heroic actions in the line of duty. On his third tour, he was captured by the Vietcong and tortured. After a daring escape, the general and two other US servicemen spent days in the jungle before being rescued by a First Cavalry Regiment helicopter which had spotted them swimming in a river.

His time in captivity had been the most traumatic experience of his military career; he had seen many good men die in prison camps at the hands of Vietcong. Beatings, starvation, torture, hangings, mock executions were daily routines during his internment. The bodies of dead soldiers were thrown into nearby streams to feed the rats. When screams and moans of the wounded could be heard at a distance, the guards would rush into their cells and beat them unconscious.

The VC had different ways to execute their captives, for instance, a group of men randomly selected was forced to sit down, stark-naked, back to back in the centre of the camp, hands and feet tied up, while poisonous snakes, scorpions, spiders, rats and leeches were dumped in their laps. VC officers, soldiers and all other prisoners stood around watching the ordeal. It was a sadistic way to execute detainees. Their tormentors enjoyed the show!

The days he had spent in the jungle, “on the run,” with other servicemen, had been very difficult. It had been “March or die”, with little food, little water, constantly hiding from VC patrols. He thanked his training in the Special Forces and the Airborne Rangers for his survival.

Men in these types of unit can handle any eventuality; they are motivated, can operate under extreme conditions, and are very resourceful and perfectly fit.

The VC moved their prisoners from camp to camp very often so that US Intelligence would not be able to pinpoint their whereabouts easily.

He still believed that many MIAs (Missing in Action) had been transferred to North Korea, Russia, or very remote North Vietnamese camps to die undiscovered.

The general talked to me in a grave tone; they were a soldier’s difficult and painful memories. Wars are cruel. Unfortunately, they will always occur.

The treatment inflicted on the prisoners in VC camps had been an aberration and a harrowing experience for the general. I knew that if we could talk about it a little more it would ease his pain and perhaps release some of the torments that had been bottled up for so long. Unless you have been a Special Forces man yourself and participated in missions behind enemy lines, unless you have seen your friends die in combat and been a prisoner, you will never understand the stress, the enormous responsibility and importance of the duties that it entails. I understood it all and the general wanted to tell me more, I sensed sorrow, anger and a smattering of bitterness in his tone of voice.

“Have you seen horror and tragedies, Sergeant?”

“Yes, I have, numerous times, General.”

“You know, the Vietnam War could never be won.”

"I think I know, and I know why."

"Why?"

"Because any country, fighting guerrilla warfare on someone else's soil has lost from day one. Remember the Algerian War with France, the French in Vietnam, the Russians in Afghanistan; and you can go back centuries, the Romans trying to conquer Gaul, the Chinese army battling with the Mongols and the Germans losing against the French resistance in WWII. They all failed because the conquerors were at a disadvantage on foreign ground. The VC knew the sites – the plains, the valleys, the mountains, the rivers – and had been at war for so long that you could not possibly win; you had to give up and pull out of Vietnam.

"General, you fought bravely and that's what counts! All those good men did not die in vain, only the credulous talked foolishly about something that they did not understand. Public opinion and American support for the troops at home were low; however each increased later and better late than never!

"You are an American war hero; very few men could have endured what you have, so please it is time to let go and tell me what eats you up!"

He did not answer, he looked at me with a quizzical expression, cleaned his throat and talked some more about his career. He had been commissioned in three different Airborne Regiments and had enjoyed the appointments.

"Nothing like Airborne, Sergeant, we were the tops!"

Most of his missions had been classified and he had been away from home, months and years at a time. His wife had raised his two daughters, always worrying if he was going to come home alive or in a coffin. Was he a little disappointed, not to have had a son who could have looked up to him and – who knows – become a military officer himself? He did not elaborate on the matter.

I was aiming at making the general talk about his demons or the incident which occurred during his tour of duty and had been haunting him ever since.

"Are you a religious man?"

"Affirmative."

He insisted that his strong will to survive combined with daily prayers kept his spirit going while in captivity. Like me he did not believe in luck but destiny. He did not die in Korea and survived Vietnam. God had wanted him to stay alive to carry on his duties. That's all. He trusted God and the Guardian Angels.

"What about you, are you a believer?"

"Yes, actually I became very religious while I was in the military."

"What happened?"

I told him about Africa and my gruelling commando training in Djibouti. The site was propitious for urban warfare and practising rescue missions with hostage-taking. Our rudimentary equipment was not as sophisticated at it is now. We trained day and night with almost no sleep at all. We were redoubtable warriors.

Suddenly we were called to the Congo on alert and we knew that it was going to be a very dangerous mission.

After we landed, all hell broke loose and carnage ensued. We had jumped behind enemy lines to neutralize the rebels' advance on the villages and capital. A battle was now raging between them, French Forces and the U.N. peace-keepers who had been attacked in the mêlée. For the next few days we had to take on one operation after the other in order to keep the upper hand in the offensive; the smell of death was everywhere. Our role was also to evacuate civilians and unfortunately many had been massacred. A few of our men had also lost their lives in the line of duty. Innocent men, women and children had been butchered for no reason at all.

We received new orders from headquarters to maintain pressure on the rebel troops and to hunt them down deep into the jungle if necessary in order to destroy their hidden caches. We did a fantastic job and did not take any prisoners.

"Did you kill them all?" asked the general.

"We did. When French Special Forces operated in unison, there were rarely any prisoners."

The general nodded, his chin resting in the palm of his hand. When we returned, I prayed with our chaplain in front of the plastic bags which had been aligned side by side at the airport. More than three hundred people including civilians and military had died in that coup d'état. Something had changed in me, I was angry and confused; it was a new emotion that had never come upon me before. I prayed the Lord to cleanse and protect the victims so that they could finally rest in peace.

"It is very honourable, Sergeant."

"I went back to work because a war was still looming and I needed all my concentration to stay alive and lead my team. While in the Congo, I did not have the time or inclination to concentrate on my inner feelings, but upon my return to France while on leave, I went to visit Monsignor Hervé at the Saint-Sauveur Cathedral in my hometown of Aix-en-Provence. I confessed and asked for forgiveness. We talked for a long time and his final advice was, "The power of prayer is limitless!" I sat in a pew and meditated for at least two hours. Amazingly I found the answer I was seeking.

Yes, General, believe it or not, Jesus and Mary took turns and answered my questions right in the chapel. As I looked at their statues, in the background their voices clear and serene comforted me and predicted some future events which would occur later on in my lifetime. It was odd but calm and very precise.

When I told Jesus and Mary that I was somehow very tormented by recent events in my life, Mary replied, "Time will heal you, please rest and enjoy your leave. As soon as you find your right path in life, all your pains will disappear at once. Now please, pray for my son and me."

I knelt and prayed. Their voices disappeared.

"Yes, General, I felt at peace with myself and I left the Cathedral smiling and full of vigour."

"You are lucky. Always remember this encounter!"

"Not lucky, General, destiny, just destiny!"

"I stand corrected, you are right, it was not luck, and it was a divine intervention, pure and simple!"

"I was in a quandary, but the voices put me on the right path. When I left the basilica, I knew that I was going to make irrevocable commitments for my future,"

He nodded, with a pensive expression on his face. "Well, they spoke to you sometime in your life; they never did to me, ever."

"General, if you are there, sitting with me today, safe and sound, healthy with a good head on your shoulders after all that you went through during your military career, it means that the Lord, Mary and their angels were protecting you and watching your every move, don't you agree?"

"Affirmative, I should not grumble, I guess that I am getting old and I have become a complainer."

"They might never have spoken to you personally, but their blessings were always with you and they heard your prayers, yes or no?"

"Yes, you are right; I certainly believe that the angels were with me in the Jungle of Vietnam."

“Now, General, I am still waiting for you to tell me your story! What exactly happened in the camp during your imprisonment with the VC?”

“Sometimes there are stories which are better forgotten than told, agree?”

“Perhaps, but in this case I feel that you are dying to tell me about some tragic events which occurred more than twenty years ago, otherwise you would not have accepted to meet me here today. Your wife does not know anything about it, am I correct, General?”

“Yes, I have never told her about my missions in Vietnam. My daughters even thought that I had died there.”

“So what exactly took place twenty years ago that changed you into an angry man? You know that I am right, don’t you?”

## CHAPTER TWO

## A DARING ESCAPE

His name was Captain Willy Henderson, US Air Force pilot, 1st Air Commando Squadron based in Bien Hoa. He flew an A-1 Skyraider plane. He was a brilliant pilot and father of two boys back in Florida. He was shot down near Pleiku in Vietnam but had jumped before his plane crashed down. The NVA had a hard time catching him and when they did, they really beat him up very hard. He never told them anything, he was a tough cookie and we all liked him a lot. The first year he was moved to a different VC Camp prior to being transferred with us. He had tried to escape on his own, got caught and had been whipped and marked with hot iron on his back. Nothing worked; he never talked and even insulted the VC at every opportunity. He had become a "problem prisoner," for them. He was highly respected by everyone in our camp. Again, he wanted to flee this nightmare.

We had no way to discuss a plan of escape; we were locked up into individual cells. However, we talked through walls, sang songs with messages hidden within the lyrics and we all volunteered for camp duties. We were a team assigned to a paddy field. There we could whisper and mumble information to each other."

*"So, General, at first you were six men altogether to break free from the camp weren't you?"*

"Affirmative, Sergeant. Captain Henderson died in that attempt; it was a tragic and terrible ordeal."

Eventually, we decided to escape because we knew that we were not going to survive our confinement. The six of us were "high profile" prisoners, the VC were either going to execute us one by one or transfer us far away, perhaps Russia, North Korea or somewhere else in Vietnam. To get the hell out of there was a suicide mission, it was intricate and risky and if we ever failed we would be tortured to death. However we still went along with the plan. Other servicemen refused to follow us because they were too scared of reprisals by the VC.

We had to cover three important steps to reach freedom. Leave the camp at night, neutralize three to four guards with our bare hands, steal their weapons and ammunition, run through a rice paddy, avoid mines which had been planted all over the place, go into a very dense forest and hide for a while. Guards, NVA patrols, dogs, VC mercenaries were all going to be looking for us, their leaders fuming over the escape.

The next step was to reach the River Cam (Sōng Cām), fifteen kilometres north of the camp. We would do it, either by walking through the jungle, or by swimming the Hăn, a small stream in Hai Duong Province, which would lead us to the River Cam. Our choppers were always patrolling the large bodies of water and we thought that our chances to be found were high. The River Cam was seven kilometres long, it was worth trying."

*"It was a good plan, General."*

"We thought so, Sergeant and we went for it!"

*"How did you prepare for it?"*

We had to stay in good shape, we ate all the crap that they fed us, did a lot of exercises and push-ups in our cells. I meditated a lot because I wanted my mind to be free and positive in case of a foul-up. We could not get hurt because a wounded man would automatically slow down the team. We were somehow worried about our physical fitness because a tremendous amount of swimming had to be performed under very hostile conditions.

*"Who were the other members of the team?"*

They were all very experienced men, who had graduated from jungle and survival training. One first lieutenant from the Big Red One (1st Infantry Regiment), a sergeant-major from the 173rd Airborne Brigade and former Long Range Patrol unit point man, a US navy pilot with two tours of Vietnam, a master-sergeant from the green berets (Special Forces) with two tours of Vietnam, myself and Captain Henderson. We were a redoubtable group of warriors, Sergeant.

We had discussed the uncertainty of the escape, the long hours spent in hiding, and we all agreed that if one of us was going to be badly hurt or wounded he would remain behind or the team was doomed. Option number one was to commit suicide because one cannot endure torture if already wounded. Option number two, the man who was hurt could choose the person who was going to shoot him and deliver him of his affliction. It was a very serious matter and we had to reach a consensus.

*"Did you, General?"*

"Yes, Sergeant, we all did, we were all professionals and some of us had already faced this situation."

*"Who was selected the leader of the team?"*

"Me. I was on my third tour and the highest ranking officer. Even though I disputed the decision, they put me in charge."

We now needed to observe the guards' daily routine and above all where they were located during the nights. The main gate, the towers, the bridge nearby, the camp's perimeter, the rice paddies where we worked were all manned by NVA guards. Mines had been placed around the camp and the rice field. Snipers were in the trees overlooking the entire area. A day-time escape would have been suicidal. We had to flee at night, maybe we could make it …we had seen many servicemen being blown up by the mines spread across the field outside the camp. Very often the snipers would shoot at us at random for target practice. The bodies were never recovered because they were thrown to the alligators.

However, we had decided to break away from this hell-hole and now it was crucial for us to do a little planning, we did not have much time, the sooner the better…

*"So, General who made the decision to go?"*

"We all did, Sergeant."

It was a Saturday night. We did not have any way to know the time or date but on Saturday night the guards always brought young prostitutes from the villages close-by and partied all night long. They were drunk, noisy and more careless about security. The VC leaders, NVA officers and politicians from the province usually joined in these activities. Our camp was considered "large", by VC standards and above all it was labelled as a "place of no return". The commandant had a very good reputation with the top brass and the local communist party. He knew how to entertain them. He was ruthless, demonic and totally corrupt. You see, my only regret to this day is that I was not able to kill him myself.

*"General, he probably has met his maker a long time ago and got what he deserved. Please continue…"*

It was a Saturday night; we could hear the trucks and jeeps bringing the hookers, the laughter and loud voices coming from the barracks and officers' quarters. A couple of choppers had flown the brass and communist party officials to the camp for the wild bash.

Western music was blaring, men were shouting and whistling. No doubt, the girls were stripping and dancing. We waited for two or three hours until they were all drunk and the security was lax.

However, the guards on the towers and the ones patrolling the grounds always remained vigilant.

First we had to get out of our cells; Henderson faked an emergency illness and started screaming. We were banging on the doors calling the guard on duty. He came rushing in and opened Henderson's.

*"What happened, General?"*

He never knew what hit him; the captain snapped the man's head and broke his neck. Now we had the master set of keys, including the key to the main gates and we quickly went around the block asking the other prisoners, one last time, if they wanted to come with us. They all refused, so we locked our cell doors not to attract attention and stepped outside. We needed more guns and supplies for survival…

If we could overpower three more guards we thought that it would give us an edge to carry out the operation successfully. Right at the moment six men following each other in an escape did not make any sense because we were sticking out like a sore thumb, so we split up and decided to meet later at the Hăn, the small stream converging on the large Cam River. It was probably going to be easier for us than marching through the jungle for days hiding from the VC and the NVA. It was a change of plan but it was reasonable and practical. The dogs were not going to pick up our scent in the water and we had more chances to get picked up by US helicopters flying over bodies of water. We also knew that PBR Riverine from the US navy was patrolling all the rivers, streams and deltas. We had to avoid the Vietnamese patrol boats at all costs; they were carrying supplies and arms for the VC – even drugs for the NVA and North Korean army – and were cold-blooded killers who would not hesitate to murder us on the spot.

It was now time to scram and we were two teams of three. I was with Henderson and first lieutenant Jason Brown from the Big Red One infantry regiment.

The guards on the towers were scanning the grounds back and forth with powerful floodlights. We hid under the elevated officers' quarters and Jason volunteered to kill the sentry manning them.

He was on the top of the stairs smoking a cigarette; Jason picked up a stone and threw it at a parked truck. The noise raised the guard's attention immediately; he walked over with his gun at the ready.

Nothing, there was nothing there, so he spat on the ground, shouldered his rifle and turned back muttering to himself.

Jason sprang up and grabbed him by the throat, pulled him down and snapped his spine. We all heard the cracking noise. We now had an automatic rifle, a handgun, a large knife and a leather belt, it was better than before.

We hid the dead body under the house and moved towards the main gate, avoiding the lights, towers and capture. The front gate was padlocked and the visitors were still partying at full blast, but we had the set of keys.

From nowhere a guard suddenly started crossing the yard cutting our exit route, I took the knife and threw it at him piercing his throat, he did not make a sound, and again we snatched his rifle, gun, knife and leather belt. We had no time to hide the body, so we sat the VC down against one of the cell blocks, away from the tower lights. We made a dash for the main gate, opened it slowly and we were free at last!

*"It is an amazing story, General. What an adventure!"*

"Wait, Sergeant, the escape will definitely take a turn for the worse."

There are no words to describe our feelings at this moment of liberty, but we had no time to rejoice because we were still on the camp ground until we had reached the river Hăn. The thrill of getting away was going to be short-lived. Mines! Mines! Mines everywhere had killed so many of our servicemen, prisoners and civilians that we had lost count after a while. Our first objective was the rice paddies but because so many bombs had been planted at random around the perimeter to prevent any escape, we decided to traverse rather than to circumvent the area. We crossed ourselves and started to walk in a straight line ten metres apart from each other. We lived through it; we did not get blown up this time! We ran into very dense woodland to hide and plan our next move.

We did not know the site, it was a very thick and dark forest but certainly very propitious for hiding. We took inventory of the equipment and agreed that we needed to save ammunition. On the first occasion possible, we had to change our prison garb, because we wore the black tops and pants of the VC. We were westerners and in any village they would shoot us on sight!

We found refuge in a small cave and we covered the entrance with branches and the trunk of a tree.

We had not heard any alarms, no sirens, but we knew that very soon, the VC and NVA soldiers were going to hunt for us and that it was going to be an interminable chase until we were spotted by our troops.

We decided to stop for a short while and then meet the other half of the team at the Hăn. Our rendez-vous was at a small boat-house painted blue with white shutters. Henderson knew the owner and had hidden there on previous escapes. The shack was safe, remote and seldom checked by the VC, he had also mentioned that we could rest inside for a few hours before we got into the water. The last time he had used it he had found some food and some fat worms and beetles full of protein. Well, we certainly needed some energy to undertake a fourteen kilometres swim.

We had a short nap in the cave and then we moved on in the direction of the Hăn. We did not meet any difficulties or interference as the VC and NVA soldiers were probably still sleeping or nursing their hang-overs. The forest was thick and its mountainous terrain almost impracticable. We progressed through it slowly but steadily. We wanted to get ahead of our enemies who would soon pursue us implacably.

Without compass or flashlight we were taking the risk of getting lost but hoped to cross this almost impenetrable woodland. Henderson was our point man and we were advancing on the target, we had to be in the water by sunrise."

*"Did you meet any patrol, General?"*

"Not right away, Sergeant, in fact we were surprised but we had achieved a very quick and clean escape, the timing, the weather and our experience in the field had played an important role in our success."

We had no fear of mines as they were usually placed on busy trails, roads, landing zones and US patrol routes.

Jason Brown and Henderson were extremely professional soldiers who could handle any eventuality and maintain their sense of humour at the same time. We needed a good laugh now and then.

The second stop was near a waterfall leading to rice paddies and a small hamlet. It was still dark, there were no sentinels guarding the perimeter so we took a quick dip in the small pond at the bottom of the cliff. We cooled ourselves off and continued our journey.

We followed the zigzagging water trail and stopped to observe the hamlet for a while. There were many similar types of villages collaborating with the VC and we did not want to face a bad surprise when passing through it. We did not know that place's name but somehow we all had a hunch that there was something unsettling about the entire area. Not to attract attention we crawled and ran up to the village's limits. We had to remain undetected because we were only the three of us and we would not have survived a violent confrontation. We hid and scrutinized the entire area…

## CHAPTER THREE

## THE VILLAGE LEADER

*"So, General, things were fine. You were on your way to the Hān stream for your rendez-vous."*

"We were very professional and correct to feel uneasy about this hamlet. Misery ensued and it did not stop there!"

*"Sometimes blunders occur during an operation and they are inexplicable. We cannot control fate and we must live with it."*

"Affirmative, Sergeant, I faced my share of errors, poor judgment and blunders as you say, but listen to the rest of the story..."

We had not seen any sign of life or any movement at the hamlet, but we could not waste time any longer and needed to set off long before sunrise so we made a dash for it.

We cautiously moved from hut to hut without making any sound; using just sign language and crouching close to the walls. We passed some shacks and a stone building which looked like a Buddhist temple. We reached a little square with a well in the centre. Water! We needed water badly.

Going to the well was going to place one of us in full view of a sniper if there was any, but we were very thirsty and we wanted to fill up the gourd we had stolen from one of guards at the camp. You know, Sergeant, that a man can survive without food for a long time but he cannot survive without water. It was a chance to take and we took it. A bucket was resting on the edge of the well with a long rope attached to it. I volunteered to get the water. I crawled quickly to the water-hole, no one had shot at me – great! – and so I filled up the gourd and drank slowly from the bucket. I poured the rest of the water on my head. It felt very good. I signalled Henderson and Jason to come over and they crawled quickly to join me. We made sure not to drink too much water but we needed to avoid dehydration. We had a very long journey ahead of us followed by a gruelling swim after that. We drank some more water and took our position against the temple again. The heat was unbearable and all you could hear around you was "BzzzzBzzzzBzzz!" mosquitoes, flies, bugs and other insects right in your face, but we were used to it, we did not pay this aggravation any attention."

*"General, could the water have been poisoned by the VC?"*

"Excellent observation, but this village was still inhabited, so the water was potable."

Many platoons, particularly from the Long Range patrol units had suffered casualties from contaminated water. When a village had been burned down either by our troops or the enemies we never drank from its well because the VC poisoned the water, even the lakes or reservoirs nearby.

In this case we knew that people lived there; we were observed, gauged and we were leery about it all. The three of us had this prescience that it was a VC village used as a cache or as a training camp. We decided to take a better look around the square and perhaps pick up something useful for our long expedition in the water. We saw some bicycles in good condition; we looked into an open barn and found corn, flour and hay, nothing else. From the main entrance of the temple we had heard voices chanting their mysterious incantation but it was not prudent to ask the monks anything, Jason had never trusted them. We were on farmland and all the domestic animals roamed loose in the backyards. They seemed well fed, these were signs that this hamlet was very much alive but we had to move on. Unfortunately we were once more empty-handed.

We followed the path leading towards the river Hān, from there Henderson was going to guide us to the boat-house where the fisherman could provide us with food, water and necessary supplies. We also needed rest before getting into the water. All was well planned to that point, Sergeant!

*"Your timing was right, no doubt!"*

The general did not reply, he only shook his head with a sombre expression on his face and continued his story.

As we were advancing deep into the forest we made sure not to lose track of the narrow river which had originated from the waterfall because eventually it was going to merge into the Hān. We had noticed some huts and shacks on both sides of the trail but we did not meet any VC or NVA soldiers. The sun was about to rise, the sky was changing colour, and it was hot and muggy. We arrived on a plateau facing a tall mountain, the sinuous river was streaming down a valley and we saw on the right side another hamlet. We made a decision to check it out fast in case we could get our hands on some food or supplies and then, we had to return to the river very quickly because in the daylight our black pyjamas were going to get us killed!

In Vietnam all villages looked alike, animals were strolling around, a donkey was attached to a wooden pole eating some corn, bicycles and scooters were parked against huts and trees.

We saw a civilian coming towards us pulling a cart with bags of rice on it. He looked at us obviously puzzled, but after a few years in Vietnam we could communicate with the population when it was necessary. He told us that he was the village leader and a farmer, he and the inhabitants were not VC, but the NVA and VC came here regularly to inspect and interrogate everyone.

The old man added that because we had been on the run, chances were that patrols had already been sent to search for us! We had to leave quickly. He took us to his house which was rather large with a barn adjacent to it. We ate; he gave us some supplies, dried food, a satchel, bandannas, bandages and another gourd full of potable water. His wife had woken up and presented us with a plate of corn biscuits and French bread.

She also said that we smelled very bad but we explained that it was ok in the bush to smell like the enemy. We had to remain inconspicuous and become like the VC in the forest. The village chief knew of our predicament, he confirmed that the previous village was definitely VC and that we had been lucky. He offered to lead us to the stream because he knew of a short-cut. Soon we were again fugitives in the jungle, the old man marched very fast for his age and knew his way around. We heard bells in the mountains across the valley and he mentioned that it was a French convent which had been located in the area for more than fifty years, a lot of nuns lived there. It was 5am and they were celebrating the first mass of the day. The old man was our guide. It was a change for us, we climbed a hill, it was steep but we soon found the small river, we thanked him profusely. Suddenly his face went blank, he grimaced and told us to hide quickly, and we obeyed.

Four VC mercenaries who were talking and laughing loudly, stopped to relieve themselves and walked on. The old man reappeared and told us that it was time for the VC to patrol; we needed to be careful and hide until night to be on the safe side. Then he asked us to follow him. We could not understand but we did. We stayed close to the water trail while moving at a fast pace, the village leader was once again our point man; he often stopped to listen or made us crouch now and then. The stream seemed to get larger and there were now some visible currents, we knew that we could use the water to lose the dogs if necessary. Again he came to a halt and crouched down, he pointed through the trees and there was a small shack guarded by two VC. Inside were guns, knives, rifles and explosives. We wanted ammunition for our guns and silencers if possible. Both men were smoking and talking to each other. We crawled very close to the edge of a bushy tree and moved behind the cache, we had to kill them, no other choice. Suddenly we heard the chief talk to the guards, he was being the "distraction", and we had our knives at the ready. He asked for a cigarette, the VC went into his pocket to pull out the package and at that precise moment Henderson and Jason jumped on them from behind simultaneously.

With our left hands we covered their mouths and in one motion pulled back their heads very hard and plunged our knives under their chins, the blades straight up to the guards and finally gave the knives a quick rotation.

They were dead before they hit the ground.

The old man searched them and with a set of keys opened the shack. The loot contained explosives, rockets, bazookas, ammunition, grenades, VC uniforms, rifles and automatic weapons mostly made in the USA but some were Russian, Korean and French dating back to WW2 and the Korean War. Many of the rifles had bayonets still attached to them. We searched, moved boxes around and discovered more arms, a few US Ka-bar knives and a leather box with silencers. We collected what we needed for the rest of the team.

Jason got his hands on a shotgun pump action and cartridges, they were noisy but efficient.

Meanwhile the leader had taken a shovel and was burying the dead bodies deep in the woods.

We noticed a trapdoor inside the shack; it had been hidden

under moss and had cases on top of it.

It was a VC tunnel, probably leading to other caches and even more tunnels.

*"Did you go inside General?"*

"No, Sergeant, we could not get another chance to escape. If we had searched this tunnel, we probably would have been caught and killed. Besides we were the wrong size for this type of operation. The US army used infantry "tunnel rats", small men trained to search and fight under these difficult conditions.

Tunnels were essential to the VC; they provided them with caches, places to eat and sleep and hospitals for the wounded. They could be hundreds of kilometres long, reaching major cities, ports and US camps. They were like spider-webs branching into more tunnels and never ending."

*"What happened to the village leader, General?"*

"We wanted his final opinion regarding our escape and chances of survival if any. So far it was really good, we had had good fortune and the old man had really been our guardian angel."

To follow the Hān into the Cām River was an excellent idea, he agreed, but told us about the VC and NVA patrol boats. Also he warned us about the fauna in the rivers; it was a very hostile environment with alligators, large crocodiles and many, many venomous snakes.

He also explained that we were going to face strong currents in the rivers and a few waterfalls. They were dangerous, it was better to avoid them.

We had to be found by our side before the Cām reached the Mekong River, because it would then be impossible to swim in such a large body of water.

He advised us to build a small raft to keep our guns and

supplies dry, we were to hold them on it, otherwise our ammunition would become useless. It was better to wear our black pyjamas, they were less conspicuous in the forest and easy to be spotted by US helicopters, he was right. He warned us again about the risks, there were many and that it was like a suicide mission, we could not go back, the VC, the NVA, mercenaries, were all looking for six escapees who had to be killed on sight or worse, "tortured to death". He had heard of the boat-house and its owner, the fisherman, he told us that it was fine, the man was honest, the VC and NVA rarely checked on him and if they had not killed him yet, it was still safe to use his services. He liked Americans and hated the VC, so we should carry on with the plan; the boat-house was our objective.

We could reach it within seventy-two hours or march through the mountains for five days. We had to stick to plan number one because we were a prime target for the enemy. We had to succeed or we were going to be dead meat! The old man fully agreed with our decision. He gave us other important advice. Should we face serious injuries, a few kilometres down the river there was another French missionary convent dating back to WW1 where all the nuns were French but spoke English. If any of us needed help it was the best place to hide.

On the way to this place, we were going to see one large and one small village. In Vietnam the VC planted spies in them and we were trained to never trust anyone we encountered. The old man agreed with our statement because he knew the collaborators in his own hamlet. If anyone would refuse to help the VC, they were executed at once. We definitely understood what to do and thanked the leader profusely.

*"Why did he help you? Did you ask him?"*

"Yes, we did."

You see, he hated the VC. He had witnessed many executions in the past and even though no one had been killed in his village, a few of the inhabitants had been taken away and had never returned. He had inquired of the VC leader regarding their fate but was told that he should not ask such questions and that it was not his business. They had just disappeared. The old man believed that they had perhaps been indoctrinated and joined the VC; it was a famous form of propaganda used in rural areas where the people were uneducated.

Until then, the VC had left him alone and they only checked on his village a few times a month but he knew that it could change and he was ready to die for his people. They stole food, clothing, and cattle or even slept overnight but he accepted it and said nothing. We asked the old man if he had any children.

He face changed expression, he bowed his head and whispered, "Yes, a daughter."

We looked at each other and felt that maybe we had mentioned a sore subject.

*"Was she alive?"*

"Yes, she was twenty-six years old, beautiful and had a degree in Political Sciences from La Sorbonne in Paris."

*"La Sorbonne, General! It is amazing! How did her father manage to pay for it?"*

He was a successful farmer with powerful connections with the Vietnam communist party. His daughter had gone to high school in a large city and spoke French very well before going to Paris. The whole village was proud of her; she was venerated by the entire community particularly for graduating in Political Sciences, which in these days added a special cachet to her reputation. Her father told us that she also spoke English fluently, she was a brilliant young lady.

*"Did you ever meet her?"*

"No we couldn't do that."

*"Where was she working?"*

The general cleaned his throat and looked at the walls of the classroom, avoiding my eyes.

"She moved around the country a lot, but was mainly working in Cambodia and South Vietnam."

*"Why there, particularly?"*

"Because she was a top leader for the VC."

*"What? A top VC leader! How was it possible?"*

While in high school, she already had some strong opinions and her own view about the country's direction and politics. In addition, her close friends denigrated the USA at every opportunity, her father tried to reason with her and open her mind on the subject but in vain.

She wanted to learn French and English fluently and to continue to study politics to become a party leader and serve her country. She was one of the best students in Vietnam and received a very substantial scholarship to go to La Sorbonne. She spent five years in France where she also studied English with an American tutor. However she mingled with radical elements that probably spoiled her mind. She was extremely beautiful and had a commanding presence in social events and gatherings."

*"What happened to her?"*

She played her cards right. Many top Vietnam high-ranking officers, politicians and leaders came to Paris to attend strategic and crucial meetings about the war, and she managed to get hired as a translator and later as a private secretary by one of the most powerful generals and military theorists of the Vietnam People's

Army. He was a top advisor to the Vietcong. She had found her niche. After graduation, she enlisted in the NVA as his aide-de-camp, demonstrating inner qualities that were far above and beyond what her superior had ever anticipated."

*"What were they, General?"*

"She was ambitious, hungry for power, and ruthless."

*"They are not really qualities, are they?"*

"Perhaps not, but for the Vietcong at that time they were essential attributes to help them fight the war successfully. She was promoted and transferred to their headquarters in Cambodia. She eventually received the grade of colonel in the Special Bureau of the General Department of Military Intelligence."

*"What was that, precisely?"*

"The equivalent of the German Gestapo if you ask me. She took charge of the task with pride and vigour, monitoring the interrogations of the high-profile prisoners, increasing the propaganda country-wide, adding more men to spy on villages, recruiting large numbers of VC mercenaries and enhancing the training of NVA officers with enforcement on 'cultural indoctrination'. She made a name for herself in a very short time."

*"What did her parents think of it?"*

The old man was crying while he was telling us the story. But all in all they did not have a daughter any more. The villages did not blame them and apparently did not bear a grudge against them. However, we understood that her family was devastated when they found out that she had turned VC and was an officer of the Special Bureau of Military Intelligence."

*"How did they find out?"*

"She came to the village with a motorcade."

*"A motorcade?"*

She came to the village escorted by full military back-up consisting of motorcycles, jeeps, trucks, NVA soldiers, VC mercenaries; and she was driven in a black government car accompanied by two army officers.

Her family had lost contact with her a long time before this. After she had graduated in Paris and worked for the advisor to the Vietcong, she stopped writing to her parents and it had caused them a lot of grief. No one knew of her whereabouts, her father had contacted his friends in the communist party, but the replies always remained strangely evasive. He did not know if foreign radicals had got a strong hold over her, or if something really drastic had happened and the Party did not want to give him the bad news. Their lives had been filled with anguish ever since; they felt that they had failed as parents and had lost face in front of their family and the villagers.

But somehow they always had a glimmer of hope that one day she was going to reappear and be their little girl again. Her Vietnamese name was "Anh," for intellectual brightness and in Paris she was called "Constance," for fortitude. The column of military vehicles roared into the village and here she was!"

## CHAPTER FOUR

## THE WRATH OF ANH

*"Her parents and the villagers must have been very surprised to see her again, General."*

"Surprised is not the word, Sergeant, flabbergasted is more like it!"

The motorcade stopped. VC mercenaries fired their weapons in the air to attract the attention of the villagers, making sure that everyone was going to attend the meeting. The old man and his wife were placed in front of everyone in a position of prominence because he was the village leader.

The driver of the black car got out and opened the rear door, Anh got out. She walked with assurance and authority to the centre of the square, she wore her hair in a pony-tail, a brown military jacket bearing her rank, a Second General Department shoulder patch, and decorations on her chest, black polished boots, black leather gloves, and she carried a horsewhip in her hand.

There were gasps of consternation, mumbles, whispers and even angry shouts coming from the crowd when they recognized her. Her parents did not say a word; they bowed their heads in sign of humiliation."

*"What happened next?"*

"The old man told us about her speech and the tragic events which ensued."

*"Did her parents ever speak to her again?"*

"No, never after that."

*"Tell me the rest, please."*

"I was born as Anh in this village, but now they call me the colonel," she announced.

Meanwhile VC mercenaries were pillaging the village and others were encircling the group who were listening to her.

She had NVA officers on either side and soldiers surrounding the perimeter, she was in full control.

"This village now belongs to me; so does your future. I decide who lives and I decide who dies. It would be a futile exercise to try to escape because punishment will be extreme. I know you all and my father is the village leader, however if you show any disrespect or disloyalty towards your country, he will be punished very harshly, do you understand?"

No one replied.

She continued:

"You will cooperate with the Republic of North Vietnam, my office represents the security of all citizens. The Americans are our enemies and I will not tolerate sympathizers, if you show such tendencies the entire community will be removed, sent to jail and the village will be razed to the ground, is it clear?"

Again, there were no answers.

"Meanwhile my men will come here to check the area and your homes and make sure that there are no traitors among you. I have ordered them to respect everyone; therefore women will not be raped, no executions will take place unless I allow it, but you will give them all the supplies that they need. This is a gesture of my heart because I was born here; I hope that you appreciate it."

*"This is quite amazing; no one said anything to her?"*

"Wait a moment, wait…"

The parents were both crying and the mother was sobbing, many villagers were looking at each other dazed and confused.

"Stop crying, you look ridiculous and you are losing face,

behave like village leaders!" she told her parents.

Then out of the blue an old woman threw a tomato at her and yelled, "You whore, how many generals did you have to sleep with to get promoted? We know your kind, you slut! How dare you talk to your parents that way? We taught you respect and morals in this small village but I guess that you forgot it all in the high society of Paris, that figures!"

A VC pointed his rifle at her but Anh made a gesture and he lowered it.

"Do you have anything else to add?" she asked.

"Yes, the Party paid for your education and we all expected you to make us proud of your success, instead you return as a VC leader and threaten our lives. We are not very educated but we are good people, we do not understand politics very well but the Americans never hurt us when they came to our village, your men on the contrary take our food, water, clothing and we do not like it. How can you insinuate that our fate is in your hands? I fed you and took care of you when your mother was ill, now look at you; you are an absolute disgrace to us all!"

*"Wow! She was brave to curse a Vietcong officer this way!"*

"She surely was but she also knew that she had signed her death warrant!"

Ahn stood motionless and looked at her with hatred in her eyes. "You talk like a traitor; you are an American-lover and a spy, aren't you?"

The old woman spat at her, the VC once again raised his rifle but was waved away; Anh approached and slapped her very hard across the face then hit her with the whip again, again and again until the villager fell down to the ground, bleeding profusely; then she kicked her in the face, the chest and then struck her with her whip in a frenzy of rage at least a dozen times.

When she finally stopped, the old lady was lying in a heap on the ground, Anh had beaten her to a pulp.

She addressed the crowd again, “She is a fool and a traitor, she will pay dearly for her arrogance, I do not understand this village, I came here with good intentions, I even told my men to treat you with respect, it was all in good faith and I have not insulted you in any way so why has this crazy woman acted so impudently? We are at war with the most powerful country in the world but be assured that North Vietnam will come out the winner at the end. My office makes sure that all villages contribute to the war’s efforts. Have I been naive to believe that my hometown would cooperate with unbounded enthusiasm?”

Once again there was absolutely no reaction from the assembly.

“Very well, I want to see this woman’s entire family, quickly!”

No one moved.

She gestured to an officer who gave her his handgun; she placed the barrel on the old lady’s temple and said loudly, “At the count of three she dies! One…Two…”

A group of people moved forward.

“I said, her entire family in front of me, everyone!”

More villagers approached the centre of the square.

She asked her father:

“I am counting twelve altogether, is that all?”

He nodded feebly.

She asked the family to move forward and began to scrutinize the group, which consisted of men, women carrying little babies in their arms, elderly people, and a few teenagers. She walked around them, stopped and looked into their eyes, checked them all from head to toe, poked them with her whip and exclaimed:

"They are filth; they are all enemies of North Vietnam and need to be re-educated!"

She ordered the soldiers to take them all to headquarters, and the body of the old lady was thrown into the back of a jeep.

She added, "Now you realize that the colonel holds your fate in the palm of her hand, do you understand me?"

There was complete silence; turning to her father she said:

"This abject attitude demonstrates a complete lack of leadership in this village, the man in charge cannot control his own people, it is unacceptable, a radical change is required or I will personally come back to make a replacement."

Anh turned around facing the villagers, clicked her heels, saluted them and in a clear voice announced:

"I belong to the General Department of Military Intelligence and cannot have dissidents in my villages. I will return but the rebellious attitude that I witnessed today will never be tolerated again. Is that understood?"

She got into her car and the convoy drove away amidst clouds of dust.

Everyone stood immobile in the centre of the square shaken and silent for a very long time, then the group dissipated with the pictures of this ghastly event still fresh in their minds.

Once alone the village leader dropped to his knees, shoulders bowed, he covered his face with his hands and cried…cried…and cried…

*"Gosh, General; that was a hell of a story and the old man remembered so many details! Amazing!"*

"Yes, Sergeant, this event had been like a thorn in his heart, he had carried it more in sorrow than in anger."

*"Do you believe that talking about it to the three of you made him feel better?"*

"It may have. Tears were running down his face as he narrated the shocking details regarding Anh's actions in the village. It was probably some kind of relief for him, yes perhaps..."

*"Tell me more, General."*

Well it was daylight, terribly hot and muggy. The four of us were in the shack and the old man advised us to find refuge and rest until dusk, and then move down along the stream while making sure to avoid enemy patrols. We all hugged him and he left furtively through the bushes. We quickly took a final inventory of water, food, ammunition and weapons. We locked the shack's door behind us and walked back to the river.

We needed to be ready in case the VC decided to engage in a river search, so we cut bamboo sticks about one metre in length and cleaned their insides; this way we could use them to breath if we had to hide under the water. It was important to be ready for any eventuality.

## CHAPTER FIVE

## A CALL FROM ABOVE

We tried our makeshift snorkels and they worked well. We decided to wait until we had reached the boat-house to build the raft to carry our equipment because the stream was still shallow and we did not need to get into the water unless we needed to hide.

The vegetation along the river was often impenetrable, the flora was thick, rocks were covered with moss and the reeds, water lilies and marshes were spread out inland.

Dense black clouds of flying insects were all around us, mosquitoes, bumble-bees, dragon-flies – you name it. As we crossed swamps we watched for alligators and deadly snakes. In Vietnam there are more than 130 species of snake, 35% of which are poisonous. We thought that if we ever got bitten, it would be a stupid way to die for a Special Forces soldier!

We were still searching for a place to hide until dark but we could not find a safe location; the first village appeared on the horizon and we remembered the old man's advice to beware of VC spies, so we decided to stay safe by only circling its borders.

As we moved forward we heard the roaring of a waterfall. We cautiously approached it and it was not a very high cliff – twenty metres at the most – two small ponds, one at the top and one at the bottom. We turned around to make a detour when..." The general stopped talking, looked at the window, wiped his glasses and stayed silent.

*"What is it?"*

"I am just gathering my thoughts, that's all!"

*"Is it Henderson? It happened at the waterfall, didn't it?"*

"Yes, Sergeant that is where it all took place."

*"Please continue, you need to talk about it, give me all the details."*

We heard loud voices and laughter coming from the bushes. We crouched down and watched...

There were five VC mercenaries going to the waterfall, they were armed with old rifles, French and Russian models, and they had bayonets fixed onto their ends. They sat on rocks by the lower pond and were passing around raw fish. They were taking a rest. One VC started to sharpen his knife on a stone and another relieved himself in the stream. We looked at each other, nodded, not a word was said.

We placed silencers on our handguns because there were undoubtedly more VC in the area and shotguns would have been too loud and signalled our position.

The sound of the waterfall also would muffle some of the noise – if any – and it was to our advantage. We moved quickly, using only sign language, Jason on the left, Henderson at the centre and I took the right. We were close and took them by surprise.

We could not miss them, impossible...

Shots to the head and the heart and three died instantly, one dived into the pond and I followed him, I used my knife to stab him in the lungs, he sank like a stone and the water turned deep red. As I resurfaced, I saw number five running down the stream carrying his rifle, I yelled at Henderson to catch him before he could warn the others. "I've got him," he shouted and made a dash for the mercenary, who was getting closer and closer, and I thought to myself, "Why doesn't he just shoot him?" All of a sudden Henderson's feet slid, he accidently lost his balance and fell on his back, the VC turned around and plunged his bayonet into his stomach again, again and again... Henderson was screaming in pain, we cut across the river and shot the VC four times in the head, we pulled the captain out of the water, and he was bleeding profusely...

Henderson was deep in shock, mumbling incoherently and losing a lot of blood.

Jason looked at me and said:

"It's over, Colonel, this is a gut wound. He will not survive it and will probably die soon. What do you want to do? Do you want me to shoot him or do you want to do it?"

We quickly looked around us, the bodies of three mercenaries were still floating in the pond but two had been carried down the river by the currents.

Jason told me, "Colonel, very soon the area will be swarming with NVA and VC after they find the bodies of their men in the river. We cannot stay here any longer, Henderson must be dead and buried before they find him otherwise you know what they will do with him don't you?"

"I know, Jason, but we cannot kill him, he's one of us, he is a hero. We must try all we can. If he dies of his wound it is another story but no, we cannot shoot him."

"So I will do it, remember that we made a deal and that the rest of the team have been waiting for us at the boat-house. Escape is our mission. So far we have kept ahead of the enemy but with Henderson slowing us down we will get caught for sure, it must be done, Colonel!"

*"So, General, what decision did you make?"*

"You know, Sergeant, Jason was totally correct but I could not resign myself to execute a hero like Henderson even though we had all agreed to kill any wounded member of our team during this mission."

*"What happened then?"*

"Negative, Jason, we will not shoot him. It is an order, clear?"

"Understood, but he will die soon, his condition is extremely grave, Colonel!"

"I know, but let's try to carry him in a safer place."

We used some of the bandages found at the shack to patch up the wounds in a very rudimentary manner and tried to stop the bleeding. We tied leather belts around his belly to hold it all firmly. He was still conscious but irrational; he was suffering a great deal and was already delirious. We carried him away from the waterfall to a shaded place and planned our next move. Undoubtedly the enemy was going to hit us very hard and soon!

Henderson was not doing well at all and once the infection set in, his traumatic condition worsened by the minute. In the bush in Vietnam any scratch, cut or wound got infected very quickly and it had killed many soldiers. In this particular case, even with the best surgical team on site and at the ready, he would have died anyway.

Before we made any further plan of action I gave Jason an option. He could go solo and reach the boat-house quickly, tell the others what had happened and pass on my orders. There was no time to wait for me, I was going to give Henderson a decent burial and reach the Hān on my own and swim to the Cām to also get picked up by the cavalry if possible. I thought that it would work well but Jason did not see it my way and got angry.

"You know, Colonel, you outrank me but now you are out of line and if you wish to court-martial me whenever we return to base, do it, but did you listen to yourself talk? Do you really believe that I would leave you both behind particularly with Henderson's injury? Why are you insulting me, Colonel? We are a team; we are brothers at arms, Colonel! No, I am not going anywhere!"

*"If I may say so, I do agree with Jason's comments and I would have had a similar reaction under the circumstances."*

"I know, but in the back of my mind I wanted to save another life. I was worried that the three of us would get caught, tortured and killed. I felt that I could save his life through this opportunity, I was wrong and it was poor judgment on my part.

We planned the remaining part of our escape to the Cām River. Henderson's condition was now a consideration and changes had to take place.

We decided to continue to follow the stream and circumvent both villages so as not to get caught by the VC.

The hamlet was located at the bottom of a tall mountain which was the home base of the French convent. To reach it we had to ascend very steep and narrow trails through various types of vegetation including a very thick forest with innumerable tall and large trees. It looked beautiful from afar, exhibiting shades of purple, yellow, orange and green.

At sundown the entire area was serene and picturesque. Looking at it, no-one could ever imagine that a ferocious war was taking place in these regions. Because of Henderson's injury, we were not in a position to confront enemy patrols; however we expected to meet a few of them on the way to the convent. The two of us were facing hostile forces who at all costs wanted to catch us "dead or alive". We had to stay "low-key," all the way.

We decided against the idea of building a stretcher to transport the captain because we were going to hide in bushes, trees, walk through a lot of reed beds, swamps and as a finale to our expedition climb to the mountaintop.

Jason and I carried the captain on our backs taking turns.

*"He must have suffered excruciating physical pain. It must have been like torture for him."*

"Yes, Henderson endured an appalling fate; actually death must have been deliverance..."

**“Mankind must put an end to war before war puts an end to mankind.”—John F. Kennedy**

He was still bleeding a lot when we reached the borders of the first village. We needed more bandages or gauze to cover the wounds but it was not prudent to penetrate into the area to get it. We were laying flat on the ground observing the movements of the inhabitants coming in and out of the locality. All of a sudden we heard voices and laughter coming in our direction, we stayed put, our faces touching the grass not moving an inch, Henderson was moaning and mumbling words so I took my knife very slowly out of its sheath and placed the handle between his teeth so that he could bite on it, all you could hear now was the buzz of mosquitoes.

Four VC, a donkey pulling a carriage full of supplies probably going to a nearby tunnel to feed the troops. We hoped that they would pass and move along quickly but…they stopped. They were on top of us, two of them urinated and I felt the warm liquid on my back while the other did it right on Jason's head. We were motionless and they were so close that I could see the dirty toenails of the man who had relieved himself on top of me. They stood there chatting and drinking rice wine for another ten minutes and then walked away.

We laid immobile long after they had gone…

We thought that it had been a very, very close call and after they had left we breathed a sigh of relief."

*"Excuse me General if I may say, they urinated on you both but look, you still made it alive, it may have been a sprinkling of holy water don't you agree?"*

"Sergeant, we can all laugh about it now but at that time…"

*"Sorry, I could not pass up the chance for a joke."*

We knew that there was intense enemy activity on the periphery of the village and because it was getting dark we were concerned about night patrols which were a common occurrence at sunset.

We continued down the stream, we had discussed the possibility of infiltrating the hamlet to find some first-aid supplies and medication to ease the captain's suffering. It was a gamble but worth the try under the circumstances. In addition we needed a rest and to look seriously at Henderson's wounds and change his bandages. The hamlet could offer a safer hide out. It was a peaceful night with a full moon and we heard the echo of the bells ringing across the valley, Jason and I looked at each other, the nuns were praying at the convent…

We stopped sporadically to wet Henderson's lips. Due to the fact that he had received massive internal injuries we could not give him food or water. He was getting seriously dehydrated so all we could do was to wet a bandage for him to suck on and it helped a little, he had high fever, was sweating profusely and his skin was waxen; he breathed with difficulty and was vomiting bile, you see, Sergeant when you added all these symptoms the diagnosis was not promising at all.

We found a large flat rock close to the riverside and placed the captain on his back to have a look at his wounds. We poured water on his face and he smiled faintly, it was not a pretty sight, there was a very advanced state of infection, pus was oozing from the holes in his stomach and the stench was horrid. We knew that his entire body had been contaminated and that the end was near but I just wanted to bury him at the convent like a good Christian, he deserved it, it was in my eyes the least we could do for a hero; we had to show him respect.

Jason went to fetch maggots in the river's silt under the rocks to help with the internal bleeding and the septic condition, we placed them over the gashes that we covered with clean bandages; we then fed the captain a large handful of the small soft creatures to combat the putrid state which was killing him so rapidly. We needed to rest and assess what were our chances to reach the convent in a short time frame, it required planning and ingenuity and in our situation it was not going to be an easy task…

In the moonlight, the shadows of the hamlet emerged from the horizon. Thirty minutes later we were crouching in the forest on its outskirts. One of us had to stay with Henderson and Jason volunteered. We placed silencers onto our handguns and we had full magazines; but we certainly did not wish to encounter confrontation, I moved quickly and silently to reach the main square. It was a quiet hot night and I could hear cows lowing within the barns. I had to approach someone and ask for medicine, there was no hospital and no nurse around; it was definitely not the right place to find help for Henderson but we had no other choice. I tried to peep into the huts without much success, some villagers were already sleeping, others were eating and the women were cooking or sewing. As I progressed toward the centre of the village I noticed a small building made of bricks with some signage on top of the front windows. One door had been left ajar so I went inside, I did not see anybody it was dark and there was a strong smell of urine, a dim light was coming from one of the rooms and the door was slightly open…

I burst in on a young woman tending to a little child who was lying up in bed with a wet towel on his forehead. She was talking to him softly; she turned around and lifted her head, staring at me and my handgun, but did not seem frightened as she asked, "You are one of the escapees of camp #1 aren't you?"

"Yes I am and I need your help."

"The NVA and the VC were here, they told us about a team of American Special Forces who have escaped and killed many of their men. They want you all dead you know!"

She spoke English fluently and I was taken aback by her directness.

"What's wrong with the boy?" I asked.

"High fever, maybe he ate some bad food or he was bitten by mosquitoes at the swamps."

"What is your name?"

"Call me Rose."

"They call me Colonel. Are you a nurse?"

"I am; and also the schoolteacher of the village."

"I have with me an American officer who is dying, I need some medicine to soothe the pain, and he was stabbed by the VC."

"Please take me to him, we will bring him back here to be checked by Dr Henri."

"Who is Dr Henri?"

"A Vietnamese surgeon who studied in Paris and London England, he is not from our village but he has his own clinic in a town nearby. He is very good and saves lives every day. You can trust him, he is not VC. If your friend can be saved, he is the man to consult. Wait a moment while I get my mother to look after the boy while we are gone and I will send for Dr Henri, we have no time to waste."

Later, as she examined Henderson's injuries she cringed, shaking her head:

"The infection has spread throughout his entire body, it's a miracle that he is still alive, Dr Henri himself will not be able to save him. He may die tonight or he will pass away tomorrow at the latest. Let's bring him back to the village."

We placed Henderson in a room next to the sick boy, it was dark and quiet and Rose brought a jug of water with cups and a wet towel.

Dr Henri arrived within the hour; he was a wiry man of small stature with long white hair and a smile on his face. He first looked after the boy and Rose had been correct it was food poisoning. It was not very serious and he gave him the proper medication.

He then removed Henderson's bandages, maggots were crawling all over his body and the smell was unbearable, he looked at Jason and shook his head. He said, "No hope, it is actually extraordinary that he has survived this long with such wounds and infection, considering also that you carried him on your backs on top of it. I have never seen a will to survive this strong before, never. The best I can do for him at that stage is to give him a large dose of morphine to ease the pain, but Rose is right he will die soon, please stay with him; you are safe here. Besides, you need the rest; you both look terrible. If you talk to him he can still understand you. Make his last moments memorable. Soldiers know how to do that, don't they?"

"Yes doctor, we do," I answered.

"Dr Henri bowed to us and left, Rose followed him outside but as she passed me by she placed a small crucifix in the palm of my hand. I found that to be a very thoughtful gesture."

*"General did you in fact have time to reminisce about the good old days with Henderson on his deathbed?"*

"We talked a little, Sergeant. Some funny events had taken place over the years and we shared them with him."

We could notice faint smiles and nods as we talked, he even squeezed our hands at times and it was simply remarkable that he still had some physical strength left into him after all that he had gone through.

We decided to pray aloud and placed the crucifix on his chest while we knelt down on the floor. We asked God to take him to the Garden of Heaven surrounded by guardian angels, his ordeal was now over and he was going to meet his maker. We prayed for peace, honour and serenity and we wanted the best for him at the time."

*"What happened next?"*

'The Lord had heard us; the captain closed his eyes, took his last breath and passed away calmly. Jason and I saluted him, kissed him on the forehead and left the room.'

Rose was waiting for us. She looked solemn and asked, "Did he die peacefully?"

"Yes, quietly, and with dignity, thank you," I answered.

# CHAPTER SIX

## A DIFFICULT CLIMB

Rose answered that she had only performed her duties of a nurse and was sorry that Henderson could not be saved.

We explained to her that our objective was to bury him as a Christian at the convent but we knew that the climb up the mountain was going to be steep and challenging because of Henderson's body condition, she nodded.

She took us inside the building again and we sat at a kitchen table. She asked her mother to prepare some food and recommended that we take a rest for the night as suggested by Dr Henri.

She then added, "Tomorrow morning I will assign two of the farmers to carry Henderson's body on a stretcher to the mission. They are strong and know short-cuts through the mountain to avoid VC patrols. They will come back to the village on their own, and you will be safe with them."

We ate and spoke with Rose about our escape, our plan for the Hān and Cam Rivers swim, our encounter with the village leader and the dreadful story about his daughter, Anh.

Until then she had been silent, listening to us attentively and not making any comments, but as soon as we mentioned Anh's name she retorted coldly, "She is a monster!"

Rose opened up to us and we learned that her village had been targeted numerous times by the General Department of Military Intelligence under Anh's directives. Villagers had been beaten, tortured, and killed, and some had disappeared without trace. Her entire family had been taken prisoners and never returned.

Rose hated the VC but had never had any problems with the US soldiers who had crossed her village. She had also studied French and English in Paris and London, England. While in the United Kingdom she had also taken up nursing and performed her internship in London's best hospitals. When she came back to Vietnam she decided to help her people by teaching and looking after the sick. She also assisted Dr Henri during surgeries. After her father's disappearance she was elected as the village leader. She felt somehow that "Anh" may have been jealous and challenged by her achievements. However, Rose, who was Catholic, strongly believed in the faith and the guidance of God in difficult times. She told us that there were no traitors in this village; the ones who had been planted by Anh's bureau had immediately been pushed away to other locales by the villagers who had kept close tabs on newcomers.

She prayed daily and had been to the convent on several occasions, where the mother superior was a very different person than we usually portray a leading nun to be. In this case she was young, very beautiful, well-spoken and possessed an amazing sense of perspicacity. Her name was Sister Marie Catherine and she came from the south of France where she had felt her calling to serve the Lord many years ago.

Rose told us that the sister would be happy to oblige in burying Henderson on the premises. She agreed that our plan of action was valid but she was concerned for our safety in the rivers where currents were strong, the patrol boats and the VC pirates numerous, not to forget the reptiles looking for their prey. She confirmed that the fisherman at the boat-house was trustworthy and had helped US servicemen in the past. She had met him personally and he had a very good reputation.

"Your team will be safe with him while waiting for your arrival but please be aware that your chances of surviving that mission are very slim.

"Once you step outside you become the hunted ones and after my men leave you at the convent, you will be on your own. By now the word is out all across the province. They have probably put a price on your head and who are you going to trust? But for now let's have some rest. You will need all of your strength tomorrow, it's a hard ascent to the mountaintop."

After some shut-eye we left the village very early with two Vietnamese farmers carrying Henderson's body on a stretcher, covered with a blanket. We gave big hugs of appreciation to Rose and soon we were on the run again…

At 5am we heard the bells ringing and the echo resonated through the valley. Jason and I looked at each other.

"I hope that they are praying for us," he said smiling.

*"How was the ascent to the convent General?"*

"Tough, very tough, Sergeant; but as Special Forces we had gone through mountain training so we could handle the challenge. We were however very impressed with the strength and agility of the two farmers carrying the stretcher. We had offered to help them but they refused."

Heavy mortar fire could be heard in the background and some hits even though not specifically directed to us had landed very close, the NVA had been targeting our troops which had completely encircled the entire valley and positioned themselves into the hills.

Screams, machine-gun fire and artillery bombardment intensified and seemed to get closer. We pressed ahead and kept moving. The NVA were on the prowl and we had to hide from them.

Suddenly our guides dropped to a crouching position and so did we. A patrol was scouring the area and coming our way…

They were still into the distance so we placed silencers on our handguns, told our guides to stay put and ran to the trail ahead of the group, hid under some rocks and waited…

There were four men in full uniform, carrying Russian-made automatic weapons.

They were walking slowly, checking thoroughly through bushes, trees, plants and vegetation on each side of the path. Some were using the barrels of their guns, others their bayonets to poke into low branches, dead trunks and layers of moss; they were cautious but unaware…

When they arrived at the trail they stopped. Their leader began to give them instructions and that is when we just bobbed up out of nowhere.

The effect of surprise was our best advantage, they did not even have time to scream, their eyes were wide open and they just stood frozen to the spot unable to comprehend what was happening.

*"Was the ambush successful?"*

"Yes, we shot them all through the head and hid their bodies deep into the backwoods. We took knives, weapons and ammunition and left the trail because it was becoming too risky to stay on it."

Our escorts led us to short-cuts since time was of the essence and we progressed along dense woodland situated on the left side of the mountain. In three hours we were going to reach the convent, we were sweating profusely and the journey was long and arduous. The scenery had changed drastically. The very tall trees, masses of leaves and branches formed a kind of protective canopy above us that the sun could not penetrate, it was almost dark even though it was day-light.

The humidity and the heat were extremely difficult to

endure but we plugged away relentlessly. In the dead silence of the forest, we could sometimes distinguish the birds chirping and the monkeys' chatter high above us.

We were advancing at a brisk pace but the ground was wet, it was thick with black mud, the smelly marsh was nauseating and everything around us was covered with moss – the trees, the rocks, the dead tree-trunks, everything…

On occasion, Jason and I were not sure of our location in relation to the convent, but the villagers knew their way around and at no time were we off-track. You know, Sergeant, amid the hostile environment a smattering of beauty emanated from the natural element."

*"Beauty, General?"*

"Yes, for instance, the colours in Vietnam were unforgettable, the sunset, the sunrise, the views of the hills and mountains at a distance, the picturesque sceneries of a traditional Vietnamese village...and the flowers! Huge flowers everywhere, they were magnificent!"

In the jungle, each layer of colour was different. For instance, swamps with huge water lilies, tall bamboo sticks, enormous plants with creepers around them and long lianas hanging from trees.

They all bore different tones of green like the palette of an artist. It was so natural and vibrant that now and then I just stood there admiring this country's charm and felt sorry that it had been destroyed by wars time after time.

"Do you think that I was wrong?"

*"Not at all, I felt the same way about Africa myself, and I understand your point of view, but we were soldiers doing our duty."*

"You know I have always regretted not having returned to

Vietnam, just to see how much things have changed since the war ended. I understand that it has been a very emotional experience for the vets who have done so."

*"Yes and I think you should do it, go back to see the places that you remember, including the camps where you were imprisoned, it will be worthwhile and therapeutic at the same time."*

The general was nodding, agreeing with everything I said.

*"Did you reach the convent on time?"*

"Yes but not before we met an uninvited guest."

*"Uninvited? Like another NVA patrol, by any chance?"*

"No, more threatening than that."

*"Wow! Please continue..."*

We had reached a middle-sized plateau, and strangely enough, the grass had not grown abundantly in the field. At the centre of the perimeter, a very large slab of rock was resting on four thick pillars with nine small square cubes of stone placed around it.

Somehow this scenery seemed out of place in the jungle and Jason and I felt that the site was spooky; there was definitely an uneasy atmosphere floating around.

Jason circled the unusual dolmen but I climbed right on top of it.

Our guides who had not yet crossed the ground started suddenly to talk and gesture vehemently; they were agitated and obviously frightened. Jason went to talk to them, meanwhile I was scrutinizing the flat surface of that strange structure. A lot of blood stains were visible on it, and hieroglyphics had been carved in the middle.

Jason returned and said that the two farmers were refusing to cross the "devil's domain," as it was called in the region.

They apologized for making a big mistake, as we were only

supposed to follow the narrow edges of that section in the forest but never to stop in the middle of it.

They also felt that carrying Henderson's dead body through the area where spirits hung around was going to irritate the angry spirits and put our lives in danger.

When Jason joined me on the top of that bizarre stone, both farmers went berserk and begged us to come down at once. But we paced the dolmen calmly, looking at the blood-stains and the unusual inscriptions. Was the blood human or animal?

"Colonel, they said that this entire area is possessed and that this large structure is used for carrying out human sacrifices and black masses. The locals call it 'the altar of Satan'. It is widely believed that demonic souls roam free and wild in underground tunnels and only come out to perform their nightly rituals."

I looked at Jason incredulously. "Do you believe that gibberish, Jason? Come on, black masses and human sacrifices in the jungle of Vietnam? I do not; we are soldiers fighting a war not believers of old women's tales."

*"General, what did Jason say to you?"*

"You know, Sergeant, something very peculiar had suddenly happened to him. He did not answer me, but looked intensely into my eyes with anger, shrugged his shoulders and stepped down from the altar."

"What is wrong with you Jason? What are you sore about? Let's not lose our focus, the convent and the mission. Yes, this place is abnormal but I need your concentration and must count on you two hundred percent, you hear?"

"Colonel, I really have bad vibes, I feel it inside my head and my stomach. This place gives me the creeps, let's get out of here right now!"

*"What was wrong with him?"*

"I did not know at that stage, I only wanted to reach the

convent quickly to bury Henderson and ask the mother superior for spiritual advice. I could have done nothing else."

## CHAPTER SEVEN

## AN UNINVITED GUEST

We wanted to reach our destination as soon as possible, and started to move on the small track leading to the convent with our farmers in tow.

We avoided crossing the devilish site not to frighten our guides who were already shaken up by the demonic presence hovering high above the trees. All of a sudden, an incantation, followed by a monotonous refrain, filled the air; words were repeated over and over again without interruption.

Jason and I looked at each other speechless and flabbergasted by this chain of events. The clear echoes reverberated throughout the forest and the tones amplified rapidly.

"It sounds like a mass, Colonel. It is eerie!" said Jason.

Both our guides dropped down to their knees covering their ears and then began to pray in their native dialect.

"Jason, I really do not know what is going on, but it's the first time in my military career that I am facing such an oddity. Please comfort the men and let's get out here on the double!"

But Jason did not reply, he was staring in the direction of the altar, transfixed and licking his lips…

*"What was the problem with him?"*

"Jason had been deeply affected by this peculiar evil encounter, and his confidence, spirit and energy had been badly bruised. He was now totally demoralized. I was powerless to save his soul."

*"General you were going through a very intricate escape, extremely dangerous, physically demanding, with little chance of*

*success overall. All of a sudden you could not rely on your partner two hundred percent anymore. What did you do?*

"I was in a quandary, but my priority was to reach the convent to bury Henderson as soon as possible, I also felt that the mother superior's perception and deep faith would be my salvation."

*"Who was the uninvited guest, General? The devil?"*

"Well, Sergeant, sort of...but wait, it is going to get more interesting and frightening somehow as my story progresses."

*"What about the incantation and refrains being spread across the woods, what did they really mean?"*

The chorus, incantation and other dicta were spoken in an unintelligible dialect which Jason and I had not understood. We did not have any idea what any of it meant. Personally, I was focusing on the tasks that I had in hand, trying not to listen to this mumbo-jumbo because I wanted to keep a clear head."

*"How was Jason coping?"*

Jason was standing, looking at the altar, continuously licking his lips, and muttering to himself. I approached the field with the two guides and called him again. He did not say a single word and began to walk swiftly towards the altar I yelled at him to stop but it was in vain. The two petrified farmers were still praying, with a rosary in their hands. I was staying close to them, reassuring them because I needed them badly. I did not want them to run away and abandon Henderson's body on the stretcher. Meanwhile I was keeping my eyes on Jason from a distance.

He climbed onto the large stone, placed his 12-gauge shotgun at his feet and raised his arms high in the air above his head. He began singing cryptic messages. When I called him again, he slowly turned his head in my direction. His eyes had no pupils, and had turned totally white!"

*"This is the most unusual story that I have ever heard. It sounds like a scene from the movie,* The Exorcist*!"*

"Quite right, and I was there to witness it for real!

The two farmers kept telling me that it was the curse of Satan; personally I did not know what to think anymore after I had looked at Jason's face. Was I in denial about it all? It's easy to lose your objectivity when you are in combat and under a lot of stress. Was Jason a very sick man, or had he been the prey of evil, and if so, why? He was as if in a trance; his voice was little more than a whisper. Looking straight ahead, with his arms still raised high above his head, he was mumbling incoherent sentences and occasionally cackling for no apparent reason.

Why had he been chosen as the victim of this possession? Who wanted his soul? My duty now was to get him out of their diabolical claws. I intended to do so, no matter what...

The forest fell silent, even the birds had stopped singing.

I approached the large stone and shouted at Jason furiously, "Come on, man! Snap out of it! Look at me, Lieutenant; the colonel is talking to you!"

Nevertheless, Jason did not reply.

He lowered his arms, knelt down on the altar, and made frightening guttural sounds one after the other; then slowly turned his head towards me. His eyes sockets were still completely white. Tears were running down his face and he began talking to himself very loudly, making erratic gestures. He seemed to be carrying on a conversation with a ghost, shaking or nodding his head, even chuckling at times; but we could not figure out what he was saying.

*"Do you think that he was suffering inside his body? Do*

*you believe that he was unconsciously in great pain?"*

"Yes, if the devil possesses you, inner pain must be intense, no doubt."

*"What happened next?"*

A resounding growl filled the forest. I just stood still, not moving an inch, but getting my rifle at the ready…

I turned around to check on the two guides who had stopped crying and were now staring at each other, totally confused. They were kneeling at the edge of the field because they were too scared to approach the large stone.

*"So you were alone in that predicament?"*

"Absolutely, and believe me, things did not get any easier. Quite the contrary!"

The growls persisted and varied in intensity. Then he made his entrance on the field, majestically: calm, imposing, and impressive. He was purely and simply beautiful.

*"Who was 'he' General?"*

"A large-sized Indochinese tiger, Sergeant."

*"And you called it a 'he,' General?"*

"Yes, he definitely was a male."

As soon as he appeared on the field, I sensed that there was something atypical and almost human-like about the man-eating animal. He prowled around the perimeter, sniffing at the cubes of stone one by one; he was really pacing the site carefully, up and down, and seemed to be searching for something in particular.

*"Why didn't you shoot him?"*

"I just could not resign myself to pull the trigger. I had my rifle pointed at him, his head was in my sight, he was very close and one bullet would have sufficed, but instead I just put my rifle down, as simple as that."

*"Was he a big tiger, General?"*

"Yes, he was a male of an unusual size, at least three metres in length, weighting about two hundred and fifty kilograms."

*"What about Jason on the altar?"*

"The tiger until then had ignored Jason's presence altogether. Somehow I was concerned about it because Jason had become very noisy."

The impressive beast circled the field looking at Jason attentively. Occasionally the growls turned into long purrs. The forest was silent and even the exasperating buzz of insects had ceased. I had never witnessed such a phenomenon before in Vietnam, never."

*"And he did not attack you, General?"*

"No, this is the point I wanted to make. I was convinced that he had smelled blood close by. He had a very muscular frame, deep green eyes and huge teeth in his jaws. Believe me, he could have had any one of us for lunch anytime! But he did not seem to be concerned, which was totally abnormal for a predator."

*"What happened next?"*

He sat and observed Jason, going through his mimics and routines. The growls became louder and louder, and even though he was getting angrier, he did not make any move. I felt a connection between the two of them and it worried me…

Meanwhile, Jason was still muttering and rambling on. His face was waxen and he was gesturing at an imaginary partner. Unexpectedly he stood at attention and started to bark orders at soldiers who did not exist, using his shot-gun to present arms and parading around the altar, shouting profanities like a drill-sergeant."

*"Did you think that he had lost it, General?"*

"Yes, Sergeant, at this stage I really believed that he had gone mad, but my primary concern was to keep everyone safe and move on to safer ground."

*"How did you come to the conclusion that there was a certain affinity between him and the tiger?"*

"Just by the manner in which the feline was watching the bogus performance, licking his lips and growling, but not moving an inch. He followed Jason attentively with his cold green eyes…

I positioned myself close to them in order to keep Jason and the tiger under my watchful eye. The farmers who were still in a state of terror were kneeling down at the perimeter of the field, a rosary in their hands, praying silently.

Jason placed his 12-gauge shotgun in front of him, looked up, and began to howl very loudly. It was a vociferous cry of pent up pain, anger, and sadness released all at the same time.

He was now sobbing uncontrollably and whispering in English.

*"What did he say?"*

"He kept saying that the number of the beast was in his head, I did not know what it meant, I could not help him, and it was very strange."

*"Anything else?"*

"He was pleading, "'Free me of him! Let me go! No more please! Take the number out of my head! I just want to rest!'

*"So, he really was suffering from this mysterious condition. He was hurting badly."*

"Yes he was, it was terrible to watch it all. The majestic wild animal rose up, shook his head, paced around, defecated, and with amazing speed jumped onto the stone of evil."

*"Did you worry about Jason's safety?"*

"Yes, at first, but an unusual occurrence took place at that moment. A voice instructed me not to be concerned about Jason's well-being, I was ordered to watch, stay away, and not become involved."

*"What was that all about?"*

"Just like I told you. The voice had spoken, in clear and perfect English.

"Then, I was told that the master was going to talk to Jason. He was no longer ours, he was theirs for good now, and I had to let him go."

*"Did you obey this absurdity?"*

"Of course not, but the series of events which ensued was quite extraordinary."

The master (the tiger) approached and circled around Jason, growling and glaring with cold green eyes. His jaws showed long and menacing teeth. His roars and grunts were actually reprimands, obediently accepted with deep apologies.

*"Did they really communicate on the altar? Could Jason honestly understand the tiger?"*

"Yes, I was witnessing the strangest episode of demonic possession in the jungle of Vietnam!"

Jason was now down on his knees. The master had scolded and butted him very hard, but he did not react at all. He simply expressed remorse, and placing his head into his hands, began to cry profusely.

The growls and roars were getting louder by the minute, the pacing more erratic and the master's temper had taken a turn for the worse. At this point his jaws came so close to Jason's face that the sharp teeth were touching his forehead."

*"General he must have been scared to death!"*

He was sweating profusely and his whole body was shaking. It was frightening. But the master never hurt Jason, he never did.

Jason stood up and yelled out, "666, 666, the great serpent is my master. Baal, you are my mentor, my soul and my strength. 666, 666, the number of the beast. Baal, I worship you!"

He repeated these sentences three times.

The master had kept his eyes fixed on him without making a move, then the chastisement stopped abruptly. The majestic beast rose up on his rear legs and placed his front paws on Jason's shoulders, licking his face with his long pink tongue. Jason reciprocated by hugging the master tightly. I could see that they were exchanging dialogue, whispering words to each other and they stayed in that position for a little while.

*"What did it all mean?"*

"I had no idea at the time, but after the convent's mother superior explained it to me, it became much clearer."

*"General it is an extraordinary story, particularly taking place in the jungle of Vietnam."*

"Yes and considering the difficulties of our operation, I did not need the devil to get involved with it at all."

*"Did you have a plan to get back to the trail leading to the convent?"*

"Yes, but I first calmly assessed all the facts in my mind. The truth of the matter was that an evil spirit had possessed Jason. The majestic tiger personified Satan pure and simple. We were standing on a site which had been cursed for centuries, propitious for demonic control. These were the facts."

*"What happened next?"*

I talked very sternly to the two farmers, explaining that the success of rescuing Jason and burying Henderson as a Christian depended on them and that we had to approach the altar at once. Unpredictable developments were going to follow and we had to be there at the ready. So we all came close to the satanic stone.

Jason was still in the erect posture of a professional soldier and had fallen totally silent. The tiger was pacing up and down the stone, licking himself and making small growing noises.

I thought that it was time for a rapid rescue to bring Jason back to the convent. I climbed onto the stone with the two farmers and we placed the stretcher with Henderson's body down at our feet.

The majestic beast advanced slowly, licking his jaws, stopping about two metres away, glaring at me defiantly. His cold green eyes scrutinized me up and down. Then he turned around, sniffed at Henderson's corpse and then resumed unhurriedly circling around me.

He was powerful and confidant and his deep green eyes looked straight through me. He did not growl nor exhibit any bout of anger. I had a hunch that I was going to have a fierce encounter with Lucifer in person. I had also noticed something very peculiar about the master. The animal did not smell bad nor was he dirty, which was very unusual for a predator living in the wilderness. Instead, I picked up a sweet scent which at the time was difficult to place and some strong traces of sulphur floating above the dolmen.

*"General were you really prepared to face the devil tête-à-tête?"*

"My answer is, 'yes'."

The master came closer and I felt that he did not want to use his enormous strength and brute force against me, instead there were astuteness and malice into his eyes."

*"How did you handle him?"*

I was waiting for some action to develop and was somehow perplexed. It was very tense on the altar. Jason had remained standing at attention, totally silent. The two guides were immobile by the stretcher and the master and I were looking into each other's eyes. That was the situation.

*"How did the confrontation begin?"*

"My goal was not to antagonize Lucifer but to save Jason from his devilish grip."

*"That was an insurmountable challenge, after all, your opponent was Lucifer!"*

"You are correct, frankly speaking I did not have a clue what to expect and how to handle it, but my duty was to save my team and that is what I did."

## CHAPTER EIGHT

## TÊTE-À-TÊTE WITH THE DARK LORD

One must follow his instincts and act accordingly, aware that the devil's best weapon is deceit. Satan's sinister existence is based on trickery, wreaking havoc, causing casualties and catastrophes, and bringing hardship and misery to the world.

The devil has many aliases: the great serpent, Satan, Baal Davar, Lucifer, the antichrist and others… At this time, he was a noble tiger who had taken Jason's soul. I wanted it back.

Jason and the two guides were standing still, their eyes closed.

The master spoke to me in perfect English, without any accent, with a very controlled tone of voice, looking straight at me all the while."

*"Were you at all a little leery or concerned?"*

"You know, as a member of the special forces, you learn to control emotions. Therefore I stayed calm and conversed with him."

"Colonel, you know who I am, don't you?"

"You are the demon from hell and I do not know what you want from us, but I am taking Jason back, he needs help to return to his old self. You have played enough tricks with his mind. Now it is time to stop these games. We need to leave this place to bury our friend Henderson, that's all I have to say. I am not afraid of you. I am a professional soldier; therefore, in a dangerous situation, I am a natural. But what about you? What's your game?"

"You are not only arrogant but very ungrateful. If you are

standing here in front of me with all the others, it is because I wanted it to happen this way. Look at Henderson! Because of my doing he is now reduced to a rotten heap of flesh. He may have been a war-hero once but is so no more. The only memory that will survive of Henderson will be that he received posthumous medals for bravery at a military cemetery in the USA. I find it ridiculous and futile. Don't you agree, Colonel?"

"No, I do not, men and women who fight for their country should receive the honours that they deserve, dead or alive."

The master burst out laughing, sarcastically and said, "A medal on a coffin! I find it cynical and shallow. You won't convince me. Because I did not take his soul for my service, you will be able to bury him with the little sisters up the mountain. That is where you are going aren't you?"

"Yes, this is my plan. By the way, how do you want me to address you?"

"I am the prince of darkness, so please call me, my Lord."

"Jesus is our only Lord."

"No, he is your Lord, in the Bible and in your prayers, but I take care of the other side, I am the malefactor, the master of evil forces, looming in the place you call hell, so please give me the respect that I deserve."

"Very well, 'my Lord' it is."

"You seem perturbed. I know that you want to ask me some questions. Please fire away. It's your chance. We may never get the opportunity to meet again face to face."

"What is this place?"

"It is one of my domains, where certain elements of our secret society meet regularly and worship. As you can see, it is tranquil here. You would not even guess that there is a war going on, would you?"

"I am curious about the inscriptions on the stone. What do

they mean?"

"You have your Bible, but we read from our own ancient manuscripts, like the Book of the Abyss, it is written in a very old language.

"Some very important passages have been extracted from the old books and engraved on the altar. Let me show you."

The master slowly approached the hieroglyphics and looked at them intensely while reciting short sentences that I could not understand. They all lit up at once with bright colours. The letters, the symbols, and the sketches were now very clear and legible to the naked eye.

"Look at it, Colonel, it is very practical at night don't you think?"

He then laughed raucously. He had flaunted his power.

"Is is true that human sacrifices have been performed on that stone, my Lord?"

"Yes, blood stains are the living proof. My devoted lieutenants take care of the rituals. Animals, humans, even small babies have been slaughtered as offerings to the various gods. We believe in male spirits with special powers, and we must demonstrate that we worship them."

At that moment one of the farmers pulled a rosary out of his pocket for no apparent reason. In response, the master swiftly moved towards him, and shouted in the Vietnamese language, "Put it back into your pocket immediately or I will burn you alive right here and now."

The man complied and apologized profusely to the ferocious predator. He was shaking like a leaf under the watchful eye of the master.

"You see, I have an aversion to holy water, ridiculous artifacts such as crucifixes, crosses, medallions, rosaries, Bibles and who knows what! How can one exhibit such paraphernalia in my presence? It is like adding insult to injury…"

"Why is it so quiet around here?"

"Because of glacial fear. This field has been the devil's retreat for centuries. It is mine and I will eat alive anyone who tries to interfere with our unrevealed proceedings. Your enemies do not even patrol this zone in the forest. They would never dare to intrude. The locals know better than to cross its limits."

"I did not see any remains. Do you bury all the victims?"

The master started to laugh loudly and mockingly. "No, you will never find any around here, not a single bone, not a single skull, nothing. We have our 'people down below,' who take care of what we call 'the housekeeping of the perimeter'. The site is always spotless; there are never any traces of our secret ceremonies and black masses."

"I do not understand the meaning of the 'people down below'".

"Troglodytes, Colonel, they live underground in caverns and tunnels and only come out at night to fetch the cadavers from the altar and the wooden areas surrounding it. They crave human flesh. They are the scariest creatures in the universe – half scavengers, half predators. They are my loyal servants, Colonel, ruthless, deadly: you could name them, 'the shadows of Hell,' and this is not a legend. Right under your feet, millions of them perform their sordid tasks and nurture my inferno at the centre of the Earth. Yes, today you met the devil and you have confirmation that Hell really exists."

*"General, your tête-à- tête with Satan seemed positive after all, the master was polite and explicit, wasn't he?"*

"Yes, Sergeant."

I made sure not to contradict or irritate him. I listened, kept our conversation very fluid, and remained calm under the circumstances. I did not know what to expect from one second to the next; but up to this point he was answering my questions obligingly.

"My Lord, if we have all ended up on your domain, it is not pure coincidence is it?"

"Of course not, I made it happen because I wanted to meet you personally and take Jason under my wing at the same time. The two farmers got lost in the forest through my power. They were not careless or incompetent. I guided them."

"What was your objective?"

"Recruiting, like the army does."

"But why Jason?"

"Two of your men, including him, are ideal candidates to join my side, but I need to give them preparatory training. Jason was soon ready."

"I do not understand why you would seek out Jason. He is an excellent soldier, a good man, and I doubt that he would ever perform sordid deeds for you."

The master was looking at me with his deep green eyes and with a sardonic tone of voice exclaimed, "No, that is where you are wrong. I chose him to become one of my henchmen. Of course he did not realize at the time that he possessed all the attributes to serve my kingdom – Hell as you call it – but soon he will be one of my best servants. I may even promote him later."

"Promote him, my Lord?"

"Yes, Colonel, your God has archangels, angels, priests, cardinals and even the pope to help him in his daily tasks, I have henchmen, lieutenants and even captains in my dark kingdom, we are extremely busy."

"What about Jason?"

"You do not know him, you were only acquainted at camp#1 as prisoners, am I correct?"

"Yes, my Lord."

"But I am aware of all that he did before he joined the army, I know him inside out, his family, his boyhood years, his strengths and weaknesses, his fears, joys, and sorrows, his habits, his most inner secrets, I know absolutely all about him. Jason has a past. Do you believe me if I say that I know you better than you know yourself?"

"Yes, I do, after all you are the devil."

The master shouted in a joyful tone, "Well-spoken! You now understand. I have been a good teacher today, haven't I ?

"You have, my Lord."

"Now, let me tell you what is going to happen, I will let you go to bury Henderson properly. He was not a good candidate for me anyway, a family man with deep Christian roots within his soul. Then you must reach the boat-house to meet your team again and get on with your rescue. It is going to be hard and it is up to me decide if you can succeed, God cannot help you on my territory. Hell is all around you, Colonel!"

"Why did you want to meet me, my Lord?"

"I was going to recruit you but I changed my mind and chose Jason instead. There is also another man on your team whom I have picked and who will make a great henchman after I have worked with him for a while."

"How do you proceed on your conversions?"

"The brain controls the heart. I know how to push the right button and one's thoughts will automatically tilt. I come to the rescue, praise, cajole, entice, and finally convince the person that he/she has become a lost soul in the universe. The mind starts wandering; the individual loses all focus and willpower to achieve anything. He or she is beyond redemption, I then perform the proper rituals from our Book of the Abyss. You may laugh, but I become their saviour, hence his or her master until the end of time. You must know that once you work for the dark Lord you become immortal and ageless. Would you care to join us? It is a very attractive proposition."

"No, thank you."

"You see, I wanted to meet you face to face because you are a great warrior, courageous, a strong leader. I like your intransigence. You are stubborn but I call this a quality, not a fault. You might wish to change your mind. You can serve as a captain, please think about it."

"Again, no chance. But who is the second man in my team that you have recruited?"

"You will find out who he is when the time is right."

"I need to know who is going to work on your side during the operation. They are my men and I am their leader. Look what happened to Jason! Such a situation will definitely compromise the escape."

"You do not need to know at the present time."

"But, my Lord…"

The master growled very loudly in my face. "Once and for all, Colonel, I tell you how it works. You all belong to me. This is my world. I decide who lives and I decide who dies. If you wake up tomorrow morning, looking at the blue sky, it is because I allow it, do you understand? Is it clear?"

"Yes, my Lord."

"If you and your team make it back safely to your respective units, consider it sheer luck. I am the devil. I started this war and right now it is raging exactly the way I like it. Since you have escaped from camp#1, you have progressed rather well towards your planned objectives; but your fortune may change very soon. You have too much on your plate and very little time to handle it all. Your men are waiting for you at the boat-house. The enemy is everywhere, trying to kill you or catch you, including one of my most devoted servants."

"Oh? Who is that, my Lord?"

"You have heard her name before; it is "Anh," a colonel at the General Department of Military Intelligence. She is soon to be promoted to the rank of general, she is simply magnificent."

"All I know is that she is notorious for her ruthlessness, but I met her family who are very nice people. Yes, she is undoubtedly looking for us."

"Your God cannot help you, he is not there, you are on my territory and this is the Vietnam War, my war!"

"What about Jason?"

"What about him?'

"Look at him, he seems to be in a lethargic state, he is not at all the Jason that I know."

"True. However, he will be back to his old self very soon, I had to let him cross the path to the dark side and it has been very trying for him both physically and mentally. Remember that he is now my devoted servant until the end of time. We must part company; nevertheless I want to leave you on a positive note."

The master ordered Jason to lie flat on his back, covering the hieroglyphics. He then came on top of him, took Jason's head between his paws and began to lick his face furiously, Satan looked at me and said, "Colonel, this is the initiation's last phase, please watch attentively."

*"So what happened next, General?"*

I can only describe it as an episode of living Hell in a Vietnamese forest. The entire area went out of control; it was a combination of mysterious happenings, a demonstration of devilish powers and psychic occurrences. I had never witnessed anything like it in my life before, nor have I since. It was an evidence of Lucifer at his best.

In the jungle, tall trees and very thick vegetation formed a protective canopy above us, and daylight did not pierce through. We were always in the semi-darkness. Without warning, six large lights, encased into the stone, appeared under our feet. They looked like projectors and shot yellow beams way up into the air.

Loud voices reciting unintelligible incantations resounded throughout the forest. They were followed by thunder and lightning, strangely enough without rain.

Laughter, howling and harrowing screams came from the four corners of the field while tremors reverberated under the altar. The large lights moved constantly, making large circles high into the trees. Occasionally we had to close our eyes, because they were very powerful and were blinding us.

All noises stopped, replaced by a strident whistle. A freezing cold temperature enveloped the perimeter, and a glacial wind, coming out of nowhere, chilled us to the bone."

*"What was the master doing?"*

He was still on top of Jason and seemed to enjoy it all; he kept looking at me defiantly, watching for my initial reactions. Then he rose up and delivered an incomprehensible monologue, while Jason lay there, motionless, his eyes closed.

The jungle was now very calm and all paranormal activities had ceased abruptly.

"How did you like the special effects, Colonel?" asked the master sarcastically.

"Very impressive, but is Jason all right?"

"I am taking care of him; he is no longer your concern, wait and see..."

A second phase of psychokinetic events ensued on the altar. Lucifer crouched over Jason again and licked his face vigorously. Jason opened his mouth wide and a flow of yellowish gelatinous substance spurted from the tiger's jaws down his throat. A strong sulfuric smell hovered above us.

Then forest was still and we were waiting for more of Satan's poltergeist demonstrations.

The tiger circled Jason's body and sat on it. He ordered him to open his mouth again and spat a long jet of blood into it. It was not a pretty sight. It splashed all over Jason's face and mouth. The master licked it clean, turned around and said, "Let's enjoy the finale, Colonel."

He moved gracefully and sat two metres away from Jason, scrutinizing the altar. His eye lingered over the two farmers, standing on the other side. He growled loudly and angrily.

"Both of them will die soon, I want to make them pay for their insolence. Exhibiting a crucifix in my presence and on my domain is an act of insubordination, punishable by death, as simple as that."

"My Lord can you show them mercy? I need to carry Henderson's body to the monastery; they are my guides who know the way and the short-cuts."

"So be it, but I will strike upon their return. Rose will never see them alive again, do you understand? I call it retribution. They will suffer an appalling fate and this matter is not open for discussion. My decision is irrevocable.

"Now let me take care of Jason, Colonel."

The altar became illuminated again, the six projectors shot their long rays of light at random into the air, spraying the tops of the trees. The ground began to tremble under our feet. The tremors intensified and forced us to kneel down on the stone. A rumbling noise, resounding like an earthquake, persisted in the background, bright flashes of lightning zapped the large stone table with full force and cracking sounds. We stood transfixed, waiting for more…

Lucifer placed himself close to Jason, looking at the sky and reciting strange invocations with a raucous voice. The bolts of lightning increased and struck Jason all over his body. I jumped forward to pull him away, but the master growled, "Stay where you are, Colonel, don't get involved!"

Jason was hit numerous times from head to toe. The extraordinary thing was that he was not burned or maimed in any way. Then a massive thunderbolt hit Jason. Streaks of purple, blue and silver lightning penetrated his skull, passing through his body and exiting at the bottom of his feet. It was so powerful that he was shaken like a rag doll. This time I thought that he had been killed instantly...

The rain of fire ceased and an acrid smell enveloped the altar. The master began chanting a refrain in a low tone of voice, nodding and pacing up and down slowly, at the same time. Jason rose up unexpectedly into a horizontal position; Satan moved closer to him, tapping his chest softly with his paw and whispered, "Good boy, good boy, relax! Now it is almost over."

The body came to a standstill and blinding lights burst all around us, a short while later they dimmed, and we could discern rows of thin glass tubes, all perfectly aligned high above the altar, full of multi-coloured liquids, their shades astonishingly beautiful, reflecting fascinating illuminations.

Then the master gave an order aloud and they all dropped down at the same time, piercing Jason's body from head to toe without causing a single drop of blood even at the exit wounds.

He remained perfectly still and silent floating into the air at the mercy of his master Lucifer. The hieroglyphics lit up once again exhibiting strong tones of red, orange and yellow; we were all looking aghast at these amazing, spectacular and magical occurrences.

The master let out a yell and all lights on the perimeter

flickered and went out. The forest became tranquil and all that we could hear were the gurgling sounds from the liquids filtering through the tubes as they passed inside Jason's body changing colour as they did so.

I asked the master about the extraordinary and very unusual surgical procedures taking place on the altar.

"You do not need to know. Just watch. But I will give you a hint – transfusion," were his words. Jason was now receiving the devil's blood...

The tiger was pacing the altar up and down mumbling a vague liturgy when he stopped in front of the two farmers. He looked at them closely and without warning threatened them in the Vietnamese language with death.

They were absolutely devastated and knelt down begging for forgiveness, but it was all in vain as he had cast a spell over them.

He then sat on the magical stone and scrutinized Jason who was being cared for in the most unusual way as he was receiving a blood transfusion from Hell amidst a rainbow of mystical glass pipes. From a distance he looked like a sea urchin floating in the air. Lucifer barked orders and the treatment stopped at once. The tubes flew out of his body and vanished mysteriously, he then lay down on the altar, his eyes closed.

The forest became alive again resonant with all its enchanted noises.

"How did you like it, Colonel?" the master inquired.

"Very impressive and most puzzling, my Lord."

The master burst laughing and said, "That's what it all about, the dominance of the Devil, the fearsome secrets of the unknown and the impenetrable forces of darkness all combined into one, isn't it tempting, don't you want to join us?"

"No, thank you, but I must admit that I was impressed by the phenomenal demonstrations."

"They merely were the gradual steps of an initiation, but yes

I made them spectacular because I wanted you to witness Satan's gradual transformation rituals."

At the very moment, Jason woke up and stood at attention in front of me, "Colonel, first lieutenant Jason Brown at your orders."

"Stand at ease, Lieutenant, I must talk to the master."

*"Did you have a good conversation with the master?"*

"Yes, and he clearly informed me of the events to come. Even though the outlook was very gloomy, I was at least warned ahead of time. A similar scenario was going to occur after reaching the boat-house, because Lucifer had already chosen one of my team as his servant and there was nothing I could do to change the situation."

Jason looked fit and ready but it was not the case with Henderson.

He was not a pretty sight, his face looked pale and bloated, maggots were crawling out of all the orifices of his body and the smell was putrid.

To carry him up the mountain was going to be a challenge…

*"But you succeeded, General, didn't you?"*

"Yes, Sergeant, but with the master's help, listen to the rest of the story…"

"Henderson looks repulsive doesn't he?" the tiger said.

"Yes he does; and I do not even know if his body will remain intact during the climb."

"Probably not, but as a gesture of goodwill, my devoted servants will prepare him for proper burial. Please do not say that the devil never helped you, Colonel," chuckled Satan.

Henderson was really a mess and maggots were feasting on his rotten flesh, I was heartbroken to think that only a few days ago this dead corpse had been one of the best fighter pilots in the US Air Force, a renowned platoon leader and a redoubtable enemy of the VC.

Lucifer talked briefly to the farmers who then carried the stretcher about 200 metres away from the altar, close to the forest's edge.

We stopped beside a tall rock, which bore large red inscriptions that I was unable to decipher, and put Henderson's stretcher down. The master growled loudly a few times. He was obviously calling for someone.

"Do not come too close, it will be bloody and not a spectacle for the faint hearted, but I would like you to know that you are the only three mortals to have ever witnessed this unique rite that I have arranged for Henderson, never forget it."

Jason was still standing on the altar, he seemed perfectly healthy and was looking straight at us from a distance. His eyes had returned to normal. Unexpectedly, whispers, gnawing sounds, chatting and chirping noises were heard all around us. What ensued next was ghastly.

Brown furry creatures, half human, half beast, emerged from under the rock. They were between one metre to one metre and a half tall, with large yellow eyes, their long and pointed teeth were protruding and they had droopy ears. Their smell was absolutely awful. They moved hurriedly, but in sequence, communicating through quick gestures, grunts, clucks, giggles and pronouncing words that were totally incomprehensible to me. Their hands and feet were just claws, long black crooked claws that were sharp like a surgeon's scalpel.

Six of them surrounded the stretcher waiting for the master's instructions. They did not carry any surgical equipment.

Satan barked orders at them.

They rushed to work on Henderson. After taking off his clothes they made a long incision along his chest from top to bottom. They sucked the blood and cleared away all the maggots; I could hear their slurping sounds and their mouths and bodies were covered in blood, with the soft, yellow, creatures crawling all over them. However horrid they were, they were absolutely amazing. They were performing a surgical operation perfectly, demonstrating the skills and precision of a professional forensic pathologist or mortician, solely by using their long, black, sharp, pointed, claws. They removed all his internal organs and prepared him for burial in record time.

Then they disappeared, the same way they had come in. The master called the two guides and we moved back to the altar.

Henderson's chest was empty and wide open.

"Let me put the final touch, Colonel," said Satan.

The master paced slowly around the corpse and said, "My team performed well, I am now going to close the wound so that you can bury him honourably with the little sisters."

Lucifer lay flat on top of Henderson and licked his face. We noticed a strong odour of sulphur around the altar.

A sizzling sound came from under the tiger's body as he was cauterizing the long incision. The master was also licking the captain's face and a faint veil of skin colour reappeared while he combed Henderson's hair with his tongue, it was absolutely amazing to watch. When he got up, the gaping wound was completely closed, being replaced by a thin, bluish, scar along the chest. As we approached closer we noticed a faint smile on the lips.

"My Lord, this is extraordinary."

"Doesn't he look a cherub, Colonel?"

"Yes, he certainly does."

"Well, he is all yours."

Jason was still standing at ease and I let him know that we were now moving on. We would both be carrying the equipment, rifles and ammunition for the team waiting at the boat-house.

The guides picked up the stretcher and we were on our way.

The master followed me and said, "Colonel, from now on all your expertise and courage will be tested to the max. This will be an epic and memorable experience, unlike anything you have faced before. A word of caution... whenever Jason decides to leave you, do not try to retain him. It would only hurt your escape. I will see you again very soon, as I have to prepare the other man who is going to join us on the dark side. Now, please follow me…

We walked a short distance into the woods and suddenly he disappeared. I called him, but he did not reply. Out of the blue, a loud and powerful laugh boomed out from across the forest. "Have a good climb to the convent!" And he added sarcastically, "Say hello to the little sisters from me." Then there was total silence.

I stood there, looking around. Out of the corner of my eye, I noticed a large teak tree on the left with smoke coming out of the trunk. I moved closer…

"666", "Baal Davar", "Lucifer" and the sketch of a large snake were engraved in it. It had been carved by the master. This was obviously another message for my attention; I shrugged my shoulders and returned to the altar. We climbed silently and under a punishing heat the small trail leading directly to the "mission", as it was called locally.

All went very smoothly. We didn't meet any enemy patrols. However, fierce fighting was raging across the valley and because we were listed across the entire province as "public enemy number one", the convent was definitely a good place to hide and rest for a while.

The large structure emerged from the top of the mountain. A towering cross stood tall into the blue sky and the chapel's bells were ringing for the afternoon mass.

"Colonel, I am not going inside," said Jason.

He remark took me by surprise, but I realized that since he was the Devil's henchman he could not possibly patronize the house of God.

"I just cannot stay around here. I must leave this place at once. I am feeling very sick."

"Fine, Jason, but where shall we meet you afterwards? It may be a few hours before we leave again. Henderson must be buried, the guides and I will eat and rest and I must speak to the mother superior to clarify some important points about what has taken place. Do you have a problem with that?"

"No, not at all. Please take your time. I will hide at the bottom of the trail. This way, if there are any enemy patrols, I will take care of them. Trust me, Colonel."

We then took an inventory of supplies, rifles, and ammunition, and I made sure that Jason had all that he needed in case of a confrontation.

I left him and went to the front door of the mission.

# CHAPTER NINE

## THE MISSION

In the very centre of the door there was a large ornate brass door-knocker in the shape of an angel; on the left, an old European-style bell-pull with a thick cord was hanging.

I used both several times but no one answered. I kept trying and suddenly I heard hurried steps coming from a distance.

"Clong, Clong, Cling!"

A small window panel encased within the main door opened.

"May I help you?" a voice inquired with a French accent.

"Yes, Sister, we are in dire need of help. May we come in?"

"Are you American?" the Sister asked.

"Yes I am." I gave my rank and unit and explained about Henderson's body.

The front door opened and Sister Marie Catherine greeted us warmly. "Bonjour, Colonel, I am Sister Marie Catherine, mother superior of the convent. Sorry for the delay. We were attending mass. We will definitely take care of your friend. But you must be exhausted, please follow me."

We were served cold lemonade in a waiting room.

Sister Marie Catherine came back and said, "I will ask Father Benedetti our chief surgeon to join us in the morgue."

I was somehow puzzled over the fact that she had mentioned the word "morgue" and that a male priest was on the premises. After all this was a convent, not a monastery.

We were led by a young Sister through a maze of corridors, tunnels, and attractive courtyards, and finally reached the lower floor of a medium-sized building.

Sister Marie Catherine was waiting for us and she opened the door of a small, compact, operating-room, which was dark and cold. We placed Henderson's body on a thick marble table and covered it with a blanket while waiting for Father Benedetti...

The father was a short man, full of energy, endowed with a gregarious personality and a strong handshake. He addressed the two guides in fluent Vietnamese and they smiled back brightly, totally at ease in his presence. A young nurse attendant came in carrying a large bucket and two basins which she placed underneath the table.

"I hope that he is not going to perform an autopsy, his body has already been treated," I thought.

The mother superior turned on the surgical lights while Father Benedetti donned his doctor's uniform and rubber gloves. He pulled the blanket away from the body, looked at it, and stood there, transfixed, immobile, his mouth wide open...

Sister Marie Catherine had approached and for one split second their eyes met. There was total silence but I caught a glimpse of mutual understanding. She took her rosary, moved into a corner of the room and prayed.

The surgeon performed a thorough examination from head to toe. With his index finger he followed the scar along the chest, looking at it attentively. He turned the body around, checking the spine, the buttocks, then once again scrutinized the face, the combed hair, the neck, and the cheeks. With a pair of tweezers, he removed some seed particles from the nose and mouth, placing them on a small ceramic tray. He went on to the next step, where he touched, pressed, and squeezed the limbs, belly, chest, feet and hands. Last but not least, he scrutinized the various cavities, closely inspecting the skin colour, abrasions and deterioration. But he made no incision. Not a single word was spoken throughout the procedure.

The Father glanced at Henderson's body once and asked me bluntly, "Who did this, Colonel?"

I did not reply.

The Sister came forward and said calmly, "Please, Colonel, answer the question. It is important."

"I will later. Right now I want to bury him like a Christian. He deserves it, he was a hero. That is the reason why I am here at the mission."

"Very well. Sister Marie Catherine is going to make the proper arrangements; meanwhile I would like to ask the farmers some questions. Is it all right with you?"

"Please go ahead. But I don't think you will get much help from them."

The two farmers were praying in the corridor outside the morgue when Father Benedetti approached them.

"Sister, may I have a few minutes alone with Henderson?"

"Please, Colonel, take your time and I will ask Emile our gardener to prepare the grave. I will also need the two farmers to help him. We will all join you later at the site to say a few words."

*"Were you happy with the chain of events?"*

"Yes, it was the calm before the storm, the real mission was going to proceed under duress but finally I would bury Henderson properly and I was eager to sit down with Sister Marie Catherine face to face. I needed that peace of mind amid all the turmoil around me."

*"I understand, please continue..."*

I held Henderson's hand and I apologized through my prayers, I was feeling guilty for sending him to his death at the waterfall. I realize now that it was not my fault, because it was combat; and fate controls everything in our lives. However there was a thorn in my heart at the time.

I cried, Sergeant, I cried for a long time, holding his hand. He had endured so much suffering, so much pain. He was an inspiration to all of us, a true war hero, excelling in many missions and a top pilot, and now he was gone…

When I left the room I had come to terms with my anger and my prayers had soothed my grief."

*"So General, Henderson is still buried at the convent, I presume."*

"No, after the war, I wrote letters to the Air Force and the White House requesting that his body be moved to Arlington Cemetery in Washington D.C. It took a long time, but the application was granted and his family and friends were very proud of the honour conferred on Willy. He undoubtedly deserved it."

*"How was your experience at the mission?"*

"Wonderful, it was a large institution within colossal fortifications. It comprised a convent, a monastery, a hospital and individual ateliers and workshops teaching trades and numerous skills to the locals, including farming. There were plenty of natural resources, large thick brick walls separated off the main areas and the nurses took care of security. The farmers and I stayed there for two days and I had to narrate my escape in full detail to the council."

*"The council?"*

"Yes, there were six top leaders at the mission. Henderson's burial was simple and discreet. His body had been placed in a wooden coffin and we threw beautiful flowers on top of it. The eulogy was performed by Father Benedetti and we took turns saying a few words.

Sister Marie Catherine, the two villagers and Emile the

gardener also attended. A wooden cross was placed on the grave, with the following inscription:

"Captain Willy Henderson

"1st Air commando Squadron

"US Air Force

"See you up there"

After the ceremony, Sister Marie Catherine approached me and said, "Let's take a walk, Colonel I will show you the main areas of the mission, it is our world you know, and we work very hard to keep it clean, functional, and as attractive as possible. I believe that Father Benedetti wants to talk to you regarding the medical examination, we shall meet him later."

We walked in silence and then I realized how serene, colourful, and picturesque the cemetery was. I remember it to this day, because it was so unusual. It actually had character and a feeling of gaiety."

*"Gaiety? In a cemetery?"*

"Yes, Sergeant, it was remotely located from the main buildings. There were a number of pathways covered in cobblestones giving access to various areas of the convent. There was a strong fresh smell hovering in the air because there were dozens of fruit and olive trees, huge flowers and vines everywhere, spread across the perimeter and beyond. I could see countless types of fruit, the plants and flowers were blooming, exhibiting extraordinary colours and sublime scenery.

I stopped, looked around and said, "Sister, it certainly does not seem like a graveyard, there is so much life around, and to my eyes this is a fruit and flower market."

Sister Marie Catherine smiled and said, "Please let me show you something."

At the end of the field, behind some low-level buildings,

appeared a very large vegetable garden adjacent to a vineyard.

"This is my Garden of Eden, my pride and joy."

The sections were neatly arranged and all the produce looked very fresh.

"In the Bible, the Garden of Eden is synonymous with beauty and tranquillity. I placed my lady's touch on both areas, the cemetery and the garden. This is why I feel strongly about the output. However, the entire department of agriculture which we manage should receive credit for their success. Our students and teachers work very hard as a team to maintain the highest standards. With what we pick daily we can feed the needy, the mission staff – and with the leftovers – the locals can make some money at the small markets in their villages. People are very poor in Vietnam. There is a war going on. We must help in any way we can."

"Sister, this is absolutely amazing!"

"Please call me Marie Catherine."

"I prefer to call you 'Sister'."

"As you wish. We are a very large educational institution, one of the most successful in Asia. Our priests are all Jesuits and of course there is a strong inclination to teach the locals and promote education. My background was business, I graduated from the Hautes Etudes Commerciales in France. I also studied English in London, England and went into the nursing profession. However, when I received the calling from God, it was stronger than anything. I came here as a mother superior, elected and admitted to my office by a formal blessing conferred by the bishop. I am the boss of the mission, as you say in America. However, all major decisions are put through the council for approval. I delegate a lot, but of course the final decision is mine. The members have specific functions and specialties; mine are finance, accounting, and productivity. Since my arrival,the mission has been profitable. We still receive funding from Paris and Rome, but we have received many accolades from his Holiness for our performance."

We walked back through the cemetery and I made an observation about the burial ground. "Sister, the more I look at it, the more I have the impression that life, beauty, and happiness emanate from the place. Am I wrong?"

"No, you are perfectly correct, why should death be a distressing occurrence? It is temporarily painful and very emotional, but after all, once God has called us, we usually go to a better place and leave behind all the sufferings that we have endured on earth. Heaven is what is waiting for us, so why be depressed? Why should our souls and remains be surrounded by gloom and pity? I am a nun in the middle of a war and I face death and its afflictions every day. This is why I wanted to create a unique place with an atmosphere of gaiety, to give our dead a cheerful and divine departure. After the passing, there is the after-life. The tombs mark mortality, the flowerbeds and the fauna exhibit the resurgence of life. Let's not be grieving for long. God has plans for us once the sorrow has faded. I created a contrast in my churchyard; once again it has a personal touch."

"Sister, I admire you perspicacity, but I would never have expected such a line of reasoning from a Catholic nun. You are really amazing and all the work that you are doing at the mission is extraordinary."

"Well, thank you, Colonel, my superiors have called me 'too progressive' and 'unorthodox' at times, but I keep plugging away, no matter what happens. You can see around us many old buildings which are in fact learning-centres with various specialties. We are totally self-reliant. We have acquired a huge electric generator; we have also built a water reservoir, a hospital and infirmary, a laundry, schools, a full service kitchen, a bakery and two refectories. Recently we opened a garage with an experienced crew of mechanics who can fix anything from a bicycle to a large army truck."

"Sister, this is absolutely remarkable."

"Thank you, Colonel. Please follow me. I want to show you a little more of what we do."

We climbed a flight of stairs inside one of the towers and exited on a small terrace overlooking the countryside.

"If you look ahead, beyond our walls, you can see our main production areas; they are in fact our lifeline. In the centre, there is a deep lake and around it are located a fish-farm and aquaculture laboratories. On the left are a stable, a cattle-ranch and a dairy-farm. Behind the two buildings at the front, we have a poultry farm and a large market-garden. At the base of the hills, there is a sizable vineyard: yes, we make good wine, Colonel! The crops are handled by locals, who are also learning the trade.

You have in front of you a good view of a very elaborate and productive domain for this province. This is an extension of the mission; God has made it all possible."

"Sister you are a dynamo, not less than a CEO working for a large corporation. Your functions are so diverse, how do you do it?"

"I pray a lot, God guides me and I delegate incessantly. I follow my operating budget to the letter. I am surrounded by several experts in their field, who report to me directly. I give them a lot of latitude. But for the most important decisions concerning finance, human resources, renovations, repairs and construction, I meet with the council once a month. We discuss each matter at great length and I make the final decision, usually based on their advice."

"Sister, you are a true leader. The locals of this province will never forget you and the mission. You will become a legend!"

"Thank you again, Colonel. Now let me show you the last sections of the complex, they are ateliers for artisans – usually elderly people – who can teach the young generation the intricacies of their specialties. They create beautiful objects that they can sell at the market and they teach their trades to the young at the same time: basket-weaving, embroidery, sewing, knitting, jewellery-making, engraving, wood-carving, dressmaking and more...

"Their arts are at risk of disappearing. They want to make sure that they will survive, and they have found the answer to the problem."

"And they can make a living at the same time."

"That is correct, Colonel. Now, you see this tall fortification at the centre of the square. It somehow splits the mission in two parts, one part is the convent, and the other is the monastery. We teach religion in both and the Jesuit priests go through the seminary. In our schools we educate boys and girls at all of primary, secondary, and high-school levels. On some occasions gifted students who have a calling to serve God can enter the orders."

"Sister, this is a marvellous place. How can you maintain such standards with a war raging around you?"

"We do not get involved in politics or military strategies. We are neutral and impartial."

"But you help the VC, I suppose?"

"Colonel this is a very poor question, if I may say so. I will answer it only by telling you this: we feed them when they are hungry, we treat their wounded, and also provide the same to their families. It also applies to the NVA. We have never refused to assist anyone in need and will never stop doing so. Families who have lost their bread-winners suffer very tragic circumstances, whether they are VC or not. God does not discriminate against anyone and wants us to help the needy. That is what we do.

"In our hospital we have treated US and Australian soldiers, civilians, VCs and NVAs alike. We are a religious sanctuary, Colonel. God cares about us all without any particular distinction, and we are saving thousands of lives through our food supplies and medical care. we have no enemies, just lives to save. Am I making myself clear, Colonel?"

I could see that Sister Marie Catherine was hot under the collar.

"Yes, you are, Sister, I apologize for my ignorance."

"Apologies accepted, Colonel."

We walked in silence for a while and then came face to face with a small church with a copper dome surmounted by cross.

"This is our chapel; we share it with a cloister within the convent walls, managed by a religious order called, 'The Order of the Visitation of Holy Mary'. They have been with us for a long time and perform missionary work worldwide; some of the young nuns join them after their studies."

"May I go inside, Sister?"

"But of course, Colonel. Would you like to pray? God will cleanse your soul of your sins. You will feel better afterwards, trust me."

*"How was the chapel, General?"*

"Sergeant, I had never seen such a lovely chapel in my entire life. It was small, perhaps twenty pews at most, but the art work and the care to detail were sublime. The ornate altar was gracefully decorated; the high ceiling inside the dome was majestic.

The frescoes depicted scenes from the Bible and portraits of the most famous Sisters of the Visitation since the establishment of the order by Saint Francis de Sales and Saint Jane Frances de Chantal in Annecy, Haute Savoie, France, in 1610.

A statue of the Virgin Mary, with an apple and a snake at her feet, had been placed close to the entrance door and a large crucifix was at the altar's right side.

The chapel was resplendent with numerous stained-glass windows interpreting the various passages of the scriptures. Their positions and shapes gave plenty of daylight inside. It was magical!

The motifs consisted of a simple linear structure from top to bottom on each wall. On one side, Adam and Eve, the last judgment, the life of Christ, the last supper; on the other, the Virgin Mary, biblical Saints and Patrons, kings and prophets, on the left side of the altar were scenes of the crucifixion, the Virgin and child in Majesty. Close to the entrance were symbolic themes, the coat of arms of France and many more…

"Sister this is stunning and so peaceful…"

"Yes, it is. In this chapel anyone can get closer to God. I come here a lot, and it inspires me. It is very small, but we also have a large church at the monastery which can accommodate our parishioners. Now I will let you pray, take your time.

"Before I leave please be aware that I have asked our staff to prepare a bath for all of you, we will also wash your clothes and repair them, as they are in shreds. Colonel, you should also shave, please, as they say you will feel better and like a soldier again.

"Sister Yvonne will wait for you outside and show you my office. Afterwards you will take a rest before meeting the council. We will have dinner together."

"But, Sister, please let me explain, I cannot…"

"Not another word, Colonel, here I am the boss. This is an order, understand?"

"Yes, Sister, whatever you say…"

*"So what happened, General?"*

I decided to pray. First, I walked around the chapel very slowly, looking at all the windows, the altar and the pews, crossed myself with the holy water and dropped to my knees and began praying. I felt so comfortable that I talked aloud to the Lord. Soon I was conversing with God, the Virgin Mary and Jesus all at once. Suddenly I heard some bells ringing faintly and the Sisters began to sing. The bells stopped after a while, but the incantation continued. I was there a long time. It felt very good to clear my mind, heart and soul. On my way out, I kissed the Virgin Mary's feet and touched Jesus on the cross, thanking them for keeping me alive through everything.

Sister Yvonne took me to the mother superior's office.

It was spartan, very clean and organized. Sister Marie Catherine was undoubtedly a good manager. She had worked hard to gain the respect of her colleagues and she carried an aura of authority with her. However, she remained polite and charming and even joked with staff and locals at every opportunity.

"Colonel, Sister Yvonne will stay with you as your aide-de-camp, please do not hesitate to ask for anything you need. From now on, you are our guest and friend at the mission. At 8pm we will meet the council and have dinner together. Father Benedetti has a lot of questions for you. So do the other members. I know that the two farmers spoke earlier at great length with him and our management committee…"

"Excuse me, Sister but I do not think that they could have told them very much. These men are shy and they get scared very easily…"

"They said enough, Colonel. Their story was baffling, to say the least, but we know for a fact that they did not lie. This evening I will introduce you to all the members of the council, we are a team of seven leaders of this mission. Now, Colonel please enjoy a good rest. We will wake you up at 7pm".

She made a gesture to Sister Yvonne and we left her office.

*"How was the hot bath, General?"*

"Sergeant, it was just divine and I slept like a log."

I was awakened at 7pm and got dressed in a new set of clothes prepared by the mission. It was time to meet the leaders of that great institution.

But I could not stop thinking about Jason sitting somewhere in a tree watching the area for VC patrols. I knew that he could handle himself without any problem but I worried about him for other reasons, such as his frame of mind and above all his new identity as 'Satan's loyal servant'.

I had to tell my story to the council, but would they believe me even though they were all people of the cloth? One way or the other, it did not matter, because I had the urge to narrate my encounter with the dark Lord and a hunch that somehow they were expecting to hear something beyond imagining!"

## CHAPTER TEN

## THE COUNCIL

*"Were they all French nationals on the council?"*

"Yes they were Jesuits and nuns who had been ordained in their respective communities."

*"Since they managed the mission, I presume they were extremely knowledgeable in their fields of expertise, General?"*

"Yes, Sergeant. Sister Marie Catherine, the chairperson, had given me a short introduction regarding their backgrounds and scope of duties; they were all highly educated with many years of experience in theology, education, business, medicine, surgery, the sciences, psychology and even exorcism."

*"It must have been a very interesting evening. What was the final outcome?"*

"Positive, Sergeant, they made me see the light and gave me strong determination and courage to carry on my mission, no matter how dangerous it was. Lucifer would interfere with my plans but they made me realize that he could never, never, beat God who had already blessed me."

We all sat at the dinner table at precisely 8pm. I was told that the kitchen staff had surpassed themselves in preparing a succulent meal, because Sister Marie Catherine had mentioned the words "special guests" to the chef.

The council numbered seven: Sister Marie Catherine, Sister Angele who was her assistant, Father Benedetti, Father Lucien his assistant, Father Romero, Sister Yvonne his assistant and Father Hervé. They were young, with the exception of Father Benedetti who must have been in his sixties. They formed an impressive team and ran the mission like a well-oiled machine.

Sister Marie Catherine asked Father Romero to say grace and we began to eat a wonderful spread of classical French and local cuisines.

"Colonel, I ask you again, who operated on Captain Henderson?" questioned Father Benedetti.

"Please answer, Colonel, it is of the utmost importance for us and for your own sake," added the mother superior.

"I will tell you everything. Even though some parts of my adventure may seem unreal, I promise you that they are true, undeniably authentic!"

"We believe you, Colonel; you are a great soldier and a man of honour and integrity. The two farmers have already told us the entire story and praised your courage and leadership. Nevertheless we need to hear all the pertinent details from you yourself, because you were the man in charge of the escape weren't you?"

"Yes I was, Father."

"Why did you choose to come to the mission?"

"Sister, I wanted to bury Henderson as a Christian."

"Any other reasons?"

"My soul has been bruised. The ordeals that I have suffered have also raised questions and doubts in my mind. Sister, I need clarification from the council."

"Continue, Colonel."

"I wanted to meet you in person, Sister. Your reputation precedes you, and I knew that you could help me spiritually, that your perspicacity was a real gift from God and that the mission would provide me with some comfort and peace before I got on with the escape. My team is waiting at a boat-house, so that we can all rejoin our respective units."

"I am aware of your plans, Colonel."

"I am perturbed by Jason's transformation and Lucifer's threats to steal one of my men again. I am a special forces officer and I feel impotent in confronting Satan's powers."

"We all understand, Colonel, but why don't we finish our dinner and after the coffee has been served you can have the floor..."

"Father, it may take a long time to tell..."

"Yes, but it is essential that we get all the facts and we shall take notes. Now, let's finish this delicious meal that God has offered us."

*"Did you tell them the entire story?"*

"Yes I did, from the time we escaped from the camp to the moment I rang the door-bell of the mission. I described, in the most infinite detail, our plan of escape, Henderson's death, our meetings with the village leader and the story of his infamous daughter Ahn, Rose and Dr Henri, and of course my encounter with the dark Lord and his demonic interventions.

I described the field with its altar and stone stools. I explained my conversations with the tiger, the transfiguration of Lucifer. I spoke at great length about Jason's possession and the rituals by which it took place, accentuated by the bizarre phenomena all around us.

I talked for more than three hours in all."

They were very attentive, took a lot of notes, nodding or shaking their heads every now and then, rarely smiling. The sisters crossed themselves two or three times. I was never interrupted.

*"Did you feel better after telling them what had happened?"*

"Yes indeed, it was a huge relief to get it off my chest!"

*"What did they do next, General?"*

It was a period of questions and answers, during which they took more notes. I got straight the point, I did not need to elaborate, and I had already given them the full story.

I noticed furtive glances among them but no comments were made.

They were particularly interested in Jason's behaviour and frame of mind, prior to the encounter with the devil and his initiation, and they wanted to know as much as possible about him.

They also asked for a lot of details about the jungle environment and of course, about the extraordinary occurrences which took place during Jason's transformation from a soldier to a servant of Lucifer.

Father Benedetti was more interested in Henderson's wound.

They wanted me to recall the details of the furry monsters. The Sisters crossed themselves once more regarding that matter.

*"Did everyone ask you questions? What about the two farmers?"*

"Yes we were quizzed by everyone. We cooperated fully with the council, and they wanted to know as much as possible in relation to their areas of proficiency. I think that the two farmers had been traumatized by it all, particularly when the dark Lord threatened them with their lives. They were really stressed, they cried, and Sister Yvonne calmed them down with some tea. It was a good meeting and they were very thorough in their lines of questioning, they wanted to help to make us feel better."

*"Did it last all night, General?"*

"Almost. At some point, Sister Marie Catherine announced that we were going to take a break. Cakes and coffee were served, the council members wanted to get together privately to review their notes. We would reconvene after a two-hour break. I was happy to oblige…"

*"What took place after the break, General?"*

"We reassembled and the members gave me their comments."

*"Was it enlightening?"*

"Very much so."

Sister Marie Catherine told me that to meet Satan was a peculiar sign of fate. She had witnessed exorcisms in the past, but had never heard of anyone who had seen the devil in person. She praised me for my inner spiritual strength to resist him. She remembered an old story about what happened in a convent in Vietnam in the mid-twenties.

*

The location was Phat-Diêm in the French protectorate of Tonquim (Vietnam). It was the novitiate of the Lovers of the Holy Cross Sisters. A young novice, Sister Marie Dien, had been cursed by a young pagan who was in love with her. But she decided to join the order, nevertheless. He went to a temple to seek revenge and asked the devil to punish her at the nunnery.

The demonic possession lasted two full years between 1924 and 1926. The entire religious community was condemned. Dom Louis de Cooman (former bishop for Vietnam), a young missionary at the time, witnessed it all, and was asked perform an exorcism. It was hard and took a long time but he was successful at the end.

Throughout the whole time, he advised the novices to pray, pray, and pray, because God was with them and was going to save them. The infestations of the devil lasted a few more years following Satan's departure until they disappeared completely.

It was painful, horrifying, and beyond belief, but Sister Marie Dien managed to endure the manifestations and was ordained at the convent. Most of the novices who had suffered during this ghastly episode joined the order at the exception of two or three who left for other reasons."

*

*"Wow, an amazing tale! Did she say anything else?"*

"Yes she did."

"You see, Colonel, the power of prayer is infinite, God, by the way, had allowed this to manifest."

"He did? But why?"

"To prove a point, he works in mysterious ways and at his own pace. Perhaps He wanted to show the jilted boy that he could not achieve his vindictive deed; by the same token he taught Lucifer, that no matter how hard he tried, he could never win against faith, prayers and the sacred heart. God teaches us lessons and tests us incessantly.

"The Sisters and young missionary managed very well, even though turmoil and a demonic presence were among them. God was undoubtedly proud of them as they passed the test.

"Life is a journey, Colonel. Fate controls everything that happens in our life. It is our engine. We drive, but fate is like jet-propulsion for us, it moves us forward. God will always help you if you also help yourself. In France we say, 'Help yourself and the sky will help you!' Do you understand?"

"Yes, Sister, I do."

"Now this old story in Vietnam changed my life, Colonel. When I was ordained I took the name of Marie Catherine because Sister Marie Dien had been my inspiration, and I volunteered to come to Vietnam. She passed away in 1944, but she is still my mentor, my motivator. She watches over me every step of the way.

"God is with you, like he is with me, Colonel!

"Colonel, we have evaluated your plan of escape. It is likely you will face a tremendous amount of aggravation because of constraints and barriers that Satan my create to make you fail. However, we will support you in your endeavour. We shall pray for you and your team to be picked up by a cavalry regiment or a navy patrol. My team here present will speak with you on various topics, but I want to make sure that you receive the spiritual help that you came here to seek.

"Always keep a cool head, be on your guard at all times. You are hunted by the VC, the NVA and Lucifer. It might be too much for one man, but we all have faith in you. Look, you have made it so far! Pray, Colonel, pray, remember that the power of prayer is limitless!

"The people you have met and who have helped you on your way to the mission are also familiar with us. We know them well: Rose, the village leader, and Dr Henri is a good friend of Father Benedetti. Am I correct, Father?"

"Yes, Sister. He is a surgeon and we have a professional relationship."

"The boat-house is a safe haven for you and your team. The owner is a friend of our kitchen chef and he sells us beautiful fish. He comes here from time to time, and Father Hervé teaches him English. Am I right?"

"Yes, Sister, he has helped many US soldiers to escape. He hates the VC. So, Colonel, do not be concerned, you and your team will be safe with him."

"You have heard about Ahn. We also know her. She despises me. This mission is highly regarded for all that we do in the community. NVA soldiers as well as the VC are treated here. The Vatican, the governments of France, the US and Australia have all praised our efforts, but she came here making totally unacceptable demands and returned empty-handed. It did not sit well with her at all. She was later told by the Communist Party to leave us alone. She chose to ignore it and returned. This time I refused to let some seriously-wounded VC go back with her. She cursed and threatened me with my life, and so I reported her to the upper echelon of her organization. Finally, her superiors ordered her to avoid the mission altogether. We have not seen her since. Colonel, rest assured that she is Lucifer's faithful servant. I saw it in her eyes. She is cruel, egotistical and callous. She might be unrepentant when she faces God. Consequently hell will be her point of no return.

## CHAPTER ELEVEN

## A SISTER WITH A PAST

"But let the others speak about their experiences with Lucifer and God Almighty, it will surely be enlightening and give you the answers that you are looking for. Are you ready, Colonel?"

"I am, Sister. Your story has been extremely informative. After all, that is the reason why I came here."

"Thank you, Colonel. Sister Yvonne, please, your turn."

Sister Yvonne crossed herself and began.

*

I was born and educated in Nantes, in the west of France near the Atlantic coast. Like Jason, I have a past. I am no longer ashamed of it. I have learnt how to live with it and use it as a teaching tool with the novices and my students here at the mission. I was raised in a middle-class family of two children. My parents worked hard to give us a good education and what we needed in the best environment possible. I was always a very good student throughout my entire academic life; I won prizes in primary, secondary and high school and made the dean's list at university. I first went to Toulouse University to study classical literature, Latin, Arts and Philosophy. By then my private life was a mess; yes, outside of the classroom I was depraved and promiscuous. I had no friends, nobody wanted to hang around with me, and people used very offensive adjectives to describe me.

It all began in high school. By the time I was fifteen or sixteen years old, I was smoking heavily, drank like a fish and eventually used drugs. My parents, who loved me very much, tried their hardest to reason with me but to no avail. Surprisingly my grades were remarkable.

My parents could not understand it, they were aware of my debauched behaviour but it did not affect my grades. Why?

We all went to meet the principal and, as expected, I was the top of my class in every subject. My attendance record was one hundred percent: for the past six years, I had never missed a single day! I was a high performer, an "A" student and I only had one more year of high school before going to university. My first choice was a very old institution in France, the University of Toulouse.

The principal was puzzled because usually students with shabby lifestyles get expelled from school quickly. Their grades keep falling, they miss classes and they usually give up studying altogether. Not me, my grade-point averages kept increasing and for the past four years I had been receiving bursaries. He consoled my parents by saying that things would be better the following year, that I was going through a teenage phase, and that I would be graduating with the highest score in the history of the school. Actually, I achieved that, but I did not have a career path yet, facing an uncertain future, and my private life was still in shambles, I liked arts, class debates, languages, and wrote English fluently.

For the past four years during the winter break and the summer holidays I had gone abroad to live with an English family in Surrey. In the back of my mind I was considering going to study at universities in the United Kingdom. As a foreigner I had to take English-language exams and I was preparing for this. My parents of course were concerned about letting me live on my own when going to university or abroad – rightly so – but that is what I wanted to do.

Why did I act in such a way? A voice inside pushed me, coerced me, sometimes cajoled me by using sweet words or forcefully ordered me to drink, smoke, shoot drugs into my veins and sleep with men whose names I never asked. When I was in England it all stopped. My behaviour was exquisite and my parents received nothing but compliments from the elderly couple with whom I lived. Once again they were confused and one summer came to visit. They were agreeably surprised by my appearance, the cleanliness of my room, my way of dressing and my table-manners. They questioned me about the change but I refused to talk about it. The voice had stopped, I was me, Yvonne, the real me, the way I should always have been. Why did it cease in England?

Each time I returned from England, it was there, always taunting me, mocking me, telling me that because I had had a nice break from it all and since I had been such a good girl for a while, it was now time to enjoy life again, to be a party animal, I deserved it and who could stop me?

The voice wanted me to obey, to do exactly as it said. I had to be bad because it suited me best. My parents had no power over me anymore. Besides, my marks were superb, I was the best student in school and never missed class. What I did with my free time was not their business. The voice had become my master. This voice was in fact my misery; it induced me to do wrong, to perform evil acts, to destroy my health and reputation, to hurt my family and even to become nothing less than a street prostitute. Very often I never changed my clothes, I did not bath for days, did not come home. My last year of high school was the worst. I slept with men for money. I told lies and said that I needed the money for my university tuition. Some older folks felt sorry for me and paid handsomely for special treatments. The voice inside me rejoiced and praised me for my cleverness. I did it many times and used the cash to buy liquor, cigarettes and drugs.

Somehow, deep inside my heart I felt ashamed, disgusted with myself because I knew that the Yvonne I was in England – the good person, polite, clean, sophisticated – was in fact the real me. Now I was a disgrace, an absolute wreck, a lost soul. But this voice kept haunting me... It prodded me into performing immoral acts and working for immoral earnings. From one part of me I wanted it to stop, but on the other side I could not. I did not have the power to do it, I did not know how! And even if I wanted to, I could not do it, because the voice was that of the Devil himself, Lucifer's voice!

I graduated with top honours and took an exam to go to the University of Toulouse; I passed it with flying colours and went for a week's holiday to the city of Chartres in northern France. I stayed at a small pension, where the concierge was a Madame Labelle. We got along well right away and on the second evening she invited me for dinner. She had prepared a homemade meal that was out of this world. We sat down in her kitchen and she asked me questions about my family, my school, my plans for the future, my boyfriends, she was a curious lady but in a nice way.

"Why did you come to Chartres, young lady?" asked Madame Labelle.

"To rest, relax a little before starting university. My parents and I do not particularly get along. I prefer to be on my own and it is a nice place."

"What exactly is bothering you, Yvonne?" Madame Labelle came close to me and for the first time I noticed how beautiful her eyes were, they were blue, deep blue and shone like crystal.

"Nothing, really nothing, Madame Labelle."

"Of course there is, my child, you are in deep trouble inside, not at school, but your life is in turmoil. He is inside you isn't he?"

"How do you know that?"

"Because I do. I am here to help you. You and I and the priest will get rid of him forever, you'll see."

"Then I burst into tears, I sobbed uncontrollably, holding on to her for a long time. She did not say a word, just caressed my hair, she held me tight and I cried..."

"Now you need to clean up and get yourself ready. We are going to the Cathedral to meet the priest. He is waiting for you; I told him that you were coming. Go on, I will make you a cup of coffee."

## CHAPTER TWELVE

## MEETING THE ALMIGHTY

After a long shower, a change of clothes and a fresh cup of black coffee, Madame Labelle and I went to the most beautiful Cathedral in France. We have many magnificent basilicas in our country, but none can compare to Chartres. It is a majestic example of French gothic architecture with dozens of stained-glass windows picturing the history of Christianity, small chapels, and staircases; and it is big, very big!

"When was the last time that you received communion?" asked Madame Labelle.

"I cannot remember, maybe for my confirmation when I was fourteen years old."

"It is time to live a Christian life, my child. Today is your day, the priest inside will guide you. You are a lost sheep who needs to rejoin the flock. Do you want to change, Yvonne?"

"Yes, I do. I cannot endure the pain anymore. But what will Satan say? Is he ever going to leave me alone?"

"Yes, my child; he has no choice. Now, inside the cathedral you may feel uncomfortable. We are here to help you all the way. Satan will be angry and is going to try to dissuade you from reuniting with us. Reject him, do not accept him anymore, do you hear me?"

"Yes, I do, but please stay with me."

"I will be close to you, you may not see me but you will feel me, my presence will be all around you. You can trust the father to get rid of the Devil, listen to what he has to say, tell the truth and only the truth because he will know if you ever lie!"

"Are you a friend of the father, Madame Labelle?"

"Yes, I do work with him every once in a while, we nurture an excellent relationship."

"Yvonne, we have arrived. The father told me to use the side door because it is already late and the cathedral has closed to the general public!" We climbed a long flight of stairs and walked into the Cathedral.

It was the most beautiful place I had ever seen, its immense size made it impressive, the atmosphere was calm and reposeful, the windows were bright and colourful, the high ceiling and murals were painted with frescoes and every column was flanked by statues. The altar was draped in white, with two gold candelabras standing on each side.

"Let's sit in the front," said Madame Labelle.

We sat in a pew and suddenly I felt a strong blow to my stomach. I was hit with such force that I folded in two and dropped to my knees. Madame Labelle picked me up and we began praying. Soon after, a nauseating feeling came to my throat but I had no time to move before a huge flow of green bile spurted out of my mouth. I stood up to leave but was pulled back by Madame Labelle onto my seat.

"Do not move, wait for the father!"

There was no doubt in my mind that Satan was acting up again and that he wanted me to suffer very much for having entered a church, his enemy's territory.

He exclaimed, "How dare you, you brat! You will pay dearly for your impertinence. What are you thinking about to come into a church!"

Then I noticed, resting on the pew in front of my eyes, a black book with a leather cover. "Book of the Abyss" was embossed on it with gold letters. It was, we may say, Lucifer's Bible.

"Open it and read the first page," the Devil told me.

I was not sure at that point what to do, but I had a very bad feeling that this black book was cursed.

I turned around to talk to Madame Labelle but she was gone. I had not seen her leave. I looked around but there was no sign of her. Then I realized that I had to hold my own until the father arrived.

"Go on, your master orders you to open it and read the first page. Are you dumb or what?" he snarled.

"No," I replied.

"What did you say to me?"

I knew then that he was very angry. There was a pause…

Whack! Whack! Whack!

I was slapped on the face three times with full force. My nose and lips were bleeding, but I did not open the book.

"You are not my master; I am Yvonne, my own person," I yelled out.

"So, that is the way it's going to be! As you wish!" he retorted.

Wham! Wham! Wham!

I was hit repeatedly with the black book: on my face, on my head, on the back of my neck. I protected myself the best way I could with my hands. More blows ensured.

I called for Madame Labelle but I received no reply. She was gone.

"Now impudent little slut to teach you a lesson…," he howled.

Suddenly, without warning, sharp pains hit me in the stomach. It felt like I had been stabbed, but there was no blood, again, again and again…

"Please stop it!" I screamed.

"Ohhh…you are not so arrogant now are you?" he chuckled.

I opened my mouth to vomit and to my horror the head of a snake stuck out, I froze, unable either to think or react. The reptile slowly slid out and dropped to the floor by the pew. I was coughing up blood. The reptile was not very long, black in colour and moving very quickly. It was hissing loudly, its yellow eyes looking straight at me, its long fangs ready to bite me…

"This is a viper from Hell, a poisonous little darling just for you, Yvonne. What do you have to say now?"

"You are doing great, Yvonne, keep fighting him! Do not let that snake frighten you, Lucifer cannot beat you, but never open that book, never, do you hear? I am with you and the father is coming soon, you'll see…"

"Madame Labelle? Is that you? Where are you?" I shouted.

"Who are you talking to? Who is it?" Satan asked.

I did not reply. I was still watching the viper. I was moving slowly from pew to pew, but it was following me, baring its fearsome fangs, hissing incessantly, and looking at me with its glacial, yellow, eyes.

Then I noticed two bare feet wearing leather sandals. The right foot moved forward, flattening the vicious creature's head with a loud thud noise.

Stomp!

When I looked up the priest was there. He had saved me from an uncertain fate. He was a tall man in his thirties, wearing a long black robe with a white collar, he had long hair and had not shaved for a couple of days. His piercing blue eyes were staring at me.

"Sorry for being late, Yvonne, I see that you are having a confrontation with my old foe…"

"Father, look at that strange book, Satan wanted me to read it. Madame Labelle instructed me to never open it. I listened to her advice."

"You were perfectly right not to open it. Let's get rid of it at once!" the father said.

He picked up the Book of the Abyss and, right in front of my eyes, it was pulverized into dust. Wow! In the space of one minute, the father had saved me from a deadly snake and got rid of a demonic manuscript.

"Yvonne, Madame Labelle wanted me to meet you because you have been having trouble with Lucifer who has been tormenting you. Let's go to the sacristy and we will be able to talk privately. He is not going to hurt you anymore, trust me."

We sat down in the small room behind the altar, where holy objects and special clothes for ceremonies were kept.

"Now, Yvonne, tell me all about you, your family, your school, your friends, and when the possession began. I want to hear only the truth. Go on!"

He listened attentively while I spoke, it lasted a long time, and he wanted details, a lot of them. I showed him the needle-marks from the syringes, my teeth yellow from nicotine stains, I told him about the alcohol addiction and my depravity. He nodded and smiled.

"Father, I feel that I am evil myself. I have told you about all the horrible things that I have done. I have hurt my family so much that I do not think that they will ever forgive me, ever!"

"Yvonne, you are already absolved from your sins and misbehaviour. You were seduced by Lucifer and were not quite yourself for a long period of time. Your family loves you and you will be received with open arms upon your return. You will pursue a very successful academic life. You have a very good mind and, most important, you are born to help people. You will serve others and God will be proud of you, so will your parents. You have a great future ahead, keep working at it."

"But, Father, I have not served God well. I am a bad

Christian, why would he want to help me?"

"God is all-forgiving. Satan waylaid you in the bloom of your youth and coerced you into a life of sin. From now on, you are going to lead a true Christian life. Please attend communion tomorrow. Father Guillaume will be celebrating the mass at 9am."

"Are you not going to be here, Father?"

"No, Yvonne. I am needed in another Parish, I help the clergy in various ways."

"Are you officially assigned to Chartres Cathedral, Father?"

"No, I often give sermons here, but I also preach in many other churches around the word. I help priests, work as a mentor for seminarians and nuns, visit monasteries and convents, and, where it is needed, try to enlarge the number of worshippers. I consider it as part of my duties to save lost souls from the claws of Lucifer."

"And it worked. Thank you, Father."

"You are welcome, he should not bother you anymore. But he is tenacious, so be on your guard! Keep praying every day, and you will be all right."

"What is your name? How old are you? Madame Labelle told me that she helps you only from time to time. Does she reside at the pension?"

"You can call me 'Father'. I am thirty-two years old and Madame Labelle is too humble. She comes to Chartres only occasionally and takes care of lost souls – sheep that go astray. It is demanding and it requires a lot of her attention. Whenever you need help, talk to us through your daily prayers."

"I heard her voice earlier. Is she still here with us?"

"No, but she is constantly watching over you,. I asked her to do so. She will never leave you from now on. We both protect you. You resisted the demon and we are proud of you, Yvonne.

You are beginning a new life, with a clean slate, a life of devotion and serenity. I suggest that you study religion at university, learn about the Bible, about the origins of our faith. It will be very interesting, probably an eye-opener."

"I will, Father, I promise…"

His deep blue eyes looked straight through me, I even felt a little embarrassed. But his presence and the tone of his voice comforted me. He was genuinely kind and thoughtful. There was also something special about him, he exuded strength, power, confidence, and authority. He was a man people would listen to attentively. He commanded respect.

"Yvonne, you need to take better care of yourself, now that your addictions are things of the past. Keep up your hygiene, show people that you are really pretty with a good disposition and you will make a lot of friends at the university.

"Please show me your arms."

He pulled my sleeves up and looked at the needle-marks. I told him that I had shot up in various parts of my body. He did not say a word. He placed his hands on mine, then he caressed my hair, my face, my lips. His eyes were closed. Then he stood up and hugged me tightly for a few seconds.

"I want you to have these," he told me.

He pulled an old book out of a drawer. The words, "The Bible", were embossed with gold letters on the brown leather cover.

"This is a token of my appreciation, you deserve it. You can read it at your leisure. It is not only holy but also depicts the most important historical facts and stories of our faith."

Then he took out a small gold chain with a cross and placed it around my neck.

"This will protect you against harm and misfortune; I have blessed them for you."

"Thank you, Father, I will cherish them with all my heart." He smiled and said, "Now let's go to pray together."

We returned inside the cathedral, and I sat at a pew. There were no traces of the viper or the grey dust.

"Yvonne, come and kneel down with me at the altar."

I did not really remember my prayers well but I recited them in my own way. The father was speaking to God in a low tone of voice and I recognized Latin at first, but he switched to a language that I could not comprehend. The cathedral being closed, the room was dimly lit, but all of a sudden a very bright illumination descended into the centre of the cathedral. There was not a sound or a word spoken, just a blinding light, over three metres tall, in the middle of the aisle.

The father stood up and walked towards the shining light, he knelt before it, his palms facing upwards.

I was curious and approached the scene.

He seemed to be talking to it, even answering questions, but strangely enough I did not hear anything.

I came even closer and now a conversation was definitely taking place. The father was nodding, occasionally shaking his head, but there was no sound whatsoever.

I saw him make some gestures and smile. Then he lifted his head, joined his hands together, and bowed. The vibrant luminosity disappeared in a flash. The apparition had lasted no more than two minutes…

"Sorry, Yvonne, it was a message from the Almighty, giving me instructions for a future assignment."

"Do you mean God was here, Father?"

He nodded, smiling.

I went down to my knees and cried.

"Yvonne, cheer up! God came personally to visit a priest and you witnessed it! That was a fabulous experience, wasn't it?"

"I will never forget that moment, never!"

"Yvonne, I must be leaving soon, and you have a mass to attend tomorrow at 9am We should go home."

"Can I ask you some questions before you go?"

"Sure, go ahead, Yvonne!"

"What language did you speak earlier at the altar?"

"I first prayed in Latin and then switched to Aramaic when I spoke with God. It is an old Semitic language with variations of Hebrew and Arabic.

"Why didn't Lucifer bother me whenever I went to England?"

"It was a game, a masquerade. He is a deceiver, arrogant, a fierce enemy, but not invincible. He toyed with you and made you believe that he had gone, that you were finally free of him. Because you never drank nor used drugs in Surrey you felt like a new Yvonne. But as soon as you went back home he had you under his thumb, because he is evil and a liar. You were strong and resisted him, he liked it and did not hurt your grades in school. Now and then he gave you a little freedom, enough rope to hang yourself. He was not in hurry to destroy your life because he already had his claws into you.

"Lucifer is extremely shrewd. He is the Devil but retains the intelligence of an angel and thinks like one in order to catch new prey. He looks for cracks in their souls, weaknesses, and bad habits, and then he strikes like a snake. That is why his nickname is the 'Great Serpent'". Yvonne, he knew all about you, and he has been following you for years."

"Father, I did not go to confession. How can I take communion tomorrow?"

"You confessed all your sins to me today. You are fine. You can take communion with Father Guillaume tomorrow morning."

“When can I see Madame Labelle again? I would like to talk to her.”

“You are going to see her very soon. She will clarify a few more things with you. I discussed it with her earlier.”

“Thank you, Father.”

“Now I must leave, it was a pleasure to meet you. You are going to do very well in Toulouse. If your objective is to study in England, just work on it! Remember, if you help yourself, the sky will help you!”

The father hugged me again and we left the Cathedral. I went back to the pension. It had been an unforgettable evening. I had been part of a sequence of events that I will remember for the rest of my life!

# CHAPTER THIRTEEN

## ON THE RIGHT TRACK

*Sister Yvonne Continues Her Story*

I walked back to the *pension*, trying to piece together all the happenings of the day. I was certainly confused, but I was happy. I had never felt so good in years. It was a quiet night, the weather was beautiful. I decided to take a stroll, while focusing my thoughts on Toulouse University, on my future courses, and trying to sort out the recommendations given by the father and Madame Labelle. I still had not chosen a career but I had time to think about it.

I was free of Satan but I had to lead a serious Christian life. I wanted to do so but I did not know how. That is why I needed more guidance from Madame Labelle. In my room I started thinking, "Who was the father? Why did God come personally to talk to him? Was Madame Labelle a nun?" While I was undressing I noticed that my arms had no needle-marks; they were all gone! My entire body no longer showed any signs of past addiction. My teeth were immaculate and the dark rings around my eyes had disappeared.

I was in a state of shock! How did these thing happen? I was sitting on my bed, crying, when I noticed in a corner the shape of a person advancing slowly towards me.

"Who is there?" I shouted.

"Do not be afraid, Yvonne; it's me, Madame Labelle"

"How did you get in? The door was locked."

"I am an angel, the angel of fortitude, who has been sent to protect you."

At that moment a halo appeared illuminating the room.

"Lucifer could never win over your soul, Yvonne. But now you have a lot of catching up to do."

We spoke for a long time, she answering my queries. I learnt that the father, who was none other than Jesus himself, had purified my body from Lucifer's demonic curse. The Almighty had suggested that I be led on a successful career-path because, "She will serve us faithfully when the time comes". Those were his words.

My resilience, my inner spiritual strength, and my hatred for Lucifer had all convinced Jesus of the need for my salvation, supported by God and my guardian angel.

When she left the room I fell sound asleep.

The following morning I was at the cathedral receiving communion, father Guillaume celebrating the mass. When he pronounced the words, "the body of Christ," and offered me the Eucharist, I was overwhelmed by a strange sensation, a combination of relief and pride. I was now a true Christian and God was with me. I felt strong and free.

The mass was over, the congregation had left the church, and I was praying at my pew.

Father Guillaume noticed me and approached. "Good morning , my child, did you enjoy the mass?"

"Yes, Father, I received communion for the first time since my confirmation. From now on I will attend church service regularly, I promise."

"Good idea, but what is prompting the change?"

He sat beside me and I told him about my destructive behaviour and actions, my family, my school marks and Toulouse University. I could not divulge any further information. Not only would it seem a rather improbable story, but I wanted it to be my personal secret. I thought that, after all, Madame Labelle was my guardian angel and she and Jesus had decided to help me. God had also given a personal message. As a result, I felt at the time that it was of crucial importance not to reveal these spiritual occurrences.

Father Guillaume nodded. He smiled and said, "My child, we need to purify our souls on a regular basis. Communion and confession take care of that. I am glad that you have decided to take a new path to success in your life. It is for the best and I wish you good luck. God be with you." He blessed me and left.

I returned home and very quickly my parents realized that I had changed for the better.

I cleaned and repainted my room, gave away some of my old clothes and went to the gym to get in shape. Once in Toulouse I continued to exercise and attended church service every Sunday. I made a lot of new friends.

It is one of the oldest educational institutions in France and the faculty was outstanding. It is listed as an original medieval university and I studied Classics with Latin and English as my core curriculum.

I had realized that to receive a formal college education was essential to give me a strong base to further both my academic and professional qualifications.

During the summer breaks, I also attended Cambridge University. Because I was a French native I was required to pass certain high-level English-language exams in order to be able to study in the UK. I lived in residence and enjoyed the atmosphere tremendously. Four years of college passed by very quickly. It was now time to embark on a new career path.

I was predestined to pursue a life of service, to serve God fully, devoting myself to help the needy. Jesus had given me a strong message and I had listened to it.

I opted for a nursing career, knowing well that it was a hard job with long hours, very few holidays, weekend duties, a lot of blood and gory details on a daily basis. My parents were thrilled when I told them that my ambition was to become a top nurse in the emergency room or the operating block.

My father introduced me to a lady who was working in that capacity in Paris. It was a very rewarding career, but required many years of studies, discipline, and strong physical fitness. She had received a master's degree in nursing and served an internship in the country's top hospitals. She convinced me to aim high. I was ready to undertake the long climb to the top. I passed all my English tests, and following a gruelling exam, I was accepted in the nursing programme at Glasgow University in Scotland.

I loved Scotland and its sublime scenery, but my studies kept me extremely busy, so I did not have much time to travel around. The bachelor's degree with honours in nursing took four years to complete and consisted of many compulsory courses, to which I added electives to enhance my major: Latin, English, Philosophy, Psychology and Religious Studies, to name a few. I applied for summer internships in the UK and abroad, whenever available. I also enrolled for the registered nurse (RN) qualification which I could complete within the time-frame of my degree. Everything went very well, I was sent to get practical experience at famous hospitals in London, Manchester, Leeds, and Newcastle. I gained a lot of experience and met a nurse in London who became my mentor. I still communicate with her.

I requested to perform research work at the University of Pierre and Marie Curie in Paris and was granted permission. It was a very rewarding internship. The staff were extremely professional and I performed analyses and tests that were of crucial importance in saving patients' lives. It was serious and hands-on and gave me a new outlook on laboratory work. It was never boring.

I was still exercising, swimming, and going to church on Sunday. I had found the Bible to be remarkable reading, but mysterious and intricate. My religious studies classes at Toulouse University and Glasgow helped me to understand it better.

On many occasions I was struggling with the content. It was difficult for me to understand the meaning of the book of God. I prayed for help. Occasionally my dreams were a source of inspiration but not sufficient to enlighten me. One night Madame Labelle visited me and helped me to decipher the complexity of this marvellous story, "the Bible".

She sat on my bed and discussed with me its origins, how it was written, naming some of the famous apostles who had contributed to its creation. All the while she was laughing and teasing me, "Come on, Yvonne, you are a great student with a fabulous memory. You can do it! But you have to peruse it many times over. It is a beautiful story that you will carry with you for the rest of your life.

"You have to interpret it in your own way, sometimes. Go through it back and forth; it is not a class manual, it is life. It deals with the rich and the poor, joy and sorrow, moral and ethical dilemmas, the struggles, wars, and thoughts of various classes in society. Even though it is an ancient book, it will never become obsolete. Relax, Yvonne, do not get frustrated, read it slowly; it will turn out to be your most interesting and loyal bedtime reading."

Then she disappeared.

I went through only a few pages at a time every day. On some occasions, I visited the local priest to ask him for advice and I found out that the Bible was in some ways a narrative written over a very long period by many people. It was not composed by God, Mary or Jesus, but by his apostles, his followers and famous personalities of their day. It includes thoughts, facts, and events that nowadays we could call "reporting". As I became more familiar with it, the chapters were easier to comprehend.

I decided to pursue my studies and work for a Master of Science degree in nursing. I stayed at the University of Glasgow because it was a very good school and I liked the environment. I took some time to visit the country and was fascinated by the scenery and its people. Scotland has an interesting history and a lot of traditions. My trips were very educational.

Internships were included in the curriculum and again I enrolled immediately. I also took courses at St Andrews University, in Philosophy, Psychology and Ethics to reinforce my general knowledge. I have nothing but fond memories of that remarkable institution.

The Master of Science programme included management courses and leadership, as some graduates wanted eventually to get into hospital administration. I enjoyed it, but preferred direct contact with patients. I also had to choose a specialty, and selected obstetrics and gynaecology. It was hard, the schedules were very demanding, but I found this area of medicine fascinating.

I was sent to London for internships at two different famous institutions, the Royal London Hospital and St Bartholomew's. I worked with top surgeons and did stints in the trauma centres.

The programme lasted two years and I graduated with top honours. I moved to St Andrews for one year to complete different courses and I received diplomas in Philosophy and Psychology. Even with all these degree in my pocket, I still needed a full-time job. I received many offers in the UK and they were very attractive. However, I did not want to rush into anything. I was contemplating undertaking something new, preferably in France. I went home, and my parents, who were very proud of me, agreed with my decision to take some time off and seek employment prospects very carefully.

L'Hôpital Général de Montpellier in the south of France attracted me, not only because the medical school in that city was number one in Europe, but because I knew that the expertise that I could acquire there would be invaluable for my career. I wrote to them and was accepted. The letter specified the obstetrics and gynaecology departments; I was thrilled and thanked God for all his help.

# CHAPTER FOURTEEN

# WORKING WITH THE BEST

*Sister Yvonne Continues Her Story*

The General Hospital in Montpellier was a foremost medical facility which could handle any type of surgery, twenty-four hours a day, seven days a week. Because it had built a solid international reputation, patients who required intensive care and/or delicate operations were flown to the hospital to be examined. We were extremely busy and I worked rotating shifts with very little rest.

Many of the surgeons were also "professors of medicine" for the medical school and were teaching their respective specialties. Students were assigned to individual departments and the interns had religiously to attend the daily patient visits conducted by the head surgeons. I was not a student anymore but I could relate to their anxieties, perplexities, and thirst for knowledge.

I was still exercising, swimming in the blue Mediterranean, and attending church faithfully.

The hospital chapel was beautiful and I prayed there often, I also became good friends with the chaplain.

My mentor in London advised me to talk to the chief of surgery about my plans and above all to play my cards right. She also suggested that doing a few stints in the Emergency Room (ER) could eventually get me a full-time position later. I followed her advice. I asked to meet in private with the Chief of Surgery; in France we call him, "Le Grand Patron".

My interview with him was short and to the point. I

explained my aspiration to work in the emergency room or the operating block, it had always been my goal even before I enrolled in the nursing programme. I realized that I needed a lot of training and practice but I was ready to make the extra effort and spend all the necessary hours in order to attain the level of proficiency required.

He listened attentively and never interrupted me.

"You will need to learn internal medicine and other areas of surgery. Obstetrics and gynaecology are a good start, but in the ER you must deal with all types of emergency, you must become versatile. It is not an easy place to work. It is very stressful and the shifts are very long, do you realize that?" he asked.

I replied that constraints came with the job and that I did not mind them.

"Le Patron" nodded and told me that he would look at my files more thoroughly and make a decision accordingly. He shook my hand and I returned to my department.

I was somehow distraught and cried in my bed at night.

"Were they ever going to give me the break that I had been waiting for?" I thought.

Madame Labelle come to visit and her presence was soothing. She reasoned with me and explained that everything took time, not to be impatient, that God was watching over me. I was fortunate enough to work with the "cream of the crop" in the medical field and soon my dreams were going to materialize. She explained that the Almighty had not made his decision yet, that he proceeded at his own pace; but to remember that patience was a virtue close to his heart and that he had his own way of helping us. With these words she kissed me on the forehead and as she was leaving she turned around and said, "please talk to Mary," and she vanished. I kept working in my department for the next three months without any further news. I took refuge from the stress in the hospital chapel.

The chaplain and I enjoyed a good conversation now and then and he was aware of my anxiety to move up to better things; but his words were, "Yvonne, I have been a chaplain in this hospital a very long time and you are one of the most gifted nurses that I have ever seen. I am convinced that 'Le Patron' has already noticed your ability and competence, so keep doing what you are doing and God will do the rest."

Madame Labelle had said exactly the same thing. Therefore without hesitation I knew what route to take…

"At night time I seem to forget to include Mary in my prayers, is it a bad oversight?"

"Yvonne, Mary is a major force in our religion and an important figure in the Bible. She brings comfort to many of us, health and resolution for our dilemmas. Yes, you should involve her in your conversation with the Lord."

"I will from now on, Father."

"Is there anything else, Yvonne, that is troubling you?"

"Do you mind if we talk about Mary Magdalene?"

"Not at all, but it is an unusual topic, if I may say so."

"I cannot tell you why, at this time, Father, but there is an affinity between her, myself and the fact that I work with women every day, some of them with very bad lifestyles. She appears fifty-four times in the Bible and was one of the most loyal and ardent followers of Jesus. Was she really a prostitute or did she only have loose morals? Jesus pardoned her sins and she became a very close friend of his mother, Mary. However, I have read contradictory statements and opinions on her past and her promiscuity prior to meeting the Lord. Can you enlighten me on the subject?"

The chaplain was staring at me intensely without saying a word. After a long pause he said, "I will, Yvonne, but is there anything that you would like to discuss, besides the mysteries of the Bible?"

"Not now, Father. Perhaps one of these days. Please tell me about her and how I should interpret her role in the Holy Book of God. After all, she has been called Jesus' right arm on many occasions. She was the apostle of the apostles.

The chaplain complied with my request. He was so knowledgeable that I felt it was like being in a catechism class all over again. What he said was extremely informative and I promised to come to see him again very soon. His teaching was totally different from what I had received at university.

One morning, upon finishing a graveyard shift, I received a call to go to see "Le Patron". I went to his office in my bloody uniform.

"Go to change and meet me in operating block No. 3," he said.

When I arrived, pliers, scissors, scalpels, tongs and an electric saw were lined up on metal trays.

Two head surgeons, the anaesthetist, an intern and a head nurse were assisting "Le Patron". I was there to observe the surgery and focus my attention on the nurse's duties.

A man's leg that was very badly infected had to be amputated above the knee. It was a ghastly sight and the smell was horrid. It was a first for me. The procedure was difficult and took a long time. I did not stand in anybody's way and observed the skills of the master.

At one point during the procedure, the leg was separated from the body and placed in my arms. I had to carry it somewhere else to be examined.

"Yvonne, this is your test, stay calm, it is only a test!" I told myself.

The surgeons worked swiftly, efficiently, with precision;

and I admired their professionalism. The master's dexterity was simply extraordinary to watch.

Once the operation was completed the head nurse whispered, "Good work, Yvonne". I felt really proud.

A few days later, "Le Patron" asked to see me.

"Yvonne, I liked what I saw the other day. I have made my decision and drafted a three-year contract, effective immediately, with specific instructions regarding your internship with the concentration, 'on the job training'. You will remain in your department, but from now on I also place you on call to assist the doctors in the ER and operating-blocks. If you want to further your career, you should consider this offer very seriously. You have three days to decide."

He shook my hand and I left his office with the papers in my hand.

I did not have much time to decide. My parents were very excited and encouraged me to accept the offer.

Down at the bottom of my heart I sought spiritual advice and I found it one night while praying.

Out of nowhere, a lady spoke to me in a soft and modulated tone of voice, "You called me because you are in a quandary. Yvonne, follow your heart. You have my blessing but God wants you to be fully responsible for your actions. Do you understand this message, Yvonne?"

"Mary, is that you?"

"Yes, I am Mary."

"I understand your message."

"You have a great future ahead of you, but at a later date we will meet face to face, because you are going to need my instructions regarding a very serious matter. But for now, good luck, Yvonne!" And she was gone!

That night I slept like a log and in the morning I went to

meet the chaplain. He was jubilant and full of praise for my proposed contract. He was adamant that I sign it without any delay. I was going to receive the best training in Europe and could not miss this opportunity. He was very insistent on the matter. I left the chapel and signed the papers.

"Le Patron" shook my hand and said, "You have made the right decision, Yvonne". He had a smile on his face.

For the next three years I only worked, ate and slept. Days of rest and vacations were sparse; on occasion I went to church in town, swam at the beach if the weather permitted it, used the gym at the university, and took communion at the chapel. The chaplain had become my mentor in Montpellier but I still communicated regularly with the English nurse. She was very proud of me and glad that I had followed her guidance. She explained that it usually took eight years of practice to become a fully-fledged ER or operating-room assistant. Since I had only been working full-time for two years, I had a long way to go! She emphasized the fact that my three-year internship was a first step in my career, I had to continue with another three additional years somewhere else, preferably a very famous hospital in Paris or London, England, only then could I get a top job in a renowned establishment. Wow! It sounded like a tall ladder to climb with no short-cut. She knew what she was talking about; she had done it herself.

I helped, observed, assisted, participated in, and was exposed to, all kinds of surgery. Very serious illnesses, traumas, and emergencies had become routine for me. I was involved in the most complex procedures, from brain surgery or a bleeding ulcer, down to rather simple operations. It was a fabulous training and this institution gave me knowledge and expertise which I could not have obtained anywhere else.

During my internship I witnessed patients with incurable

diseases, car accident and drowning victims, men maimed in bar fights, battered women, and little children tortured by their parents.

In my opinion the geriatric ward was the most depressing. Quite often I was the only comfort the elderly ever had. Many did not receive any visits; so they enjoyed talking to me and I did my very best to make them laugh and give them a "happy day".

Sometimes I just held their hands and they smiled at me. It made me feel good, proud, and worthy to be a nurse.

Modern medicine, new surgical tools and procedures were continuing to evolve at an amazing pace and I was at the forefront of progress in the field.

I soon realized that the job had taken over my life. The chaplain saw it too and suggested that I rest for a few days periodically, just to recharge my batteries. I went home to Nantes but slept most of the time…

One day I decided to go to Chartres to see the cathedral again. As soon as I walked inside, a feeling of serenity came over me. I attended Father Guillaume's service and took communion. He remembered me and was very happy to hear that I had turned my life around completely. He praised my dedication to the nursing profession and my friendship with the chaplain. "He will always be a loyal and precious friend. Keep him close to you," he said.

After spending a couple of days in Chartres, I returned home to Nantes to be with my family. They were very happy for me that I had found a good career and a unique training-ground, but they were worried about my health, concerned about a potential burn-out because I was working so hard.

I reassured them by explaining that I was now leading a very healthy and clean lifestyle. I was also doing a lot of sports to control my stress level.

I enjoyed my mother's cooking for a few more days and slept like a log. I jogged, swam, and prayed daily, until it was time to go back to work.

Upon my return to Montpellier, I found that my department was as hectic as usual. In any hospital, gynaecology and obstetrics are the busiest areas and that is why I enjoyed being part of them. I could put into practice what I had learnt in the classroom and use all my skills to make the sick women and the new mothers feel better. Many had had traumatic experiences and I was always ready to listen to them.

Actually the counselling and psychological help that I gave my patients made me a better nurse and a more rounded professional.

Surgery was carried out at a fast pace and my skills improved drastically year after year.

"Le Patron" was very happy with my performance and so were the head nurses of the various departments.

My job evaluations were full of praise and extremely positive. My internship programme was going to end very soon. It had flashed by so quickly that I had lost track of time. I was a professional ER nurse in one of the best hospitals in Europe but I did not know what my next move was going to be. It was time to pay a visit to my mentor, the chaplain.

"Do not be concerned, Yvonne. 'Le Patron' is looking after you and you are a very experienced and popular employee of this hospital. Yes, you still require three more years training but I am convinced that the administration is going to transfer you to one of the best institutions in France. They are going to take care of your training accordingly.... When does your contract expire, Yvonne?"

"At the end of next month, Father."

"Well, I have an inkling that you are going to be called into the boss's office very soon…wait and see…"

"Thank you, Father."

"And please, talk to Mary in your prayers."

And so I did.

I prayed, asking for more strength as well as clarity of vision for my destiny and purpose in life. I wanted Mary to accompany me in my "inner sanctum" to converse privately.

Prayers often get answered when we the least expect it, if answered at all. Three weeks later "Le Patron" called me in to his office.

"Yvonne, you are going to Paris to complete your internship. You have a three-year contract with the American Hospital. I wrote them a letter of recommendation on your behalf and called the chief of surgery to explain the details regarding your programme. This institution is renowned worldwide. I changed your order of specialty from gynaecology and obstetrics to general internal medicine. You will assist the surgeons and will also be at the helm of the novices' instruction. These next three years will be a turning point in your career.

Meanwhile, you still have one month left with us and I have placed you under my watch. This will conclude your training with us. Please do not fail this assignment as it will be vital for your future. I have scheduled you to attend my procedures and help at the emergency room in any way you can. You will carry a pager and be on call twenty-four hours a day, seven days a week. I know that you will perform very well in Paris but we will talk again before you leave…"

I was so overwhelmed by the news that I could only give him a, "Merci, Monsieur". We shook hands and I left his office. I called everyone I knew, my parents, my English mentor, Father Guillaume in Chartres; and they all congratulated me. They were proud of my achievements. The nurse in England advised me to work closely with all the department heads because they had to report directly to "Le Patron" and it was his way of keeping track of the interns' performances in addition to his own observations.

Later I had lunch with the chaplain.

He was exhilarated, full of praise, and gave me a lot of advice about my future occupation. Then he said, "This is the work of Mary. Have you noticed that, since you have been talking to her, things are better for you? Yvonne, think about it..."

At night, I chatted with Madame Labelle. She often gave me a lot of energy, peace of mind, and spiritual counselling. She also encouraged me to speak with Mary; she knew that the mother of God was very pleased about my new job and that she had plans lined up for me, which would materialize at a later date. But what plans? What were they? Madame Labelle would not say. However, it seemed that my own future had been mapped out by the Virgin Mary.

The last month in Montpellier was hard. I worked and worked incessantly. My pager's vibrations never ceased and my name called over the intercom resonated in my head anytime I tried to catch a little shut-eye. In fact I ended up losing my sleep altogether. This is a phenomenon which often occurs in the medical profession, particularly for interns who work horrendous schedules.

I hated this small electronic device with passion and cursed many times over whoever had invented it.

"Le Patron" gave me a gruelling test, the "seventy-two hour stretch", usually mandatory for medical interns, future physicians, or surgeons. But I was selected for it and I was going to be evaluated on it. I was on straight calls in the ER and operating-theatres. It was extremely difficult to stay alert, focused, and amicable with everyone, without any sleep.

Moreover, I had to maintain perfect accuracy in the operating-theatre during difficult procedures, including one that lasted sixteen hours with "Le Patron" in charge. In addition, I helped the patients, smiled at them, cajoled them whenever required, and moved on to other duties, all without sleep. At the end I felt like a robot, but finished the test with top marks.

Time out, my internship had ended, I had paid my dues. I could call myself a seasoned ER nurse and keep my head up.

I was called into "Le Patron's" office but this time I was not nervous.

"Yvonne, we must say goodbye but I hope that we shall meet again, you may even decide to work with us in the future."

"You are running an amazing institution, you are an eminent surgeon and my five years at this hospital have taught me more than I could ever have expected. To work for you has been an invaluable experience. I really mean it."

"Thank you, Yvonne. It is a nice compliment."

On his desk were four envelopes perfectly aligned and he handed them to me, one after the other, explaining their content.

"This is a bonus; it will help you settle down in Paris."

The second was a remarkable letter of reference signed and stamped by "Le Patron" himself.

The third one was a sealed envelope addressed to the chief of surgery at the American Hospital in Paris.

"We are friends, he and I. This letter will probably make things a little easier for you down the road. It is 'for his eyes only', but be assured that with this letter your 'Patron' in Paris will take you under his wing."

Finally, I received the results of my internship including the final marks and transcripts.

"Your total average for the past three years is 98.89%. It is unheard-of, but you have achieved it. Let me say that it was an honour to teach you."

With these words he hugged me and I cried. We shook hands and he told me, "Please do not be a stranger, come back and visit us. I personally will follow your progress closely. Remember, in three years time you will be looking for a full-time position and our doors are always open for you."

"Merci, Monsieur."

That is all I could say because I was still emotional.

I had two weeks holiday ahead of me prior to starting my new job, I wanted to see my family but there were a few people that I needed to talk to in order to clear my soul. Honesty is one of my virtues. That is why I had to see the chaplain, and Father Guillaume in Chartres, and there were questions that I wanted to ask the English nurse in London.

"So, Yvonne, are you ready for the city of lights?" asked the chaplain.

"Yes, Father. I believe that the move will be extremely beneficial for my career and 'Le Patron' wrote me a very reference letter commending me highly. He has also drafted a training-scheme to be approved by the American Hospital of Paris and I am supposed to be the leader of the novices. It is a very new experience for me. There are a lot of beautiful sites in the capital. I have promised myself to attend mass at Notre Dame Cathedral."

"I will miss you, Yvonne. Please keep in touch."

"I certainly will. After all you are my mentor and my friend. Before we part, I need to talk to you. It may take some time, however."

"Sure, Yvonne. I am ready to listen. What is on your mind?"

"Honesty and truth, Father. I want you to know that I was not always the person that I am now. That is why I asked you questions about Mary Magdalene when I came to this hospital."

"I do remember; please tell me more. I am all ears."

So I told him everything, describing all the most intimate details.

My early teenage years, my torments, my vile and shocking lifestyle, the suffering I brought to my family, my schooling, my guardian angel, Satan's possession and the Lord's intervention in Chartres, my conversation with Mary. I wanted the chaplain to know that God had saved me from the claws of Lucifer and that I would forever be grateful for my transformation.

The chaplain was looking at me intensely, not saying a word and when I stopped he took my hands and kissed me on the forehead.

"You are blessed, Yvonne. I am honoured to know you. You are a true child of the light. Heaven is watching over you and all your endeavours will be successful. I am proud of you. You managed to fight and escape the grip of the demon. Not too many people could have done it. God saved you because he knew that you were special with a tremendous potential."

"Thank you, Father. I wanted you to know. I am going to Chartres to tell the same to Father Guillaume. He will be pleased but surprised, I am sure."

Before I went to Chartres, I made a small detour to Les Saintes Maries de la Mer. It is a very famous and religious site in the south of France, close to Montpellier, where gypsy communities celebrate their festivals and symbolic masses. It is very small and quiet when out of season. I went to pray at the local church, a very tall and large structure with a history dating back to the eleventh century.

I was alone inside when I noticed a beautiful statue of the Virgin Mary in an alcove on the left-hand corner of the altar. I walked towards it and gently caressed our mother's bare feet.

"Thank you for all that you have done for me, I know that I am not worthy of your kindness but I promise you to try harder," I said.

I went back to sit at the pew. There was a calm and relaxing atmosphere everywhere and I must have been snoozing when the sound of a woman's voice woke me up.

"Do not apologize for your hard work, we all know what you do and how you save lives day after day. Your heart and soul are in the right place and you should know that we are very happy for you. In Paris you will again be a brilliant success, Yvonne, and there I will meet you for a tête-à-tête. I bless you We are all here to protect you."

Her voice was clear, without accent, and filled the room. Was I dreaming? It seemed so real!

The following day I took the train to Chartres.

Father Guillaume hugged me and exclaimed, "Bravo, Yvonne, look at you! You are now a star nurse. going to work at the best hospital in Paris with the top surgeons in their fields. I am proud of you!"

"Please, I am still in training with three more years of studies in front of me."

"For you, it will go smoothly. You are going to be at the top of your class again," he said laughingly.

"Father, I need to talk to you but I would like to sit by the altar and you can consider it a confession if you like."

"Would you prefer the confessional?"

"No, Father, just you and me by the altar. I insist."

"Very well, let's go."

We sat at the same pew where Jesus had saved me from Lucifer who was trying to take over my soul.

I narrated again the details of my past, without missing any detail, including the apparitions in the Cathedral. He was looking deep into my eyes, not saying a word and he had a sort of puzzled expression on his face. I showed him the spot where God talked to his son and where the bright light was shining, illuminating the entire church. I told him about my guardian angel and my conversations with the Virgin Mary. He took my hands.

"My child you brought a miracle into this basilica. Be assured that the Pearly Gates will be open for you. Even if Mary unveils her secrets, you probably will still have questions. I am amazed by what happened right here. If you had not told me, I would have never guessed. More than ever, I am very honoured to be the leader of the Cathedral of Chartres. My child, you are well protected. Satan was no match for the Lord and he cleansed you of his diabolical presence."

Then I asked Father Guillaume a very important question, which had been nagging me for quite a while. "How difficult is it to take the veil?"

He did not reply immediately. He had a blank look. Then he whispered softly, "May I ask why? Yvonne, are you thinking…?"

"I do not know yet, it is just an inquiry at this stage. You are the best person to advise me, along with my friend the chaplain in Montpellier."

"What did he say?"

*

"The chaplain insisted that I complete my internship in Paris, then find a position as an ER/OR nurse in one of the country's best hospitals. He was flabbergasted by my inquiry, but did not dissuade me from taking the veil. He only wanted to reason with me."

"'Why, Yvonne, why now?'" he had asked.

"'So much has happened in the past few years and God

saved me from a life of debauchery and gave back my family honour, pride, health, and happiness. I owe it all to him. He gave me a new sense of purpose and I feel that I must repay him,'" I had replied.

"'Repay? Like a debt?" the chaplain had exclaimed. 'No, Yvonne, you have it all wrong, God does not do things or perform miracles to be repaid. He does it because he loves us all. There is no need to repay anything at all. You are a nurse. You have already been serving him for years. You are helping people from all walks of life and doing as much good as any nun would in the circumstances. To take the veil at your stage in life would be a terrible waste, particularly when you are so close to getting the job that you have dreamt about for so many years. Please reconsider your decision. I am always here to help. But for now, becoming a nun should be out of the question. You have too much to offer in the nursing profession.'"

"We also discussed the vows, the different orders and the rigid life of a convent or a cloister."

*

Father Guillaume was smiling and nodding at the same time; he took my hands and said, "Yvonne, I could not have explained it to you any better; the chaplain is your mentor and true friend. He is perfectly correct, you should give serious consideration to your thoughts, because to join an order is to find a vocation very much like nursing. It is not a career or a job. You take vows for the rest of your life. You serve God into infinity. Please think things through.

"But, firstly, complete your internship; then find a good position and keep helping people, saving lives; and if at a later date, you still think about becoming a nun, I will help you find a novitiate and a vocation director, I promise. Now, I am going to be blunt, but I must tell you the truth. You have not yet had the true calling to serve God, it is only an idea in your mind. You were predestined to become a nurse; that is your calling, my child."

Of course, both the chaplain and Father Guillaume were correct. We hugged, Father Guillaume blessed me and I went back home to Nantes.

I spent time with my parents, swam many lengths of the pool, went to the gym, and got back into shape. Thanks to my mother's cooking I was full of energy again. Now and then, I talked to Madame Labelle, who boosted my morale; she was preparing me to work with "La crème de la crème" of the medical field in France.

When I was on the train, I made the decision to plunge into my studies again and perform to the best of my abilities at the American Hospital of Paris.

In my compartment I shouted, "Paris, here I come!"

I was thirty-five years old but I still had a lot to learn…

## CHAPTER FIFTEEN

## A TURBULENT INTERLUDE

The colonel looked at Sister Yvonne, bewildered, and shook his head. The council members in attendance were nodding and smiling.

"Sister, this was not only a fascinating story but you are truly an extraordinary person. By the way, when did you decide to take the veil?"

Sister Marie Catherine interjected.

"Colonel, Sister Yvonne will definitely finish her story, but it is already very late. Let's get some sleep and reconvene at 10am. Breakfast will be served from 8am onwards. I want you to listen to the anecdotes of our council members. It will be very informative. Is it going to create a problem with regard to meeting your team at the boat-house?"

"No, Sister, because my orders were to wait for each other no matter what. The delay will give them more time to rest, to get ready; and they will be safe at that location."

"Very well, then. Please focus your attention on these stories and you will realize who you are going up against."

"Is there anything I should be aware of in particular, Sister?"

"Lucifer will pursue and hunt your team relentlessly until you are all annihilated. All of us around this table have had direct experiences with Satan and the after-life. You must consider your mission the ultimate challenge!"

"Please remember, Sister, that I have met him in person. I saw his powers and how he destroyed Jason!"

"Yes, Colonel. But unfortunately this is only the beginning.

He has other cards up his sleeve."

"I wanted to thank you and your team for all that you have done for us. Personally I needed your spiritual support and I received it. By the way, you must be very grateful to the Lord for having Sister Yvonne at your side. She is a precious asset to the mission!"

"Yes, she is!" roared the group in appreciation.

Sister Marie Catherine was beaming with satisfaction. "I am happy to support your mission to the fullest and I want our collective expertise to protect you from Lucifer. Yes, Sister Yvonne is very special and has already achieved a great many remarkable deeds at her young age. She is working as a surgical aide to Father Benedetti, she teaches religious studies to the novices, and assists Father Romero during exorcisms.

"Exorcisms? Did you say exorcisms?"

"Yes, Colonel. The Devil has no frontiers. Be assured of that."

"I heard that these ceremonies can be very dangerous..."

"They can be, Colonel, but Sister Yvonne has dealt successfully with the demon in the past..."

"Sister Yvonne, you really have a lion's heart."

She was smiling, shaking her head, exhibiting humility.

"I would like to check on Jason outside before we retire."

"Please, Colonel, go ahead, because you may be with us for a little longer if you do not mind."

"I will be back soon."

I walked down the trail to meet him...

*"General, what a beautiful story! Sister Yvonne must have been a real dynamo. It seems almost impossible to be possessed by the demon, meet your guardian angel, Jesus, God, and the Virgin Mary, all at the same time!"*

"Somehow she did, she really did.

"I will tell you how she became a nun and was sent to the mission in Vietnam. Until then we could perhaps take a break and reconvene tomorrow morning because my story is far from over, and it is getting very late…"

*"I agree, General. Let's meet after breakfast. I want to hear the rest of your fascinating adventures in Vietnam. How could you remember so many accurate details of your exploits?"*

"Well, I do not think that I could ever forget them, but it was soothing to talk about it."

*"I am glad that it has helped, General. You are a true hero!"*

"I do not feel like one, Sergeant. In my opinion the true heroes have their names engraved on the wall in Washington DC."

*"Good night, General."*

"Good night, Sergeant."

*

*"Good morning, General. Did you get a good rest?"*

"I did, Sergeant, and in addition I received compliments from my wife!"

*"Oh? Why is that?"*

"I told her about you and the reminiscences of my Vietnam days, but left Lucifer out, of course. She was very supportive and felt that I should have done it many years ago. However I explained to her that only a soldier who had faced combat could understand the meaning and the horrors of it all. She is now happy that we are sharing our experiences and encouraged me to join you again today."

*"Good for you, General. Well, I am all ears. Sister Yvonne was finishing her story. You still had to face the council, but firstly you went down the trail to check on Jason. Am I correct?"*

"You are. Yes... Jason…"

*"What is wrong, General?"*

"Jason was totally unrecognizable!"

*"What do you mean, General? What was wrong with him?"*

*

My rifle at the ready, I was approaching the intersection down the hill below the mission. I could hear only the buzz of the mosquitoes and the screams and sounds of the battle raging across the hills. There was a full moon; it was easier to see from a distance in the dark.

He was wearing a bandana around his head, his eyes were bright red and he had a raucous voice.

"I came to see if you needed anything, Jason."

"No, Colonel, you can go back to the little sisters."

"I am going to stay at least one more day at the mission, but we can make up the time by taking short-cuts with the help of the two farmers. We should reach the boat-house within three days. Anyway, the team is safe there with the fisherman. Will you be OK with that Jason?"

"Of course, Colonel. Look at my lunch for tomorrow!"

He showed me a big fat rabbit that he had just killed.

There was a very foul and recognizable odour at close range.

"Bodies, Colonel, over there," pointed Jason.

He had been living in a large tree, surrounded by dense vegetation. I walked behind the bushes and saw corpses piled up one on top of the other.

"There are fourteen VCs. Patrols cross this trail at least three times a day to bring supplies to the troops fighting in the hills. I do not know how long our boys will be able to hold on to our positions, the way things are going. The NVA's artillery barrage is too powerful for our troops, I guess. Can you hear it?"

I nodded and I noticed a necklace with bloody ears around

his neck. "What are those Jason?"

"Ears, Colonel, what do you think? I cut them off the poor bastards who are lying there, they won't need them anymore will they?" exulted Jason, raising his voice.

"Jason, why did you do that?" I questioned.

He shook his head, circled around me and suddenly burst out laughing, loudly; he laughed and laughed, waving his arms around.

I stood there speechless; looking at the bodies while Jason was making fun of me. Even though it had been common practice for some long-range reconnaissance patrol units (LRRPS, pronounced "lurps") during the Vietnam War to mutilate the enemy, I considered it totally unacceptable.

I wanted to tell him that I had never condoned such a practice in my platoon and that I judged it immoral and sickly.

He had been completely wrong but he did not care anymore; he was a loose cannon. I knew for a fact that I would be flogging a dead horse if I tried to reason with him.

He was dancing around, mimicking me, and pointing his finger singing.

"Why, Jason, why did you do it?" I glared at him and he approached. "Jason your behaviour is insubordinate; you are disrespectful and out of order!"

His face was almost touching mine, I could smell his breath, his eyes looked straight through me and I froze in horror. The pupils were red and dilated with orange flames inside them.

He groaned with a twisted mouth and said, "You are scared, Colonel. You know who I am. You saw it in my eyes, didn't you?"

I did not reply.

"Didn't you?" he yelled.

"Yes, Jason. I know what you have become!"

"Do not lecture me, Colonel, it is not the time nor the place!"

"What you did was morbid and unholy."

"What did you just say?" he exclaimed.

*

"Then, Sergeant, he went crazy, he just lost it and I thought that he was going to kill me, right there and then. His red-hot fiery eyes had widened. He was foaming at the mouth, hurling insults and profanities. My comments had angered him and he pulled out his handgun, pointing it straight at me.

*"General, the demon had surfaced; Lucifer's servants cannot handle orders and criticism, can they?"*

"You are correct, Sergeant; only the master can tell them what to do."

*"What happened next?"*

*

Jason had killed fourteen men without firing a single shot, using only his bare hands and the knife. He insisted that I look at the cadavers, and claimed that as the team leader I should have done the same. He taunted me, spat on the bodies as a sign of victory and complete disdain, and I noticed that he had already urinated and defecated all over his victims.

"I want to shoot you in the head for insulting me, Colonel. How can you tell me how to deal with our communist enemies? They are VCs who wound, torture, and kill US soldiers in the field. How dare you come up with such remarks? What kind of Special Forces officer are you? A wimp? A coward?"

Then, without any warning, he placed his handgun on my forehead and pressed the trigger.

"Click."

Nothing, I did not even have the time to flinch.

He pressed again, "Click, Click, Click".

I had not moved one inch. The gun had misfired four times.

I saw the puzzled frown and angry look on his face. At that moment a resounding roar and a loud voice filled the hot night. "Jason, let the colonel return to the mission, I do not want any harm to come to him, do you understand?"

"Yes master," replied Jason bowing his head.

The Dark Lord had saved my life again, but why did he do it?

"You did not really intend to offend Jason, did you?"

"No, my Lord, I was just emphasizing some rules of combat, military etiquette, I should say."

"Never again, Colonel. My loyal servants only follow my orders. There is no etiquette in jungle warfare. You especially should be aware of that. We do not take criticism from mortals very well, as you can see...do you understand?"

"Yes, my Lord."

"Now, go back to the mission at once, because I have already called the 'shadows of Hell' to perform housekeeping duties, and if you stay here they will eat you alive. Please leave, we shall meet again..."

I ran back towards the front door of the mission, but at the top of the hill I turned around and saw the troglodytes rushing towards the corpses. I heard the grunts, the chirps, the slurps, and the bones cracking. They were cutting up and devouring them in a frenzy. Jason was standing upright in the middle of them, laughing hysterically.

I remembered those terrifying, furry, monsters with large, yellow, droopy, eyes and razor-sharp claws. They craved dead flesh, but occasionally enjoyed eating people alive. They were the fearsome predators of the Abyss!

## CHAPTER SIXTEEN

## AN AMERICAN IN PARIS

I was devastated by what I had just witnessed. Moreover Lucifer was now in full control of my destiny. Would I ever live to complete the escape?

I rang the bell and Sister Marie Catherine opened the door. She just looked at my face and asked, “Is there something wrong, Colonel?”

I told her about my ordeal with Jason.

She shook her head and whispered, “Please come inside and we shall talk more at the meeting.”

The eight of us were served a copious North-American style breakfast. Father Benedetti inquired about my encounter with Jason. I did not leave out any detail. Everyone listened silently. Some members were nodding their heads, and others kept silent.

Sister Yvonne crossed herself at the mention of the furry monsters.

“Lucifer seems to enjoy toying with you, doesn’t he, Colonel?”

“Apparently so, Father…” I replied.

“Well, we should begin our meeting where we left it before we broke up. Sister Yvonne, you may continue…,” said Sister Marie Catherine.

*Sister Yvonne Continues Her Story*

I was now working at the American Hospital in Paris, one of the most prestigious in the world. I met my new boss who already had my files on his desk and gave him the letter of recommendation written by, “Le Patron”. He read it silently.

He was a tall, wiry, man, wearing gold-rimmed spectacles. He looked at me with a faint smile and, waving the letter, said, "Your former 'Patron' is my best friend. We go back a long way and worked together under very difficult circumstances. He is the best surgeon in the nation, if not in Europe.

"As the final chapter of your studies, I am requested to take you under my wing for the next three years, and make you the best surgical nurse in our institution. Yvonne, I will be honoured to oblige. Your grades have been exceptional; you are a young lady with a bright future ahead. You are going to work on my watch in the General Surgery Department. Obstetrics and gynaecology are your fields of expertise, but to become a professional ER nurse you need to be exposed to diverse procedures including how to handle the calls of the emergency ward.

"You will also demonstrate some of your skills to the new interns. You will always have them in tow but they will not interfere with your work.

"You will attend training-sessions and meetings with our doctors at all levels.

"Welcome, Yvonne, to the American Hospital in Paris. Please get a beeper because you are now on call twenty-four hours a day!"

We shook hands and I left the office smiling. It was Montpellier all over again…

My schedule was drafted by the head nurse and approved by the assistant administrator of the General Surgery Department. Surprisingly they gave me some free time to relax. I had not had any full day's rest for an entire year, only half days occasionally.

Whenever I called them, my family and friends were very supportive of my experience.

The diabolical beeper was ringing incessantly. Very often I

did not even have time to eat lunch.

The chaplain, who had communicated with his counterpart in Montpellier, was a very nice and funny man, a real motivator. We had an excellent rapport.

When things were tough, I went to pray at the famed Notre Dame Cathedral and spoke with the bishop, Monsignor Dominique.

Madame Labelle kept giving me courage, wisdom, and resilience. I also knew that Mary was omnipresent and watching over me.

The American Hospital in Paris was a unique institution and a fabulous training ground, it was so busy that I did not have enough time in the day to complete my tasks. I guess that is the life of an ER nurse. I learnt how to cope with it. I still managed to visit some of the most popular tourist attractions in the City of Lights. I took long walks by the River Seine and visited small picturesque neighbourhoods. Paris is a magical place!

Later, I found a gym and a swimming-pool for exercise. Many of the hospital patients were not French citizens but Americans, British, Australians, or Canadians. A few were members of the "rich and famous", or leaders of European countries.

I was happy to practice my English, not only with the patients, but also with the international surgeons. We could take care of any medical emergencies. The hospital had a staff of five hundred physicians, some full time, others on call. I was exposed to incurable diseases, cancer patients, epidemic and venereal illnesses, heart and brain surgery, transplants and amputations, deformities, body deficiencies, bleeding ulcers, and more.... We had ultra-modern equipment, the staff were polite, efficient, and dedicated; and I assisted brilliant surgeons from all over the world.

I could not have expected more from any medical institution; once again I felt that I had been blessed.

On the first year, I was given two evaluations from "Le Grand Patron" himself and the head nurse.

The results were excellent.

They praised my accomplishments, stamina, and overall conduct, and decided to increase my workload gradually over the next two years.

"Le Grand Patron" (as he was called) was very respectful, with a good sense of humour. To watch his work was like a dream. He was simply extraordinary, his speed, skills, dexterity, and accuracy were unparalleled. No wonder that surgeons worldwide came to Paris to learn from him! When I assisted him, he always made it a point to give me his opinion when it was over. "Good job, Yvonne." "Improve your speed." "Focus, focus, concentrate more." "Pass me the instruments without looking at me; you should know better."

I really appreciated his constructive comments; they made me a better ER nurse and reinforced my weaker abilities.

My mentor in the UK, the British nurse, told me, "Yvonne, you may even get two job-offers." Would it be Paris or Montpellier? It was too early to decide…

I really enjoyed coaching the young interns; they were conscientious, funny, and respectful. They demonstrated a keen interest in the medical profession. The novices were often shocked by the sight of blood, pus, and open wounds. They would faint during surgical procedures, thus realizing that medicine might not be the right career path for them. After my first year, the numbers had dwindled from twenty-two to a group of eight students.

Le Grand Patron was not perturbed at that ratio and told me that medical studies are a vocation, not a job. You must have the love and the heart for it, and only the best can graduate. It was a long road to the top.

"Yvonne, the interns have made very positive comments about you. Just keep doing what you are doing."

"Merci Monsieur," I answered.

*

*"General, when did your Sister Yvonne find her true calling?"*

"Well after her internship programme in Paris. But even then she still hesitated because she knew that once she had joined an order there was no going back. It required a lot of soul-searching and it was a major decision to make. Let me tell you the story..."

*

"Sister, you were once again the hospital All-star!"

"No, Colonel, I was just a nurse, learning her skills among top-notch doctors. They were the champions, not me."

"Did your time in Paris have an influence on your decision to become a nun?"

"Not really, it was a gradual process which is hard to explain, you go through transformations both at the psychological and physiological levels, concurrently. It usually takes a long time to develop. In my case, something extraordinary happened while I was working in Montpellier, two years after my graduation in Paris. I will tell you the details imminently."

"I am all ears, Sister Yvonne..."

*

I did not take my holiday during my first year in Paris.

The chaplain tried to convince me to visit my family in Nantes, but I decided to carry on with my hectic schedule and prepare for my upcoming final exam. It was going to be extremely challenging and I wanted to be ready.

I was called into "Le Grand Patron's" office and he announced, "You will attend your final exam next week. It will last three days, during which time my assistants and I will grade your work. The results will reach you very promptly. Good luck, Yvonne!"

"Merci, Monsieur..."

"I plunged into my books, notes, and handouts with frenzy; I had heard that the oral presentations could last two hours! Madame Labelle came to visit me; she was in a jovial mood, reassuring me, giving me courage... I needed it more than ever!"

*

*"Was it difficult, Sister Yvonne?"*

"Gruelling, Colonel, very, very hard! It comprised written tests, assisting 'Le Grand Patron' during surgery, laboratory analysis, practical work with the patients, diagnosis of ailments, question and answer sessions with a panel of doctors, two very long presentations on different topics, and more..."

*"You passed your final, I believe?"*

"Yes, Colonel, I did."

Sister Marie Catherine interjected, "Failure is not a word in Sister Yvonne's vocabulary. However, she remains humble and will never boast about her success.... Please continue, Sister..."

*

The chaplain knew that I had passed with flying colours, he had prayed the night before and asked Mary to be by my side all the way...

"Yvonne, 'Le Grand Patron' wants to see you," the head nurse said.

Five long days had passed and now the results had finally arrived....

"Le Grand Patron" invited me to sit down.

"Yvonne, your results are extraordinary, your final mark is 98.2%. Congratulations!"

"Merci, Monsieur".

"Are you happy with us? Is everything all right?"

"I am, Monsieur. The staff facilities are remarkable, and I enjoy the use of the chapel. But, above all, to work as a nurse with you and your team has been a privilege. You have given me invaluable opportunities to improve myself. I can never forget that, monsieur!"

"Good, Yvonne, but the head nurse told me that you have not yet taken any vacation time. Why is that?"

"I am following a frantic schedule and wanted to prepare well for the final, that is why I cancelled my holidays."

"You need a rest. As a nurse you know the risks of a burn-out. There are two long years ahead and it will be hard. You cannot keep this pace up until graduation, it is impossible. I am giving you, effective immediately, two weeks off, paid in full. No arguments. Relax, enjoy yourself! I shall see you upon your return, refreshed and rested."

"Merci beaucoup, Monsieur."

He handed me two forms, one for the paymaster, the other for the head nurse's time-tables. I was totally unprepared for this kind gesture and I left with a big smile on my face. No beeper for two weeks, Hurrah!

It was July, the weather was beautiful and I was on my way to Nantes.

My parents were thrilled to see me and we stayed up until the wee hours of the morning. My mother cooked my favourite dishes and I slept in every day.

I decided to pay Father Guillaume, my mentor the chaplain, and "Le Patron" in Montpellier a visit. I believed it was the right thing to do.

Father Guillaume hugged me tight and we talked like old friends. Later I went to sit at my favourite pew by the altar. On my left was the statue of the Virgin Mary looking straight at me. I got up to touch her feet. The church was empty and quiet but a clear voice resounded deep inside me.

"Yvonne, you are a fine woman who needs to balance her life better. There are times to work, study, play, rejoice, and pray. By the way, read the Bible a little more, you need to know it to serve God later. We shall talk again…"

Father Guillaume could not make any comments regarding Mary's interventions. He told me to remain calm, to listen to her advice and wait for future signs.

I left Chartres for Montpellier.

The chaplain and I sat in the chapel and we talked about my family, my work, my studies and he asked me if I had prayed at the Notre Dame Cathedral. He had seen it as a young man and had never forgotten its beauty and prominence.

"Yes, I have occasionally," I replied. "And I also met Monsignor Dominique, the bishop of Paris. The cathedral is his responsibility. He is very nice and a very powerful man in Paris."

Then I told him about my new experiences with Mary.

"They seem to be few and far between but keep coming back, don't they?" he said.

"Yes, I am really confused about the messages. Father Guillaume told me wait and follow her advice. What else should I do?"

"He is correct, but here are my ideas about these apparitions. She and her son work at their own pace which is usually very slow. We have all heard the saying, 'God works in mysterious ways'. Well, these are prime examples. Mary is not ready to tell you her plans for your future, not yet.

"Presently she is just helping you in your daily tasks,

always watching over you. She loves you very much, she is supporting you all the way. At a later date you will both sit down together to finalize serious matters. I am sure of it. For now, please follow her advice to the letter, and enjoy life. If you have any difficulties with it, you can call me, but Madame Labelle will be delighted to clarify matters for you, I am sure. That is all I have to say."

"Thank you, Father, I am thankful to you once again, you have made me feel better."

"It is a pleasure, Yvonne, and please go to talk to Monsignor Dominique. He is a church leader. He will be happy to give you his opinion. He is a bishop respected by the Vatican."

"I will, Father, but he might not have the time to see me."

"Nonsense, call him up, make an appointment. But, Yvonne, you have to tell him the whole truth, do you hear?"

"Of course, Father, he will hear it all, but do you really think that it is a good idea?"

"Yes, do it, you are now in dire need of advice and support, it is the perfect opportunity. Father Dominique is a great bishop, he will understand..."

I left the chaplain to go to "Le Patron's" office. After warm greetings, we discussed my work in detail. I praised the American Hospital in Paris and its boss at great length.

He was all smiles while listening to my stories.

"Yvonne, at the end of your internship you will have had eight years of nursing experience at the two most famous hospitals in Europe. You also have a very high level of education. You are fluently bilingual, therefore you could work anywhere in Europe, the UK, or the USA. But personally I believe that your dream job is here, with us in Montpellier, am I correct?"

"It is too early to say, Monsieur. I still have two more years of internship to complete."

"You are right, Yvonne, but if in two years time a position did open with us, would you be interested?"

"I might. I am really focusing on gynaecology and obstetrics as a career."

"I understand, well let's leave it at that for now and good luck in your studies. Let's keep in touch; you are one of the most talented nurses that I have ever seen."

"Merci, Monsieur. Coming from you it is more than a compliment."

We shook hands and I was soon on my way back to Nantes thinking about my mother's cooking.

The remainder of my vacation evaporated in no time. I felt rested, energetic, and ready to start my second year of internship on the right foot. My schedule was as busy as ever, "Le Grand Patron" expected me to attend all of his procedures and the head nurse increased the number of interns under my wing to twelve.

Twice a week, I went to the Pierre and Marie Currie Hospital to work in the department of epidemiology. I wanted to familiarize myself with the tests and analyses of viruses and foreign infectious diseases. It was only a temporary assignment but I enjoyed it. I had worked there when I was a student in the UK and I had only admiration for this institution.

I had some difficulties with two interns on my team, sons of prominent surgeons. I had nothing against them, except that they demonstrated signs of arrogance and even spite towards me. I had to stop it at once before it festered. The chaplain suggested that I talk to "Le Grand Patron."

"Monsieur, I have some problems with two interns under my supervision and I need your advice."

He listened attentively to my complaints, frowning and shaking his head slightly at times.

"Well, Yvonne, what do you intend to do about it?"

I replied, "I am thinking about bringing them both to the boardroom. I will be frank and strict, expecting not only apologies but also the promise that such incidents will never happen again. If they do, I will send them to 'Le Grand Patron's' office with disciplinary letters from the human resource department. At this stage that is all I can do to prevent any recurrence."

"Excellent, Yvonne, I like your style. Go ahead and do not be concerned about any repercussions from their fathers. I will call them right now. Let me know how it goes."

Later that day the three of us met and I guess that my approach was correct, I never had any more problems with them afterwards. I received a very complimentary letter from "Le Grand Patron" which was placed on my personal files.

My second year of internship was a success, even though the hours were horrendous. I enjoyed the challenge and got along very well with everyone. The chaplain and I had many interesting discussions about religion in general, and he also helped me to understand the Bible, which was giving me tremendous difficulties.

"Do not be concerned, Yvonne, that is why it has been called, 'the mysterious book of God' he told me.

I had a lot of support from "Le Grand Patron" and the head nurse who taught me medical and management skills "on the job", which is in fact the best way to learn.

My group of interns remained twelve in number and were progressing rapidly with good grades.

I really needed a rest and I went home to celebrate Christmas with my family.

I turned off the black demon, "the beeper". What joy!

Upon my return, the head nurse took me under her wing to teach me scheduling and work distribution. I also had to evaluate the twelve interns by giving them "face to face" interviews. My part time job at Pierre and Marie Curie Hospital being terminated, it was replaced by additional administrative duties. "Orders from Le Grand Patron," I was told. In addition, I was studying for my second year final. I already knew the workload that I was going to face and did not want any bad surprises.

Even though I felt confident, this exam was going to be the turning point of my entire internship. The second year is seen as the "hub" of the programme. Compulsory questions were going to be added, such as: administrative and clerical duties, laboratory and analysis, leadership, ER trauma procedures. I had to be ready.... Madame Labelle promised to give me her full support if I was in any difficulty.

Time flies and the second year finals were already around the corner. To avoid burn-out, I jogged, went to the gym, and swam laps.

I prayed in my room and at Notre Dame Cathedral. I felt healthy, confident and ready to conquer any challenges thrown at me.

The chaplain asked me, "Did you talk to Monsignor Dominique?"

"I am sorry, I did not."

"Are you scared because he is a Monsignor?"

"I am not as close to him as I am with the other priests including you; I guess I am wrong..."

"Yes, you are, please go to see him, it might erase the anguish that you feel about your finals. He is a brilliant educator himself, he taught in Rome at the Pontifical Biblical Institute. He will give you sound advice, I am sure."

"I will, Father, I apologize."

I made an appointment to meet Monsignor Dominique at his office over the week end.

"Wise decision," said Madame Labelle.

*

*"How was your meeting with Monsignor Dominique?"*

"Colonel, it was an unforgettable experience that I have carried with me ever since. I will not divulge anything, because the advice given was under the secret of the confessional. Monsignor definitely had an aura about him. His Holiness regarded him highly and he is now a cardinal in France. To meet him was a solemn moment in my life and I will always cherish that memory."

*"How was the final, Sister?"*

"It lasted a full week, ten to twelve hours a day. I slept through the following week-end and I was back at work on Monday."

*

Two weeks later I was called in to "Le Grand Patron's" office.

"Congratulations, you passed with 97% average. You obtained the highest grades, I am proud to have you as my student!" he said.

I took two weeks rest during the month of August, before the third year began. I did not travel and spent time in Nantes with my family. I needed peace of mind and a lot of sleep.

Upon my return, I was assigned to a new group of interns. There were only six of them and they appeared very motivated.

I received extra hours at the emergency department, "orders from above," said the head nurse.

The devilish beeper was doing its routine, night and day. Sometimes I thought that whoever had invented that apparatus should be hanged…

Surgery with "Le Grand Patron" was getting more intricate and lasted longer. In some cases, procedures took up to sixteen hours to complete.

I visited cancer patients and drug addicts, observed physiotherapy sessions, helped people with behavioural problems, and young mothers without partners – some of them as young as fifteen years old, which was a tragedy for their families. I enjoyed visiting the department of gynaecology and obstetrics, where I felt confident and knowledgeable.

I helped a British orthopaedist to repair fractures and deal with traumas caused by accidents and sports injuries. – Patients who suffered broken bones were always in great pain and at times required surgery.

In the autumn, I was sent to the psychiatric ward. I did not have much experience in that discipline. While at university, I had taken courses at the minor level and at the general hospital in Montpellier I visited the department only a few times.

I can say that it was a first in my professional career. The physicians made it clear that I was only an observer and was not supposed to say a word when attending doctor-patient sessions.

It was very enlightening and made me realize the extraordinary complexity of the human brain. Group therapy included people of all ages and walks of life. The interaction was oftentimes frustrating, depressing – even scary – but those meetings titillated curious feelings and questions in my own mind, "Why do people do what they do?" I could not find an answer.

Science and religion have always conflicted on certain views. During my stint at the psychiatric ward, a prominent visiting neurologist argued with me that the Devil did not exist, that it was only a fallacy in Scripture and that he could not have taken over someone's mind. Frustrated, I walked away, putting an end to that conversation.

"Time flies, Yvonne," the chaplain told me.

Christmas was around the corner, and I realized that it was my last year in the capital. I was working, exercising at the gym, swimming, praying, reading the Bible, or walking around Paris playing the tourist.

I loved that city, it was an enchanting place, but did I love it enough to reside there permanently? I needed more time to think about it.

"Yvonne, tomorrow we are proceeding with your semi-annual evaluation," Le Grand Patron told me.

"Oui, Monsieur."

I was not concerned because the last four appraisals had been exceptional. We met at 9am in the boardroom with the head nurse, Le Grand Patron and his assistant. The last performance review would take place in July before the final exam.

I wanted to go home for the Christmas break so I straightened out my projects ahead of time. I evaluated individually the six interns who had performed extremely well.

Upon my return, I was going to work on my final. I did not want to leave anything to chance. My semi-annual evaluation had gone flawlessly.

"Le Grand Patron" shook my hand and I was on my way to Nantes.

When I called all my friends to wish them a Merry Christmas, the main question was, "Where do you plan to work after graduation?"

I did not have any answers, I was keeping all my options open, the final decision was going to be mine and mine alone.

Madame Labelle was a source of comfort and told me, "Yvonne, please focus on the final, it should be the only priority in your mind, one step at a time."

Meanwhile I was exercising daily because my mother's cooking was adding weight on my waistline.

The Bible was my bedtime reading but the Old and New Testaments were now clearer; it was slowly making more sense. I called Montpellier.

"What is wrong, Yvonne?" the chaplain answered over the telephone.

"I have again the desire to serve God, it is giving me bouts of anxiety, the feeling is nagging at me and I do not know what to do, Father."

"Wait for the Lord to guide you, Mary is going to meet you face to face and then you will be able to discuss it all with her."

"Yes, Father, I will wait…"

"Merry Christmas to you and your family."

"Same to you, Father, thank you for your advice."

My family and I went to the cathedral at Nantes to celebrate midnight mass. Afterwards we all went home to eat the traditional French onion soup. There is nothing like Christmas!

*

*"Did you ever discuss the signs of the calling with your parents, Sister?"*

"No, Colonel, I did not want to worry them unnecessarily, beside I was not sure myself what it all meant. I talked about my work, my studies. They were very proud of me and waited anxiously for my graduation. I did not disappoint them."

*

*"General, Yvonne was an extraordinary person, you were very fortunate to have met her. The mission was surely relying on her versatile skills and she must have been a precious asset to them."*

"Yes, Sergeant, she was indeed."

*"I wish that I had known her."*

"Her life-story fascinated me, Sergeant. This young lady had spent seventeen years after high school studying at the best universities, including internships, training, and special courses to become a top ER nurse, not counting the novitiate to take the veil."

*"This is true willpower!"*

"Yes, Sergeant, and you would never have known just by looking at her. She was very humble, quiet, reserved, but she had a lot of stamina."

*"You admired her, didn't you?"*

"Yes, I did. She was not afraid of Satan anymore, even though she had to face him again during exorcisms."

*"Is it true General? Tell me more..."*

*

Upon returning from vacation I went straight back into my hectic daily routines of difficult surgical procedures, teaching the six interns, and attending to emergency calls.

I want to add that two particular occurrences took place during my last months of internship. It was somehow a challenge for me but I managed to deal with them the best I could."

*

*"Tell me, Sister."*

"Colonel, I will discuss it later at the meeting when the council presents other cases to you."

*

It was July and my last semi-annual appraisal had been processed. Madame Labelle had helped me revise for the final.

"Look what a guardian angel can do," she had said laughingly.

"The final of all finals," "Le Grand Patron". had called it.

"The six interns scored top grades in their last evaluations."

*

*"Well, Sister, how did you do?"*

"Colonel, I received the highest marks in the programme for

the entire three years combined. I was relieved; it had been a long journey and an unforgettable experience. I was now officially a fully-fledged ER/OR nurse, and in addition I had received the UK national registered nurse (RN) qualification.

"The long working hours, the many years of study, the blood, sweat and tears and the arduous road to the top had all been worth it!"

*"Did your parents come to Paris for the graduation?"*

"Yes, a lunch ceremony had been organized by 'Le Grand Patron' and they were invited' as well as the Dean of the nursing school department of Glasgow University, the head nurse' and the hospital's surgical teams' who were all in attendance. It was time to say goodbye with a lot of hugs and kisses.

I wanted to spend the rest of the summer with my family and take a long vacation. I was not ready to speculate about my next move even though job offers were pouring in.

We all took the train back to Nantes.

# CHAPTER SEVENTEEN

## PRIVATE REVELATION

*Sister Yvonne continues her story*

Vacations are marvellous, being a lady of leisure was so wonderful! I was sleeping a lot, I went to the gym and swam every day; work was the last thing on my mind because all doors were open for me, possibly in France, the UK, or even the USA.

My parents were thrilled to see me healthy, positive and optimistic about my future.

Came September, and it was now time to get back to work!

International medical trade magazines were advertising very highly paid positions abroad, but because money had never been my motivator and because the countries listed did not attract me, I decided not to apply for any of them.

Unexpectedly, my father received a call from "Le Patron" in Montpellier, who wanted to see me about a job that was available, but at the same time I received a registered letter from the American Hospital in Paris, where an operating-room nurse was needed as soon as possible.

My mentor in the UK had been right on the dot, I now had two job-offers simultaneously.

Madame Labelle said, "Yvonne, the choice is yours!"

I wanted to sleep on it for a while and not rush into anything.

My parents and I had a long conversation about my career. They usually did not get involved with my work and always trusted my decisions, but they saw that I was in a quandary and gave me some advice.

I called the chaplain in Montpellier who of course wanted to see me back like yesterday.

"'Le Patron' will receive you with open arms. I believe that he has a very good job for you. Please come back!"

My mentor in London was more pragmatic and told me to consider all the angles of what was offered. Because I was now thirty-eight years old, I should consider what the possibilities for future promotion might be. She also suggested that leadership roles should be taken into consideration. She certainly had a point and I made note of it.

I called "Le Patron" to find out more details about the job in question.

"I have the ideal position for you, a supervisory responsibility in the operating theatre, where you will oversee a group of four ER nurses in the department of gynaecology and obstetrics. That is your forte, I believe?" He was certainly right.

I called "Le Grand Patron" in Paris and we discussed the position available at the American Hospital.

The duties were similar to the ones that I had performed while on internship in the general surgery department.

All in all, I was leaning towards Montpellier.

The historical city, the climate, the relaxed atmosphere of the south of France and its casual lifestyle were favouring my decision. On the professional side, I was very enthusiastic to lead my own team.

After talking it over with my family one more time, I opted for the general hospital.

"Le Grand Patron" was not angry and understood the reasons for my decision:

"Let's keep in touch, Yvonne, and remember that, if you need any help, I will always be there for you. Good luck in your new venture!"

I was on my way to a new challenge. In the empty train

compartment, I knelt down and asked Mary for her blessing. My eyes were closed and I had a vision of her beautiful face smiling at me. Was she giving me a sign?

It was like coming back home. I recognized familiar faces in the corridors and was able to find equipment quickly, at the same place as before, wherever I needed it.

"Le Patron" took great care of me and I was allowed a lot of latitude in implementing new systems in the ward. My team was very professional and we shared mutual respect. The hospital was as busy as ever and I had taken up an excruciating schedule with the little black beeper ringing incessantly.

I was visiting my patients regularly and enjoyed the smile on their face when I walked into the room.

Many women had very difficult lives and they shared openly the most intimate details of their tragedies. However, the birth of a child always brought a sacred moment of pride and joy; it was a magical time for them. I helped them in various ways: finding a name for the newborn, drafting letters or filling in forms for the ones who were illiterate. I even brought legal advisors to the few who were in very dangerous relationships.

Some were desperate and needed psychiatric help. I tried everything to give them comfort and make them happy. I considered it to be part of my job and I reinforced this philosophy with all the members of my team.

"Yvonne, I hear very positive comments from your patients. They even call you "Sister Yvonne" and are wondering if you are a nun, did you know that?"

"No, Monsieur"

"You have been passing on your skills and knowledge to your team, I believe?"

"Oui, Monsieur. You see this is my philosophy about nursing. It is very hard to bring a child into this world. For some women it is even traumatic, while others have more serious gynaecological problems. Therefore I feel, if I can spend some extra time with them, I might ease their pain, give them peace of mind and even heal their souls in some cases. With good service they will surely nurse themselves back to health more quickly. It might be above and beyond the call of duty, but we should all try to contribute to a sense of well-being for our patients."

"Bravo, Yvonne, well spoken! I will report your comments at our next council meeting. I knew that to hire you back was the right decision."

"Merci, Monsieur." I smiled and left his office.

"My life was great, I enjoyed my work and my colleagues. The city and its beaches were marvellous. But for no apparent reason, when I walked alone on the golden sand, I felt a knot in my stomach and emptiness in my heart. When it occurred, I sat down and cried, cried, cried, uncontrollably..."

*

*"What was wrong with Yvonne, General?"*

"She was getting calls from above; nobody knew it because she had kept it a secret. It would be two years before she would take the veil, but spiritual messages were sent to her over long periods of time..."

*

*"Sister, did you notify the chaplain?"*

"Not immediately, Colonel. I thought that I was overtired and they were signs of burn-out. I did not pay much attention to it at first. But when more symptoms began to appear, it concerned me. I asked 'Le Patron' to perform some tests and I went through a full physical check-up to know the status of my condition.

"There were no problems at all and I was perfectly fit. However, deep inside my heart I knew that something else had caused some of these ailments.

"You see, Colonel, God calls his flock selectively. He knew me well, but wanted to get my attention without interfering with my work. I was a nurse and in the past many nurses were nuns who combined their skills with serving the Lord. He definitely had plans for me…"

*"What about the signs, Sister?"*

"They were sporadic and did not disturb my routine. For instance, I had an urge to pray, my moods could change on a whim, I talked to angels and apostles in my sleep, saw Mary's face in mirrors and met the Lord in an elevator. These apparitions became familiar to me after a while.

"I also dreamt a lot, had conversations with the Virgin Mary and the crucifixion of Jesus appeared on the wall of my apartment.

"I asked Mary what it all meant but I did not receive any reply.

"I discussed these phenomena with Madame Labelle and the chaplain. When I spoke with them, they both agreed that what I had been experiencing was very positive. Very soon, I was going to find out what Mary and the Lord had planned for my future."

*"Did you keep having visions, Sister?"*

"Yes, Colonel, and now and then I conversed with God when I least expected it.

"Madame Labelle clarified the many events that I could not understand, particularly the meanings of the dreams.

"The whole thing went on for the next two years, until I sat down with the Virgin Mary for a long discussion, regarding my new life at the service of the Lord."

*"Please, Sister, tell us how it happened!"*

"Well, Colonel, I kept seeing some images in front of my eyes and they became clearer day by day. I had an intuition that something out of the ordinary was going to take place. I did not know how and when, but I did know that it would change my life forever.

"The signs and apparitions did not fluster me anymore. I focused my energy and attention on my work and the patients' welfare.

"Soon my prayers would be answered."

*

It had been a hard day's work. I needed peace of mind and decided to take a stroll along the beach. I had taken off my shoes, the sand was warm, it was a truly magical night, with all the shining stars scintillating around the full moon.

The summer season had ended and the entire area was quiet and deserted.

I stopped and listened to the seagulls feeding from the fishermen's nets and watched the tides gradually ebb and flow. I fully enjoyed this scene of serene tranquillity.

I must have been walking ankle deep in the water for at least two hours. A cool breeze blew in from the coast-line and the clear sky was sprinkled with shiny diamonds.

There was no need for a flashlight, as the full moon took care of that. All I could hear was the monotonous sound of the waves crashing against the reefs. On my left there were tall sandy dunes and cacti plants but still no one in sight.

I sat down on a large, flat, stone, closed my eyes, and smelled the fresh air. "I was right to have returned to the south of France and Montpellier. There is no place like it. It is paradise on earth," I murmured.

There were some activities far off. I observed the reflections of the "lampareaux" dancing with the waves. – This group of small fishing-boats, with large lamps at their sterns, specialize in catching sardine, and are very common in the region.

The flashing lights of a huge tanker attracted my attention. It was probably going abroad and honked its loud siren into the night. The other ships reciprocated in sign of acknowledgement of the maritime safety procedures. “Have a good trip, big boy,” I muttered to myself.

I was not on duty for another twenty-four hours and had a lot of time to spare; I decided to keep walking for a while longer.

I was not tired anymore and walked briskly into the night. I had found a new source of energy and my head was clear and rested.

But what was that luminescence up ahead? I wondered.

At a distance I noticed the faint glow of light flicking on and off, but I was not sure what it was. I decided to come closer to find out.

Perched on a small sand dune, was an old rowing-boat leaning against a rock. In the centre, an illumination was spinning very quickly in circles; there were shades of blue, pink, orange, and red. It was hard to distinguish them. It was simply beautiful, like the painter’s palette with mixes of pastel colours moving around, up, down, left and right. I gazed in awe at the light-show, and stood transfixed in shock and disbelief.

“Close your eyes, Yvonne,” a voice asked.

“What? Why?”

“Please close your eyes, Yvonne,” the voice asked again.

I turned around and obeyed.

“Now open your eyes,” the voice said softly.

A tall lady stood in front of me, smiling gently. She was wearing a long brown dress and a light blue headscarf, there was a cord used as a belt around her waist and a white sleeveless blouse was draped over her shoulders.

Her hair was tied in a pony-tail and she was barefoot. The Immaculate Conception opened her arms, her eyes fixed on mine, looking straight through me. She was the most beautiful woman I had ever seen.

"Let me hug you, Yvonne. We finally meet."

As soon as she squeezed me into her arms I felt a surge of energy spreading over my entire body, I could not speak, cry, or even move a muscle. She let go of me and said, "Please sit down, let's talk."

"Mary what happened just now? I feel very strange all of a sudden."

"I just renewed vigour into your system; you are working too hard and are on the verge of a burn-out. Please relax now and then. You should walk on the beach more often…"

We exchanged small talk for a few minutes and then Mary asked me bluntly, "What is troubling you, Yvonne?"

"Mary, I am very happy right now. I may be working too hard but I lead a clean lifestyle and I thank the Lord for it."

"Please answer my question and let's be honest with each other."

"Quite frankly, I feel that something is lacking, I do not know what it is, I have this strong desire to do something more, I want to serve the Lord but I do not know how. Should I take the veil? It has been nagging me for a long time."

"Have you talked about it with anyone else?"

"Yes, my mentor the chaplain at the hospital and Father Guillaume at Chartres cathedral. They both confirmed that I already serve God because I am a nurse and they do not want me to reach a decision hastily. They suggested that I ponder about it before making a final choice which would be irrevocable."

"They are perfectly correct, Yvonne. Very soon you may have to make the most important decision of your life. First and foremost, your heart must speak, then your mind will analyze the pros and cons of becoming a nun, and finally you will reach a decision. I know that you want to come with us and serve our Father, but, Yvonne, only do it when the time is right!"

"Mary, I really enjoy my job very much, and to be a nurse has always been my dream; but the calling to assist God seems to be getting stronger and stronger, what am I to do?"

"Wait and see, until the time when you realize that you need to act upon your vision. At the present time, you are exhibiting great devotion to your nursing duties; but if you take the veil, your loyalty will be to the Lord. Do you understand, Yvonne?"

"Yes, I do, Mary."

"You have a lot of people helping you. You should be thankful, Yvonne, and they are correct: to become a nun and serve the Lord is a very intricate soul-searching decision. It requires devotion, sacrifice, and a lifetime commitment. Are you ready for it, Yvonne? If you had the chance, would you join a convent tomorrow? If I would ask you to walk away with me at that very moment and serve God without hesitation or equivocation for the rest of your life, could you do it?"

"Perhaps not, Mary, I would like to think it through in the first place..."

"You see, Yvonne, to devote your life to God is an honour. It will bring you unimaginable joy, serenity and fulfilment. You must ponder on it now, but very soon you will reach a conclusion and your soul will finally be free of torment. I am supporting you fully."

"Mary, I still want to be a nurse."

"Of course, you are very good at it and you have a promising career ahead of you. Yvonne, many nuns around the world are also nurses and you can become one of them."

"Thank you, Mary. I feel that by taking care of my patients, relieving their pain, discomfort, stress and anxiety, it symbolizes in some way the grace of serving God, doesn't it?"

"It does, and you are an honour to your profession. You also talked face to face with my son Jesus and met the Almighty in Chartres. You fought Satan with all your heart and never despaired. You have a lot of offer; you are a young woman with a wealth of experience and an inspiration to all. When you are ready, Madame Labelle will guide you; I have discussed it with her."

"Thank you, Mary, I do not deserve so much praise."

"Oh, but you do! And from now on I personally consider you one of my angels."

"But, Mary…it cannot be…I am not an angel... Why? What are you telling me?"

"The truth, Yvonne, only the truth. This message comes directly from the Lord himself."

I was flabbergasted, went down on my knees and cried. Mary was smiling and caressed my hair.

"Do not cry, Yvonne, it is a very happy disclosure and now you and I will work on your new role."

"My new role?"

"Yes, Madame Labelle and I will train you to become an angel, it will probably take years."

"I do not know what to say, Mary."

"Say nothing, learn, listen, observe, and ask questions. Practice and your intuition will be critical factors in your success as an angel. Madame Labelle and I are your coaches, so it is 'on the job training' from now on. Good luck! I trust you fully. Do not be concerned, you will do very well."

Mary was smiling, she got up, and she hugged me tightly and whispered, "I am proud of you, you deserve to be my angel!"

"I started to talk to her because I had so many questions to ask. I was confused and did not know where to begin. I covered my face with my hands and sobbed. When I looked up, Mary had gone. I was all alone on the beach and the old rowing-boat leaning against the rock was empty."

*

*"General, this is absolutely extraordinary. Did Yvonne really have an encounter with the Virgin Mary?"*

"Yes, Sergeant, she did. She was very calm and collected when she told us all the details. The team at the monastery accepted Yvonne as an angel of God and did not treat her differently from any other member of the council."

*"Was she still under Madame Labelle's guidance when you met her?"*

"Oh yes, Sergeant. She mentioned that it takes years to become a fully-fledged angel and that only after the Lord's approval could she perform accordingly any divine functions."

*"How do you feel about having met a messenger of God, General?"*

"Well, Sergeant, in fact I met two opposite forces, Lucifer and Yvonne, the angel. It was quite ironical in a way, wasn't it?"

*"Do you think that it played a role in your staying alive during your escape?"*

"I do not know for sure, it may have had an impact on the operation, Sergeant, you never can tell, can you?

*

*"The more you tell me about your life, Sister, the more I want to bow down to you. You are simply an extraordinary person."*

"Please, Colonel, do not say that, you are embarrassing me in front of the council. I am merely God's servant helping poor people in a convent up in the Vietnamese mountains."

Everyone at the table was laughing, when Sister Marie Catherine interjected, "Colonel, Sister Yvonne is very humble and, I may say, a little shy. We are aware of her gifts and qualities but here we all share duties and our devotion to God. We are actually very proud to have an angel among us. Still it will take many more years before she can be called 'angel'. Now, Colonel, let Sister Yvonne finish her story about how she took the veil."

*"Please, Sister, forgive me, I did not mean to embarrass you."*

"No harm done, Colonel."

*

I was forty-one years old with a great career but unfulfilled ambitions in my heart and soul. I wanted to serve the Lord, not only through my job, but as a nun. That is what I wanted. I went to see Father Guillaume in Chartres. He promised to help me with the novitiate.

It was the most important decision of my life and this is why I called the chaplain, wrote a letter to Monsignor Dominique, spoke with my friend the nurse in the UK and sat with Madame Labelle, to be sure that I was not making a mistake in coming to this decision.

Well, they all supported me but I had not yet discussed it with my parents and "Le Patron". I was a little hesitant because I did not know how they would react to the news. Madame Labelle coaxed me into calling my family and telling them the truth. I did and they were very proud of me. My father insisted that I pursue my nursing career but had no problems with my becoming a nun.

Le Patron was looking at me with a pensive expression on his face, he was caressing his chin with his right hand, not saying a word. My file was on his desk right in front of him.

"I believe that you have thought things through, haven't you?"

"Yes, I have, Monsieur."

"What do you want to do, Yvonne?"

"Keep working here until you find my replacement and then move on."

"Very well, I appreciate your professionalism and wish you good luck in your new venture. Not everyone can be a nurse and a nun at the same time. You must follow your calling and be happy. You deserve it, Yvonne! You can count on me for anything you need, do not hesitate."

"Merci, Monsieur."

Well, it was not that hard after all.

I worked in Montpellier for eight more months and prepared for my novitiate.

Everything fell into place. Father Guillaume arranged for my novitiate at the convent of the Sisters of St Joseph of Chambery, Department of Haute Savoie (Savoy) in France, surrounded by very high mountains.

The discipline was very strict. – The rule is based on that of St Augustine. – There were two years of probation during which we made an annual vow. After that, we bound ourselves by perpetual vows. I was forty-four years old when I became a nun.

I enjoyed my time in Chambery, studied very hard and finally the Bible became more understandable.

"Le Patron" had called the local hospital's Chief of Medicine and I kept assisting in surgery wherever they needed me. Monsignor Dominique had also contacted the Mother Superior to let me practice my nursing profession during the course of studies, so that I did not lose my dexterity, which was essential for my future.

Times flies and finally I was Sister Yvonne.

It was time to be assigned to a new destination. I was thrilled because a lot of different experiences and challenges awaited me.

The Mother Superior called me in to her office. She was a stern person but a very astute psychologist with a formidable reputation. She ran the convent with an iron fist and it was ranked number one in the country, sending nuns all over the world.

"Yvonne, it is time to part. Have you enjoyed your novitiate with us?"

"Yes, Mother, I learned a lot and it is with you that I have found my true vocation in life."

"But you are a brilliant nurse, isn't this profession also a vocation?"

"Yes, Mother, it is. But I had the calling to serve God. I had to fulfil this obligation; the signs pressed me daily into taking the veil. These thoughts magnified my curiosity. I had been eaten up by the aspiration to enter a religious order for months. Here, with your help, I have finally achieved peace of mind. I even improved my knowledge of the Bible, which has always been a problem in the past."

"I know, Yvonne. I believe that you have now grasped its significance.

"I have a very special assignment for you that is right up your alley. There is a large convent combined with a monastery called 'the Mission', but it is far away. They are looking for a nun who is a very experienced nurse. The Mother Superior is a young French woman, a great leader and a brilliant strategist.

"The management team calls itself, 'the Council'. It is comprised of Jesuits and local nuns who perform various functions and make sure that the religious institution runs efficiently. It has received a lot of praise for its performance from his Holiness.

"You must be very flexible in your new role. You will be

assisting Father Benedetti, the Chief Surgeon at the mission, and occasionally a local doctor, Dr Henri, at a nearby village, which has its own clinic. You will also teach English, French, catechism, religious studies and nursing. There is a great need for education in rural areas. The monastery is situated on the peak of a mountain but it is still accessible by following a trail.

"This is a great opportunity, Yvonne, and you are very highly recommended.

"Your references are absolutely remarkable, even gleaming. Your former employers and mentors, including Monsignor Dominique in Paris, have all praised your attitude, dedication, and professionalism in your work. You can be proud of yourself, Yvonne."

"Mother, have you checked my past?"

"I knew all about it before you even joined us."

"Mother, I know that it has not always been that…"

"Stop, the past is past; let's look now at the bright future ahead and the opportunity that is offered to you. God is on your side, my child. I will do everything that I can to help you; but please, as one says, do not miss the boat. Do you agree?"

"Yes, Mother, it sounds fantastic, but you said that it was far away. Where exactly is it?"

"In a very dangerous place where war has already broken out and will continue raging for years to come…"

"Where?"

"Vietnam. I may add that the Monastery is located in a strategic location, right on the border between North and South."

"I see…"

"Sister Marie Catherine, the Mother Superior, insists on taking care of everyone indiscriminately. It is quite an unusual place with American or Australian soldiers being treated beside Viet Cong Mercenaries and NVA officers. Between the four walls of this monastery there is no war.

It is going to be very hectic at times, Yvonne."

"I am used to it, Mother."

"How do you feel about this assignment?"

"Positive, I always strive for a challenge and the mission satisfies that criterion."

"You are leaving in forty-eight hours. I will give you the details of your journey. Please notify your family at once of your departure."

"Mother, I must ask, how did you learn about my past?"

"Contacts, connections, referrals. Father Benedetti has worked with your former 'Patrons' and I have known Father Guillaume and the chaplain in Montpellier for more than twenty years. Monsignor Dominique has been a guest at the novitiate on special occasions. It is a small world, Yvonne."

"I want to thank you again for this great opportunity. Please be assured that I will perform to the best of my abilities."

"I know, Yvonne; I have no doubt about it. Now it is time to say goodbye, let me hug you and wish you good luck in your new venture."

Then, out of her pocket, Mother Superior pulled a little pouch containing a gold chain with a cross that she placed around my neck.

"This will give you strength when you face hardship and please always remember us, my child."

"I always will, Mother."

Then she whispered in my ear, "You are blessed. You are not going to Vietnam alone. Mary and Madam Labelle are holding your hand."

"But Mother… How do you know about Mary and Madame Labelle? Who told you?"

She smiled at me and closed the door.

*

*"General, Sister Yvonne must have performed brilliantly at the mission during the war, am I correct?"*

"You are; and she remained in her position for many years after that."

*"What happened next at the meeting with the Council?"*

"Sister Marie Catherine asked the members to narrate some of their experiences about Lucifer as compared with divine apparitions. All of them had personally dealt with Satan, while only a few, including Sister Yvonne, had witnessed interventions or inexplicable interferences from guardian angels.

"There were stories of exorcisms, resuscitations, and diabolical possessions. It was an informative session, chaired by the Mother Superior, who wanted to demonstrate the Machiavellian tricks and dishonest methods the Devil can use to achieve his aims. All the stories were true, disturbing and scary at times, to say the least."

## CHAPTER EIGHTEEN

## EXORCISMS AND THE BRIGHT LIGHT

"Sister how long have you been in Vietnam?"

"More than two years, and I have enjoyed every minute of it. This mission was exactly what I needed to fulfil the dream of my life. I serve God spiritually and professionally and enjoy helping the locals, who are very poor but talented. I work hard, teach, learn, and pray a lot. This is very good for the soul, Colonel."

Sister Marie Catherine announced, "Colonel, you know all about Sister Yvonne's history and it has demonstrated that the Devil can be beaten on his own ground if one has faith. Everyone here present, including myself, has had dealings with the Great Deceiver in one way or another. Please listen to the stories, they are true testimonies that will help you understand him better, discern his remarkable cunning to persuade people to join him in Hell."

"Sister, before we begin I have some questions about religion and beliefs that I want to ask the Council. They have been nagging at me for a long time, do you mind?"

"Not at all, shoot!"

"Did Jesus go to Hell after the Crucifixion and the Resurrection?"

"We believe at the Council that he did, however not all Christians agree. We leave it open to the opinion of believers. The Catholic interpretation of the Bible is slightly different from other faiths on the matter," answered Father Lucien.

"I have seen abominable furry monsters in the forest close to the dolmen and Satan told me that they are the housekeepers of Hell. Do you know what they really are?"

"Yes we do. They are the servants of the Devil and eat dead bodies. They are creatures of the abyss. Rumours circulate that they have eaten babies alive, taking them from their cots or their mothers' arms. Never approach them, Colonel, they are extremely dangerous," said Father Hervé.

"Lucifer has placed a curse on the two farmers who are accompanying me, because they offended him. Are they in real danger?'

"They surely are. This isn't some idle threat. He will kill them and you will not be able to stop him. When it happens, it will be swift, right in front of your eyes. He has already made up his mind," explained Father Romero.

"What do you say to an atheist?"

"Nothing, people are free to have their own ideas regarding faith and belief. However, when the Lord calls, what does one do? I have witnessed many situations when people were on their deathbed and it was time to go. They all prayed intensely for forgiveness of their sins as they felt that they were in a state of perdition, having been an atheist all their life. They wanted a priest to perform an act of contrition and give them the last rites. The closer you get to God, the more you start thinking about your next journey and realize that the power of prayer is absolute. They all asked for salvation and redemption. That is why Jesus Christ is our saviour," Sister Angele stated.

"I met Satan and he was a Vietnamese Tiger, is there a reason why he chose to appear like that?"

"You see, Colonel, Lucifer has the power to become whatever or whoever he wants. However some specific animals represent Satan in the Catholic religion. He probably decided to be one of them."

"What are these animals?'

"The crocodile, the dragon, the serpent, the rat, the wolf, the bear, and the leopard," said Sister Marie Catherine.

"I should therefore be watching out for them when I resume my escape; am I correct, Sister?"

"Yes, and I may add that insects, locusts, spiders, maggots and flies are all signs of the Devil's presence. You have a lot to worry about, Colonel."

"Was there a particular significance in the Crucifixion of Jesus Christ? I am very curious about the 'mystery of the Cross'."

Father Benedetti answered, "For centuries, theologians and ecclesiastics have debated, written, and made assumptions about this particular historical event, but without any concrete evidence. According to the witnesses of the day, Mary the Mother of God and Mary Magdelene cleaned away the blood after Jesus was brought down from the cross and many people, including Roman soldiers, touched the cross to purify their souls. They all knew who he was and the miracles that he had performed. From that moment on, the Cross became the symbol of suffering, penitence, and Christianity.

"The High Priests, politicians and local rich merchants did not want to accept Jesus as the Messiah, and this is why they made an example of him in front of the masses. He was a scapegoat and wrongly accused. To diminish his status he was placed between two common thieves. But, Colonel, you know the rest..."

"I do, Father."

Father Benedetti continued, "Crucifixion was a common form of punishment used by the Romans. The way Jesus was nailed to the cross has long been a subject for debate. All in all, Colonel, he died to save us all. The cross, I believe, played only a small part in the event."

"But he is the Redeemer, Father."

"Yes, Colonel, he is; and this entire council can vouch for his generosity, forgiveness; and guidance. We all have witnessed the power of his actions."

"I would like to ask your views about Purgatory, Hell, Paradise, and the Pearly Gate."

"Sister Yvonne, can you please answer the Colonel?" asked Sister Marie Catherine.

"I will sum up what has already been written in the Bible. Many call it mythology or legend, but it is the book of God.

"Paradise is simply beautiful, calm and peaceful. By contrast, Hell is horrifying, putrid, a place of debauchery and death. Purgatory is a transitional and unpleasant place where mortals suffer and must repent for their sins; otherwise they are doomed to perdition. However, nobody has ever returned to give us all the details.

"The Pearly Gate is Heaven's official entrance, closely monitored by its gatekeeper, St Peter himself. Hell is controlled by Lucifer, assisted by his henchmen: rogue angels, hard-core sinners, slaves, and satanic servants, including the furry monsters. Remember, Colonel, that Satan was God's favourite archangel, a perfect creation, who is cunning, brilliant, charming, and cruel, with the mind of both an angel and the demon; above all he is a deceiver. He is the most dangerous creation in the universe.

"Many Christians do not believe that these places really exist but the council has come to the conclusion that they are individually a 'state of mind' for one to ponder on and reflect how to receive redemption and God's pardon for the sins of the past.

"When we look at the after-life objectively, we see it more as a time spent in retreat to meditate, pray and search for the core of our soul.

"Undoubtedly there is a feeling that Paradise and the Dark

Abyss exist and that only with the Lord's permission can St Peter open the Gate for us. For the unrepentant who have made their choice, Hell becomes their habitat.

"Jesus knows what Satan's domain is like, because, after his crucifixion, he went down for three days into the inferno, trying to reason and convince the sinners there to repent, but all in vain.

"The concept of the end of life and the resurrection, the passage to eternity, the interpretation of the rich poetic imagery painted by illustrious artists over the centuries, is unequivocally personal; after all we shall all meet our maker, who will decide for us if we must go up or down. We have no choice in the matter."

"Bravo, Sister Yvonne, it was very informative and to the point!" stated Sister Marie Catherine.

We all applauded in unison.

Sister Yvonne thanked the council with a timid smile.

"Now, I give the floor to our members," she announced.

The Colonel then asked Sister Marie Catherine if she could narrate her story.

*Sister Marie Catherine tells her story*

Following her novitiate she lived in Aix-en-Provence, south of France, where she worked as a nurse, assisting a midwife performing births. On the day when the event took place, the patient was a woman in her early thirties who had a bad reputation, loose morals and was unmarried.

Somehow they were worried because the lady did not show any signs of pregnancy and was not suffering from contractions, but nevertheless complained of an acute pain moving inside and around her belly.

Sister Marie Catherine found it an abnormal situation and

talked to the patient privately.

She learned that the woman had a one-night stand with a stranger whom she met in a bar and later found herself pregnant; the man vanished.

Over the next four months her symptoms had not manifested normally and she felt on occasion a strange sensation of something foreign in her stomach, it did not seem like a baby but it was smaller, creating annoying abdominal discomfort. She had not consulted a physician because of embarrassment and had even considered an abortion. However her inner religious beliefs prevented her from going ahead with this and she mentally welcomed the child. Yes, her heart had spoken. The newborn would be a real blessing in her life. She wanted to redeem herself after her previous pathetic and miserable existence.

The lady was twisting on her bed; the severe pains had started again. Her screams were a loud howling and her entire body was shaking and breaking out in a sweat.

The midwife went to check the foetus, but all of a sudden she stopped and turned towards the sister with a frightened look on her face. She moved away from the bed, got up, speechless, immobile, her eyes wide open.

"What is it?" the sister asked,

"My God, oh My Lord, how is this possible?" she replied.

She was holding her bloody hands in front of her and tears were running down her face.

The nun was confused and wanted to know what had happened. The patient was sobbing, asking to see her baby.

"Is there something wrong with the baby?" whispered the sister to the midwife who did not respond and only shook her head. She was in a daze, paralyzed with fear.

Sister Marie Catherine realized that this pregnancy had gone terribly wrong and took charge of the situation at once because the life of both patient and child were at stake. The nun asked the midwife to leave the room and to pull herself together.

The lady was breathing more easily and had calmed down a little; these were positive signs.

The Sister wiped the patient's face and body with cool water and encouraged her to push hard to help the baby out of the womb.

After a few minutes the nun decided to check the baby's position inside the uterus, but...but...

Oh Gosh! There was no baby but instead a large black hairy spider crawled out of the vagina and jumped onto the sister's chest. With a scream she brushed it off. The creepy creature moved with the speed of light all over the furniture, the walls, the doors; it was everywhere. Finally it stopped on a ceiling beam, facing the lady directly.

She was yelling, "Why? Why? Why? God, why did you do this to me? Why are you punishing me this way?"

The midwife walked back into the room and when she saw the spider, she dropped to her knees, stammering and mumbling a prayer. Sister Marie Catherine tried to keep everything under control but it was definitely a difficult situation. She gave the lady some relaxant, and made a vain attempt with a broom to push the creature out of the wide-open window. Why then didn't it leave? Instead it waited, immobile, looking straight at the patient.

It was a large creature, with a body as wide as a dessert plate, comprised of eight thick legs, at least fifteen centimetres in length, with two big, bright, red, eyes on the top of the head. Its mouth opened and closed constantly. We all looked at it silently. It bore no colours, no stripes, it was pure black. It was hissing sporadically, which was quite strange because arthropods do not usually make any sound. The eyes formed two, big, red, circles, moving left to right and vice versa.

It was a frightening sight and Sister Marie Catherine never forgot this occurrence.

The lady was transferred to the city hospital where she was put through a battery of tests. There was absolutely nothing wrong with her physically.

She was in perfect health and of course had never been pregnant. As a precaution she was sent for psychological evaluation. She did not fare well; she failed many of the tests and was diagnosed as severely depressed. Of course she had been traumatized by the experience and was still in shock.

Sister Marie Catherine had grown to like this lady and tried to help her through her ordeal. She visited her at the hospital and talked to the doctors about her case. They all agreed that it had been an awful experience for the patient and very, very bizarre, to say the least. Experts were called and the description of the spider did not fit any known species. Why did a spider grow inside her womb? Many assumptions were made but none could really be regarded as valid.

Specialists from Marseilles were called and once again all the tests and examinations proved negative. The lady was in perfect health and the experts concluded that perhaps a tiny small spider could have penetrated into her vagina and grown inside her. It might have come from a swamp, a field, a garden, a lake, or even a swimming-pool. The lady totally disagreed with their diagnosis.

Sister Marie Catherine was deeply concerned for the lady's state of mind. She could not come to terms with the fact that what she had experienced was "a freak of nature", if it could be described that way. She blamed herself, she incessantly brought up tales of the past and told Sister Marie Catherine that the strange man who had got her pregnant was the Devil himself. As a result, she was now possessed.

Satan can take many forms and appearances and in this case it had been a handsome stranger with dark hair.

She cried all day and all night repeating, "God punished me and Lucifer will take me. I deserve it. I can feel him inside me, he even talks to me at night!"

The medical team wanted to send her to a sanatorium in the Alps, where tranquillity, peace, and the fresh air would do her a lot of good. She categorically refused. She wanted to stay where Sister Marie Catherine could be at her side; she insisted that she was the only friend that she had ever had in her life. She confided in her the most intimate secrets.

Over the next few weeks her physiological condition deteriorated drastically and there was cause for alarm. She did not take baths anymore, her skin colour was like wax and she swore like a trooper. She had stopped eating solid food and lost a lot of weight.

She had bouts of anger and even attacked the orderlies at the hospital for no apparent reason.

Sister Marie Catherine seemed to have a soothing effect on her and during her visits the lady was calm and relaxed.

There was definitely a tumultuous affliction inside her, causing her physical and psychological pain. But what was it? Why did her appearance and mental condition change so rapidly? What caused it?

The nun wanted to know why her friend maintained that she was possessed by Satan?

"He tells me that he is my only salvation, that I deserve hell because I am a whore, and that I must serve him for eternity to pay back my life of sins and debauchery. He ordered me not to shower anymore; he insults me and calls me a waste of life, a piece of garbage and a disgrace of humanity. He ordered me to stay alive to serve him and not to try to commit suicide. He wants me to suffer.

After a few more days of observation, Sister Marie Catherine went to speak with the Chief of Psychiatry; and they discussed the lady's case and her symptoms in detail. She had no physical ailments and was definitely not mentally disturbed. However, the medical team insisted that some aspects of her behaviour, her attitudes and short temper had become problematic. Her actions were very unpredictable and it had been difficult to make a diagnosis.

"She is a lost soul, Doctor, she has surrendered all senses of spirituality, and she insists that she is possessed by the Devil who switched her baby for a large spider."

"Do you believe a story like this, Sister?"

"At first I ignored it, considering the pain and trauma she had suffered, but you know, subconsciously, I now believe the lady."

"What do you plan to do?" asked the doctor.

Sister Marie Catherine divulged her plans to the Chief of Psychiatry who listened attentively.

She felt that the patient had genuinely been possessed and that an exorcism was the only way to give her back her life. The ritual had to be authorized by the local bishop of Aix-en-Provence.

In the Catholic Church the request for an exorcism can be a lengthy and complicated application procedure. A medical certificate stating the psychological condition of the patient must first be issued. The local priest will then put in writing a demand to the bishop of the area, who, if the exorcism is authorized, will address an official entreaty to Rome for approval. All documents are scrutinized before being sanctioned. Finally the Vatican will send a licensed exorcist to perform the ceremony.

Once Sister Marie Catherine had received the written medical status, she went to visit Father Edmond the parish priest. He listened attentively, now and then asking specific questions, and even reiterating some of the words that Sister Marie Catherine had just said.

"I need to know every detail, even your inner thoughts on the matter, Sister. The bishop will need to present the most comprehensive aspects of your case to the Vatican for the rite to be approved. An exorcism is a very delicate procedure; a failure in the ceremony can cause grave harm to the subject or even death. Do you understand?"

"I do, Father."

The subject had been tied down onto her bed and all loose objects had been removed from the room before Father Edmond's arrival. He was going to make an assessment as to whether an exorcism should be performed.

Sister Marie Catherine could not recognize the lady. She was pale beyond belief, her hair was stringy and turning gray, she had sunken eyes and spoke with a cavernous tone of voice. When Father Edmond arrived, all hell broke loose. The bed started jerking up and down; deafening whistling sounds and loud laughter filled the room accompanied with pungent smells of urine and faeces.

The lady was throwing insults and profanities at the Father. When a person is possessed they can get an aversion to anything or anyone involved with the Catholic Church, such as priests, nuns, artefacts, crucifixes and cathedrals. What was very odd, however, was that the subject continued to talk to Sister Catherine and had no animosity towards her.

Satan addressed them mockingly. "Why did you come here? Do you really believe that a little sister and an insignificant priest can take away a servant of the Dark Lord? Get out, let her be, she is mine now, there is nothing you can do about it!"

Father Edmond sprinkled holy water all over her body, she screamed and writhed in pain. She turned her head towards Sister Marie Catherine and whispered, "Please stay with me, make him go away. I cannot endure it any longer, I am suffering too much, take him out, please."

"We will, don't worry," answered the sister.

Father Edmond approached the lady and recited some parts of the rites and made the sign of the cross on her forehead.

The subject spewed up a flow of bile at the priest's face and laughed hysterically, "That will teach you, Priest, your God has no place in this room, get out!"

They both left flustered and Father Edmond said, "She is definitely possessed; I will contact the bishop without any further delay."

"Father, why isn't she turning violent or angry towards me? I also represent the Catholic Church but she still recognizes me and begged me for my help. I cannot understand it, can you?"

"I am not a licensed exorcist but I have assisted at a few rites over the years. On some occasions a subject who had strong affinity with family members or good friends still maintained lucidity through their torments, and – as in your case – asked their loved ones for release from the devil.

"It is rare. but not impossible. The devil takes possession of a soul in various ways, and he is cunning and a deceiver. He likes to toy with peoples' souls. Demonstrations of possession differ. A few similar manifestations have been noted, but each ceremony is different.

"I will request your presence as a second assistant; you will be very useful during the rituals, since the subject has such strong and positive feelings for you."

"But, Father, I don't know anything about exorcism; I might

be in the way, more than anything."

"You will be fine. I promise you it will be the experience of a lifetime, you'll see..."

Sister Marie Catherine nodded apprehensively.

Father Datria had been trained by Grabriele Amorth, a renowned exorcist of the diocese of Rome. Father Edmond knew him well and Sister Marie Catherine was appointed second assistant for the ceremony. Upon entering the room Father Datria placed the stole over his shoulders and raised his crucifix high above his head. Father Edmond sprinkled blessed water on the subject's body.

"ECCE Crucem Domini (Behold the cross of the Lord)," Father Datria kept repeating.

The lady screamed, swore profusely and vomited green bile all over the bed.

Then a verbal exchange ensued between Lucifer and the exorcist.

Sister Marie Catherine recalled that it was more colloquial than formal. Satan even used good humour and sarcasm through it all. Datria did not flinch from his duties. He followed the Roman ritual to the letter, reciting the prayers, asking Lucifer to leave her body at once, admonishing him for making her suffer unnecessarily. He knew that the devil was playing his usual tricks. Father Edmond, meanwhile, kept reading verses of the holy Bible aloud while sprinkling the room and the subject with sacred water.

Sister Marie Catherine was holding her rosary with one hand while wiping the sweat off the lady's forehead with the other.

The subject was in terrible pain and shouting profanities too horrid to describe.

Green bile flew out of her mouth with such force that it

splashed all over the sister's face.

The smell emanating from the lady's body was nauseating. She was still tied up on her bed that was soaked with urine and faeces. Her eyes had turned completely white in their sockets and her gravelly voice was stammering incoherently.

After a while the whole room became shrouded in a thick mist and it was cold and damp.

Meanwhile Father Datria was carrying on with the rituals and ordered Satan to go back to his dark abyss.

"We are not afraid of you, Demon, you are in no position to fight us and to challenge God the Almighty. You will lose, leave at once!" he commanded. We are mocking you, you unclean spirit with no soul. We shall stay with the possessed until you return to hell and never come back!"

"I will make you pay for you arrogance," retorted Lucifer.

"Try me, Hellion, I am ready for you," yelled Datria.

All of a sudden, dozens of little black spiders invaded the room, crawling rapidly everywhere.

Sister Marie Catherine screamed, but Father Datria advised her to stay calm and to control her emotion.

"Satan is showing off again. Don't pay him any attention, it's a devilish trick!"

The lady was now convulsing, her white eyes were dilated and black spiders came out of her open mouth, running all over her body.

"Father, look, look!" shrieked Sister Marie Catherine.

Datria gently placed his crucifix on the lady's chest and gave the sign of the cross on her forehead.

Father Edmond knelt down beside her bed and recited from the Holy Bible.

"Lucifer, you are no match for me. Give up! She is no longer your servant, God has taken her back and assigned her a guardian angel, Sister Marie Catherine," the exorcist cried out loudly.

"The little sister should fear the wrath of Lucifer," Satan replied.

"No, she is one of us; an angel of the Lord and the Virgin Mary has blessed her and welcomed her calling."

The spiders had multiplied and covered the walls, the ceiling, and the furniture. The priests were now redoubling their efforts to fight off Lucifer, who was very angry. He did not want to lose a prospective servant and was using the oldest trick in the book to keep his prey.

"Go away, despicable creature of the abyss, you cannot win. We are three against you and you will not take her away from us, you hear?" shouted Father Datria.

"How dare you, Priest, oppose me?"

Then in unison, Father Datria, Father Edmond and Sister Marie Catherine harangued Lucifer vociferously, pacing the room, spraying blessed water all over the lady's body and reading the Bible aloud. Datria was holding his crucifix high above his head, Sister Marie Catherine was reciting her prayers at the top of her lungs, and Father Edmond was reading passages of the rituals, with the rosary in his hands. They were loud, powerful, and focused to overpower the Devil.

"You cannot conquer the kingdom of the Lord, you are banished from God's circle, as you have betrayed him, and you do not belong to the family of the Lord. Go away, leave at once and never return! We command you, the Lord commands you, return to the dark abyss. You belong to the inferno of hell, and God commands you! At that moment a howl of rage filled the room. Father Datria opened the window and a brisk wind passed through with a whistling sound.

"Gone at last," he whispered.

The lady lying down on the bed had her eyes closed.

"I am going to clean her up and move her to another room. I want to make her comfortable for when she wakes up," said Sister Marie Catherine.

"You did well, Sister," said Father Datria.

"Thank you, Father."

*"Did the lady recover from her ordeal, Sister?"*

"Yes, Colonel, the physicians gave her a thorough check-up and did not find any trace of trauma or mental illness. She was perfectly fine and did not remember the exorcism."

*"What became of her, Sister?"*

"She went back to school, became a teacher but never married. We kept in touch over the years and she leads a happy life."

*

"You see, Colonel, Satan cannot win all the time, he is not invincible. We have all had our battles with him; and you, Colonel, you will have to face the toughest fight of your military career when you leave this monastery, not with the VC, not with the NVA, but with Lucifer himself. Please take our advice and do not let him con you with his sordid stratagems," said Father Benedetti.

"I know, Father, and I am aware of his tricks, I cannot afford to drop my guard."

*

### *Sister Marie Catherine tells another story*

Sister Marie Catherine had another interesting story to tell. She was not the protagonist in this case, but narrated events that had made headlines throughout her country when she was a young novice.

In a small hamlet in Alsace, in the eastern part of France, an old woman, who was nicknamed "the witch", was rumoured to live with the devil in her home. Very often foul smells emanated from the house, incantations were heard at night. No one dared to investigate the hearsay and the local priest advised his parishioners to stay away from the area. When she passed away, on the same night, terrible noises could be heard, and there was great commotion inside.

On the following day, the gendarmes went to look in the house for clues.

The furniture was all over the place, the floor was littered with broken glass and chinaware. It looked as if the place had been ransacked.

Oddly enough, silverware was hanging upside down from the ceiling, which was dripping with blood. They found a book with a black leather cover, embossed with silver letters, entitled, "Book of the Abyss". The local priest urged the policemen not to open it under any circumstance.

The house was carefully searched and finally padlocked for safety reasons. The mysterious black book was left inside on the top of a dresser.

About two weeks later, on a very cold night, the property was engulfed in flames. The firemen battled against the fire with all their might, but in vain. It continued to rage until the small hours of the morning. The fire chief gave the order to let the house burn down to minimize the risks. The locals claimed to have seen the face of Satan in the flames; others had heard the demon laugh in the middle of the night. But these stories were probably not true.

It was the kind of blaze that was very unusual. The chief had never experienced such a fiery combustion. It would not stop, no matter how much water was poured over it. It burned and burned and burned throughout the night. The heat was unbearable.

Suddenly, around 6am, it stopped. The firemen looked at each other baffled, aghast. It was as if someone had turned off a switch. The inferno had completely ceased. After the smoke had dissipated, everyone could see the house still standing, smouldering but erect. The Chief ordered his men to douse the structure and called the gendarmes and the priest to come to the site.

The padlocks were opened, but what a shock! The inside of the house remained intact. The temperature was cool and there were no traces of a fire having taken place.

The old lady had never married. She had no family and was known to be unkempt. However, the house was tidy and clean, the bed was made up and there was no foul smell any more. It was very different from the last visit, before the house was padlocked.

"Who did this?" asked the captain of the Gendarmerie.

"We do not know, Captain," replied an officer.

"Last time I was there, it was a pigsty," said the fire chief.

"Yes, that was the way the old lady lived, but look at it now, you could eat off the floor," replied the priest.

All of a sudden, voices, chanting their mysterious incantation, could be heard throughout the house. No one could understand what was said because it was in a foreign dialect.

"Father, look at the dresser," said the gendarme.

The Book of the Abyss was still there, untouched, unscathed, at the same place.

"Please do not touch it, do not open it! It is the book of Lucifer, it is demonic reading!" said the priest.

"Let's go now, put the padlocks back on the house, place safety fixtures on all the doors and cordon off the entire area! We do not want any children playing around the house. It could be very dangerous," the captain of the gendarmes said.

"Yes, Sir. Right away, Sir" replied the officer.

"Father, could you come with me to the hospital morgue?" asked the captain. "I want to look at the old lady's body, just to be sure".

"Can I join you?" inquired the fire chief.

"Sure, let's go," said the captain.

"What happened over there, Father?" he asked. "Do you know? The fire, the house in top-notch condition, the chants. It is very strange, very bizarre, I must say.".

"Captain, it was the work of the Devil. Satan wanted to show his power. He possessed the old lady years ago, and he did not want anyone to take her house away after she died. He owns the property in his own right. It was a message from the crypt or from Hell, whatever way you want to interpret it."

The fire chief listened, attentively nodding and the captain cleared his throat a few times. Nothing else was said until they reached the local hospital.

"We want to see the body of the 'witch'," said the captain.

They were shown to the morgue.

The old lady was known as the 'witch' in the entire region. Nobody in fact knew her real name. "She is the devil's advocate," murmured the locals at the corners of the bistro. Her past was hazy. No one could be sure of her age, her background, or her means of income, and she did not have any relatives. She was a recluse.

The pathologist in charge at the hospital accompanied the three men to the morgue to show them the old lady's body.

"I have not conducted a post-mortem yet because I need an authorization from a family member or a city official. It is the law."

"I will sign the forms, Doctor, she did not have any family," said the Captain.

"Very well, her body is over there," pointed the doctor.

An assistant pulled out the metallic drawer, and to their astonishment, it was empty – bare – the body had vanished!

"Is this a joke, Doctor?" inquired the Captain.

"I... I... am sorry, I cannot understand. The body was right there, I saw it myself this morning."

"Maybe someone misplaced it, please check the drawers to be sure," the fire chief requested.

"Yes, yes, let me verify the log, it is unbelievable. I am sorry for the confusion, please give me a minute," replied the doctor.

Two assistants came to help the pathologist to review the list and inspect all the drawers.

"No, Captain, there is no mistake, the body is missing for sure," the doctor confirmed.

"So, it has simply vanished into thin air? How could this be possible?" retorted the fire-chief.

"It has never happened before, I have no explanation for it. Again, please accept my apologies," the pathologist responded uneasily.

"Father, you keep silent, don't you find the situation peculiar, to say the least?"

"Not if Lucifer is involved, Captain."

"What is that gibberish, Father?" I am a Christian but I have difficulty in placing Satan at the heart of a problem, when there is possibly a more logical explanation, like in this case when a body has disappeared from the town morgue. Why blame the Devil? It could have been a clerical mistake, or a human error. I am convinced that the doctor here present will find the old lady's corpse soon enough."

"Sorry to disagree with you, Captain, all our files and

drawers have been thoroughly checked, the body is not there. It is gone, nowhere to be found," interjected the pathologist.

"Don't you believe in the Devil, Captain?" asked the priest.

"I am a sceptic and I have never met anyone who had dealings with him personally, Father."

"Please pray never to meet him, Captain," replied the priest.

"What did really happen, Father?" inquired the fire-chief.

"The old lady was a recluse with no friends, family, or relatives. She was nicknamed 'the witch', and no one knew her real name. She could have been more than one hundred years old and still lived all by herself.

"Yes, she could be odd at times, but she never hurt anyone; she just did not mingle with her neighbours. One thing is for sure; she was a long-time servant of Lucifer and maybe she was his mistress in the past; that is why she was left alone and did not have to fulfil any obligations towards him. The Book of the Abyss was her bedside reading and proof of her creed.

"The Dark Lord did not want the house and its land to be destroyed and sold. It was his gift to her, and still is. If God works in mysterious ways, so does Satan!

"Now she is gone, no one knows where she went and what she will do. We all should leave it at that and stop speculating about things we cannot comprehend. I have said my piece. Now you know what I think."

Everyone kept silent, nodding and looking at the priest with a perplexed expression on their faces.

"You have made your point, Father, let's not waste any more time. Doctor, I will sign the forms required by your supervisors. You will not get into trouble," said the captain.

"Thank you, I'll send them to your office this afternoon."

The house still stands today on its piece of land. Occasionally the gendarmes check inside and nothing has been touched. Surprisingly, it is spotless and tidy, the smell of roses perfuming the master bedroom, with the Book of the Abyss on the top of the dresser, the way it was left just before the fire...

*

A standing ovation was given to Sister Marie Catherine.

*"Great stories!" applauded the Colonel.*

*

*Father Lucien tells his story*

Father Lucien was the next person to speak. He remembered a man who had a devastating car accident while under the influence. His eight-year-old daughter died from her injuries but he survived the crash. He never got over his loss. He drank even more to drown his sorrows because he could not live with a guilty conscience.

One night he saw his daughter standing in a very bright tunnel – it was not a dream – and he sobered up very quickly. She spoke to him calmly, she looked radiant, and was smiling at her father. She had forgiven him, she told him not to worry about her because she was now in a very beautiful place where peace and love were omnipresent. She begged him to stop drinking and get healthy.

However, he could not escape his torment, he was never going to be able to reconcile himself to the fact that he had killed her while drunk-driving. He just wanted to die because he felt that he deserved hell and nothing else. His drinking spiralled out of control and soon all of his body functions ceased altogether.

The end was near and his wife was at his bedside.

Suddenly a stranger walked into the bedroom.

"Who are you? What are you doing here? You cannot walk into my room uninvited," she yelled.

"Quiet, woman! I came for your husband, it is none of your business. Leave at once!" snarled the stranger.

He was very thin, pale, wearing a large black hat, a long dark overcoat, and pointed boots; and the lady said that his fingernails were unusually long and painted red. His sunken eyes were cold and he had a raucous voice. The lady remembered that the man was extremely tall with a creepy appearance.

Both men were locked in the bedroom for a long time. When they came out, her husband seemed cured of his fatal disease.

"What has happened?" she asked.

"He is fine, he will not die and you should say good-bye to him because he will not come back. You will never see him again," the stranger replied.

"Where are you taking him? He cannot leave me just like that, he is my husband," she implored.

"Enough, I don't have the time to discuss it, he is mine now, he belongs to me," snapped the tall stranger.

"Let's go," he told the husband.

"Yes, my Lord," he replied.

"What did you call him? – My Lord?" asked the wife.

"I am the Dark Lord of the Abyss, just remember that," replied the stranger sardonically.

They left without another word. She never saw her husband again throughout her whole lifetime. Satan had taken him into his diabolical inferno. She met a designated exorcist from the Vatican a few months following the incident. He asked her pertinent questions relating to the stranger's visit.

"The room became very cold, a thin icy mist floated around the apartment and the man had a strange smell about him. It was like gun-powder; yes, very strong," said the lady.

"Sulphur?" suggested the priest.

"Yes, that's it; sulphur, Father!" the lady acknowledged.

"Do you believe that it was the devil, Father?" the woman

inquired.

"Yes, it was, you will never see your husband again and this is the painful truth."

"Where did he go, Father?"

"To hell, plain and simple. Lucifer took him under his wing, cured him of his critical condition and made him a servant; but that is what your husband wanted. There is no way out for him anymore," explained the priest.

The lady was sobbing, she hugged the father tightly and left the room.

The priest stood facing the window, looking at the blue sky, trying to sort out painful thoughts that troubled his mind. The poor, the sick, the dying, teenagers, the destitute and the homeless, they all were prey for Satan who constantly seeks new recruits to fill his ranks.

There was nothing that he or anyone could do to stop it. Satan lurks at every corner looking out for weak and troubled souls.

The father needed to pray...

*Father Lucien tells another story*

Father Lucien introduced his next story to the council and the Colonel.

He was a student at "Le Grand Séminaire" in the north of France, and following an internship, he was assigned to be a teacher at a boys' school. It was during that particular time that he discovered how perniciously Satan worked.

One of his students became Lucifer's victim quite rapidly, gradually crumbling in front of his eyes, until he was taken to the trenches of no return. The priest had been powerless to save him. Sebastien was a handsome sixteen-year-old with a great disposition; he was brilliant academically, and a top-notch athlete.

His favourite subjects were Catechism, Latin, Sports and Philosophy. He was a rising star at the Lyceé and a prospect for France's "Grandes Ecoles". Nevertheless, Lucifer had other plans for the young man.

Suddenly his outgoing personality changed dramatically and Father Lucien noticed frequent mood-swings and bouts of anger.

Germain became increasingly irritable and even violent. His grades fell to the lowest score and his parents were at a loss to understand what had happened to him. They were alarmed by their son's behaviour. Moreover the boy had become unkempt. His personal hygiene left a lot to be desired. He was very rebellious and rebuffed any form of authority.

One day Germain had a fight with a classmate at a nearby public park. He totally lost control. He kicked the other boy to death and left him lying there in full view.

Germain refused to answer questions from the police. Because of his age and his father's influence he was released on bail.

The last time he was seen, he was walking in the red-light district of his hometown with a tall man who was wearing a dark coat and a large black hat.

Witnesses confirmed that the young man seemed jovial and talkative with the stern-faced stranger.

Somehow he seemed totally unconscious that he was on the road to perdition and that Lucifer was showing him the way…"

*

The council clapped in unison.

"Father, your stories are mind-blowing, that's all I can say," exclaimed the Colonel.

"Remember Colonel that they are all true stories," interjected Sister Marie Catherine."

"I know; and I am enjoying them all. Please continue!" said

the Colonel.

Father Benedetti began to talk. He was next to tell his stories.

*Father Benedetti tells his first story*

While working as an intern at the Bellevue hospital in New York City, USA, the priest met a compatriot from the island of Corsica – a man in his forties who was suffering from insomnia and migraines.

The man's soul had been bruised and his heart ached to tell the whole truth to a man of the cloth. He was a professional assassin for the Mafia. He was the best in the business with at least seventy-two kills to his name. The other Mafiosi did not want to associate with him. He received his contracts through registered mail because no one wanted to talk to him face-to-face, he could put the fear of God into anyone.

He had killed men, women, children and the elderly, without showing any remorse for his crimes or pity for his victims.

"A contract is an obligation to your client which must be completed in full because it has your name on it," he said.

He could hit a target at a distance of more than one kilometre with his US army DMR (designed marksman rifle) and he favoured dum-dum bullets that exploded on impact causing irreparable damage.

*

*"Father, why did he tell you all this?" asked the Colonel. "A contract killer is usually very discreet about his work."*

"Because he had gone to hell and back, that is why."

*"You mean to tell me that this man had seen hell and returned to the living, Father?"*

"Yes, Colonel."

*

After an altercation with the New York City police, he pulled out a gun, but was shot four times. His heart stopped beating and he died in the ambulance. He was in the Dark Abyss almost immediately. He recalled the experience vividly and maintained that it had been more frightening than anything he had done or seen in his lifetime. When he spoke with me I could see terror in his eyes. Retribution for the wrongs he had done had eventually come. He knew that sooner or later he would have to return because he was an enforcer for the underworld. He always worked alone and it was only fair that he paid for his sordid deeds. He knew only too well the Cosa Nostra saying, "Spilled blood never dries." However, he had never imagined the horrors of Hell!

When I asked him to describe Hell, he sighed heavily and said that upon entering a very dark tunnel, he found every single person that he had killed lined up, silent, looking at him with hatred in their eyes.

Loud metallic clangs resounded incessantly throughout the entire place, the stench was horrible. The heat, dampness and humidity were unbearable.

Most of the action was taking place in a circular kind of arena. There were tunnels and caves situated above, bonfires had been set alight at random, and extreme violence could be seen everywhere.

Whipping, torture, mutilation and executions were being performed by monstrous beasts from mythology – centaurs and minotaurs. Anubis and Osiris carried long sharp pikes and whips with lead balls at the end of large leather straps. They forced men and women to fight to the death like gladiators. Small furry creatures were roaming around eating the dead bodies with frenzy, making slurping noises.

Blood was everywhere and cadavers were rotting away in

every corner. There was no light at all; only torches placed on the walls. To be sent to Hell means eternal darkness and unbearable suffering, that is what he had witnessed in the short time that he had been there.

When he was resuscitated in the operating-room, he was told that he had been lucky to survive death after being unconscious for such a long time, but he did not feel that way. What he had experienced was going to be a traumatic and indelible stain on his soul and spirit.

There was no possible solution. His fate was worse than death. Satan had chosen a new prey and he was now a marked man.

It was too much to bear even for a villain like him!

*

*Father Benedetti tells another story*

Father Benedetti recalled another experience.

In the mountains of Corsica, a woman living in a hamlet was hit by a bolt of lightning during a severe storm.

She survived with minor burns and the doctors thought that it had been a miracle, considering that she was already in her sixties.

When she returned home she began raving at everything and everybody around her.

She yelled at her husband and neighbours and claimed that Satan was taking to her incessantly. The doctors could not find anything wrong with her and sent her back home.

The symptoms got worse and she was transported to Marseilles to be examined by specialists. Everyone in the region thought that she had lost her marbles!

Even though she was behaving very strangely there was no trace of illness or dementia in her brain. She was in perfect health and the physicians were puzzled. The diagnosis tested negative.

All of sudden she started to eat broken glass. When the time came to pump out her stomach, she spat it out time after time.

They gave her plastic cups to drink from. Then, one day, she broke a window and swallowed the shards. She died instantly from internal bleeding.

In the morning she was placed in the hospital morgue for an autopsy to be performed.

The same afternoon, the pathologist on duty saw a tall man coming into the room where the woman's body was kept. He was wearing a long dark coat and a large black hat.

The physician asked him to leave immediately because the premises were forbidden to the general public. The stranger answered, "She is ours now, and she is coming with me!"

At that particular moment the doctor lost consciousness. When he woke up, the drawer was pulled out, empty, and the body was gone. It was nowhere to be found. The local priest insisted that it was the work of Lucifer.

The case was closed by the administrative department of the hospital.

*

*Sister Angele tells her story*

A group of young people driving in a large powerful automobile were speeding when crossing a bridge. There was two-way traffic. The driver made a terrible mistake, deciding to overtake the car ahead of him and colliding head-on with a big truck, a horrific accident.

The car burst into flames, the doors jammed and the petrol-tank ripped open on impact. The shock was absolutely devastating. Witnesses of the accident recalled that two of the passengers tried to get out, but in vain. Soon a fire spread rapidly.

Screams could be heard and there were flames everywhere.

The fire department was on site very quickly, dousing the car, while the police closed the bridge to traffic. The smell of petrol was very strong and undoubtedly the vehicle was going to explode at any moment. The chaplain of the fire department was reciting prayers while holding a crucifix in his hands.

The media had been notified and were already speculating on the tragedy.

Were the passengers dead? Was it a drunk-driving accident? Was the person at the wheel speeding carelessly?

Suddenly, coming out of nowhere, a young man with long blond hair calmly walked into the flames and opened the car doors with his bare hands; he was not wearing any gloves.

He pulled the passengers to safety one by one and even gave them some words of comfort.

The car blew up but no one died.

The victims were treated at nearby hospitals. Witnesses – including emergency services – were flabbergasted by the turn of events and everyone was asking who the blond hero was.

The local TV channel had been able to catch a glimpse of the rescue but the face and the features of the brave young man did not show on the tape. The technicians were at a loss. The saviour had disappeared from the scene of the crash as fast as he had come into it. Everyone looked for him and inquired about him. Advertising was placed in the local media to find him, but there were no results. He was a mystery man, a good samaritan who for many people was a hero who had saved five teenagers from a horrible death!

The accident could have been quickly forgotten, had it not been for the chaplain of the fire department. For him, there was a lingering mystery that had to be solved. He decided to do his own investigation and talk to some of the witnesses including the victims.

The fire chief said, that to walk into a fire without protective gear was simply impossible. But the young man was wearing only blue jeans, a grey T-shirt and black sneakers. The door handles of the car had probably reached one thousand degrees celsius in no time, but he just opened the doors bare-handed even though they were jammed.

The police chief insisted that the unknown rescuer had dragged five persons to safety from a crash that no one could have survived.

The truck-driver, who was sitting in his cabin, had been more protected, and escaped with only minor injuries. He had witnessed it all and was still baffled by what had occurred.

"Father, I do not know what to tell you, only that the good samaritan was an angel sent by God to save them all."

The chaplain nodded with a smile. He agreed with the truck-driver. Over the next few weeks he interviewed policemen, fire-fighters, taxi-drivers – anyone who had been on the bridge when the accident took place. The reports coincided closely with the official statements and what the press and other media had reported.

The chaplain had no doubt regarding the young blond hero's identity, but to obtain confirmation, he wanted to talk to the five teenagers.

All had experienced a major spiritual change. Their belief in God and angels had deepened. Their faith had been restored.

Three had died immediately on impact, two remembered vividly the divine intervention in detail.

"The doors could not open, flames were already spreading inside the car; we knew that the end was near. Three of our friends were dead and the thought of dying of burns was too horrific! Suddenly he appeared, calmly opened the doors and said, 'Let's go.'

"He sat us near a fire-truck. He told the emergency services to wait for a few minutes as he needed to talk to us privately. They all looked at him confused but they obeyed his request. He went to get the others. He brought them back alive!

"They were alive. Father; how was it possible? They had died on impact, we all had suffered broken bones, burns, cuts and bore contusions and wide open gashes.

"He lined us up. He kissed us on the forehead, hugged us tightly, and gently massaged our limbs. All wounds, pain, fractures, and internal bleeding disappeared almost immediately.

"'Pray to Mary, Pray to God. They have given you a second chance at life. My name is Sebastian, I am your guardian angel and will escort you through your long journey. Please be good Christians, serve others, think of the needy!' he said and he was gone…

"He was handsome, in his twenties, had long blond hair, shoulder-length, his eyes were deep blue, and he spoke softly without an accent.

"When he touched us we could feel heat and inner strength, and we knew that something had happened to us. It was a special and extraordinary experience. Even though he was young, he commanded authority, respect, he was a leader. He saved our lives. How can we repay that gift, Father?" they asked the chaplain.

"Do what Sebastian asked you," was his answer.

*"Whatever happened to these young men, Sister Angele?" asked the Colonel.*

"They all followed the right path, Angel Sebastian had preached right to them. One became an army officer, one a search-and-rescue specialist, one a policeman, one a fire-fighter, and one joined the clergy"

*"It's an extraordinary tale, Sister".*

"Yes, Colonel, it is, considering that God himself had spoken to the victims. Right after the crash they remembered floating high above the bridge, and amid a bright light, a voice had told them, 'You are now returning where you came from, it is too early, it is not the right time and you still have a lot of work to do on earth. Sebastian will take care of you!'

*"They had seen the light and angel Sebastian took them under his wing."*

"Yes, it is a beautiful allegory," said the Colonel.

*

Sister Angele received a round of applause and began her second narrative.

*

*Sister Angele tells a second story*

On a frozen lake in Canada, a man and his young son were driving their snowmobile at high speed, they were laughing and joking and the little boy was telling his dad, "Faster, Papa! Father, I like it when you go fast. I am not scared."

They were really having a good time.

Unexpectedly, drama ensued.

A portion of the body of water was still in the process of freezing, so the ice was thin and fragile. The man did not seen it in time, he was going too fast. He could not stop, and they plunged helplessly into the icy water.

The man managed to untie their seatbelts but they were wearing a lot of heavy clothes, including boots, and the water was so cold!

Hypothermia strikes within the first minutes in freezing temperatures and the end was coming. It was late afternoon and there wasn't a soul to be seen. Nobody had witnessed the accident. They were drowning and going down quickly to the bottom. The little boy was the first to lose consciousness, his father holding him tightly.

Before passing out, the man remembers darkness all around him. He was reaching deep below the lake's surface, and he had no more air in his lungs. He was still holding his son against his body and then… nothing…they both had drowned.

A deep voice resonated with power and authority. "You are safe now, look at me, open your eyes!"

A man was kneeling down in front of them and was pressing on the boy's chest.

"My son, is he alive?" asked the father.

"Yes, he is. He needs to spew out some water and then he will regain consciousness."

The father vomited and do did his son.

"Good, you are both fine, help is on the way."

"Who are you, Sir? You saved our lives, but we did not see anyone when we were on the lake."

"My name is Adrian, I am your guardian angel. Thank God and Mary in your prayers, they have given you a second chance at life! Always remember this day. Be kind to your fellow-man, help the needy and the sick. I will always be there when you need me. God has great plans for you and your son."

Sirens could be heard far away.

"I must go now. Please remember my words."

The father wrapped a blanket which Adrian had brought with him around his son's shoulders, he kissed him on the forehead, the boy smiled.

When he turned around the angel had disappeared from sight.

After a check-up they returned home. Of course the media wanted to hear about this extraordinary rescue by a guardian angel. The believers and the atheists had a field-day. However, the man never changed his story and both father and son became men of the cloth.

*

"They became priests, Sister?" asked the Colonel.

"Yes, they did and that was God's plan. The encounter with Adrian proved fruitful."

"Did the man describe Adrian, Sister?"

"Yes he did. He was a young man in his early twenties. He spoke without an accent and was extremely handsome. He wore his long blond hair shoulder-length. The most intriguing fact was that he was only wearing blue shorts and he was barefoot.

"In the Canadian winter it is extremely unusual don't you think?" The Sister was smiling.

"I would say so, Sister, but Angels are not like us, am I right?"

"Yes, you are right; Angels are the messengers of God and particularly Guardian Angels, who have – in layman's terms – super-power. Is it an acceptable explanation for you, Colonel?"

"Yes, Sister, and I would like to say that after discussing the Dark Lord, your stories were refreshing and demonstrated that God is known for his wisdom and goodness."

The council gave Sister Angele thunderous applause.

*

*Father Romeo begins his story*

Father Romeo was the next member of the council to speak.

He was a young priest in a small Sicilian village when he was asked to assist with an exorcism to be performed on a young shepherd who had been whipped repeatedly while working in the field.

At first women circulated the idea that perhaps his father had been the culprit, because he was a heavy drinker, but the local bishop insisted that it was the work of Satan and he called

Rome to send an exorcist because he feared for the boy's life.

The local farmers had witnessed the cruel attacks and it was as if the boy had been hit by a ghost!

Ultimately the father had been exonerated, but the assaults continued…

Sometimes howls could be heard from a long distance away, blood was spattered everywhere, and the boy bore hideous scars all over his body.

He could not understand why he was going through this ordeal. A resounding voice kept repeating, "More, More, More!" throughout the whipping.

After speaking with the young man at great length, Father Romeo and the exorcist agreed to perform the prescribed ceremony after the bishop gave his full consent.

The priest wanted to see the location of these incidents. It was a hot day and he was wearing a short-sleeved shirt with his collar.

A farmer showed him the area in question.

He began to pray aloud, crossing himself, standing in the middle of a field, surrounded by grazing cows.

All of a sudden blows hit him with brute force.

"Whack! Whack! Whack!"

His arms were bleeding profusely.

"Go back where you came from, Priest, you have no place here, this field belongs to the forces of darkness!" a raucous voice shouted.

He had fallen to the ground but the invisible whip kept striking, it was unstoppable.

Local farmers who witnessed the attack in horror came to the rescue.

Father Romeo spent a week in hospital with multiple lacerations but he fully recovered.

It did not dissuade him from helping the young shepherd and freeing the demonic field from its possession.

Satan was successfully chased away, but Father Romeo still bears the scars of his encounter with the devil.

He eventually became a renowned exorcist, highly regarded by the Vatican."

*

"Did you perform exorcisms in Vietnam, Father?" asked the Colonel.

"Certainly, there are no boundaries for Lucifer, he prowls through the jungle, lurks around villages, searches and seeks for prey to become his servants. He took Jason from your team and he will probably steal another man before you complete your mission.

"Our stories describe in detail how he operates slyly to carry out his vile deeds.

"Unfortunately, people – including young children – get possessed by his diabolical powers. Exorcisms can save their souls and restore their faith."

Before starting his new story Father Romeo explained that each exorcism is not only different, but requires patience and perspicacity.

Now and then he had had to face Satan's fury and brute force. In one particular situation, he was thrown around the room and slammed against a wall. Sister Yvonne was the father's assistant during the ceremony and bore the brunt of Lucifer's wrath. He lashed out profanities at her and even tried to strangle her. He mocked her, reminded her of her past, and spat up green bile in her face. However, the power of the Lord was with them and the Devil was cast out.

Father Romeo and Sister Yvonne formed an impressive team and they exorcized many residents who had been possessed by the forces of evil.

The power of prayer is an absolute allegory that Satan cannot combat and win. He will never triumph against God.

*Father Romeo tells another story*

Early in his priesthood, Father Romeo was sent to a small city in the state of Iowa in the USA. Almost immediately he built a loyal congregation and worked very hard to keep the teenagers out of trouble, to help the needy and the poor, and instigated a church programme motivating the youth to focus on sports and education, rather than dealing with drugs and roaming the streets brandishing guns.

He was very well liked and respected in the community.

Even though he was a young man, he had already acquired expertise in exorcism and the Vatican was sending him across the nation to battle the devil.

Father Romeo was a highly-regarded professional in the field. His Holiness had praised him for his dedication to his work in a letter of commendation and had sent him a small golden cross that he wore around his neck at all times.

Soon he was going to be the witness to the strangest occurrence of his lifetime.

The church was located in the downtown area, opposite a very large department store at the intersection of two major avenues. An office building was adjacent to this popular spot which created an occasional traffic jam at peak hours. However, the locals seemed to be attracted by the hustle and bustle of the city centre.

The emporium was famous for its discounted prices, it had an excellent reputation and a loyal clientele. A petrol-station, combining a minimart and a diner, "The Lustre", stood alongside the city's main artery further down the block.

The restaurant was very busy, it served home-style cooking and the portions were very copious.

One day, Father Romeo was on his way to lunch at The Lustre. While crossing the street he had an intuition that something out of the ordinary was going to happen... He was not wrong... He was walking in the direction of the diner when a gigantic explosion took place. A fire had started at The Lustre restaurant spreading rapidly to the minimart and the petrol-station. Explosions and balls of fire ensued.

Father Romeo was thrown on his back by the force of the blast.

Within minutes of the accident, emergency services rushed to the scene. The sirens of ambulances could be heard everywhere. There was pandemonium, screams, and shouts. The security services were shouting directives and many passers-by had been hurt by flying debris.

Father Romeo had not been injured. He got up and looked at the devastation. Bodies were lying everywhere. Flames were shooting up into the air. Cars, buses and the minimart were now engulfed in flames. He went to help the injured and used his robe to wrap some burning victims, he gave the last rites to the dying. People had been decapitated by falling glass, others were very badly burned because their clothes had caught on fire. Rescue teams were picking up limbs and other body-parts and placing them in black plastic bags. Chaplains from the various local institutions and all catholic priests had been called to the scene to help in this dramatic emergency.

Father Romeo took a brief look at the church. It had remained intact from the disaster, being at a safe distance. However, the department store and the adjoining business tower-buildings had been extensively damaged.

Father Romeo continued to help the wounded and many

died in his arms.

Fire-fighters were trying desperately to protect and save the petrol-station from a major blow up. They were spraying a large amount of fire-retardant foam all over the petrol-pumps to prevent a deadly outcome.

The fire chief and three of his men had formed a circle around the perimeter and were winning the battle. But Father Romeo thought that they were too close for comfort and that they could be badly hurt if there was an explosion. How right he was!

"Boom! Badaboum! Baaang! Wooosh!"

It was a cataclysmic flare-up. The detonation was so loud, so powerful and deafening, that it was heard many miles away. The petrol-station's pumps had exploded, spilling jets of fuel everywhere. With the surrounding fires, it created a very large inferno. The fire department was now totally overwhelmed.

In this absolute mayhem Father Romeo witnessed another tragedy, the fire chief and his three men had now become human torches, rolling on the ground trying to extinguish the flames, screaming in pain, burning alive, writhing in agony.

The team rushed to the scene, spraying them abundantly to put out the blaze, but in vain.

Father Romeo tried to approach the victims. but was kept at a distance by the firemen for safety reasons. They continued to douse them until all flames had disappeared. The station's leader spoke to Father Romeo. "Please, Father, can you accompany them to the hospital and perform the last rites? They won't survive their burns, they are too serious."

At the city hospital the priest asked to see the victims to pray with them and bless them for the last time.

"Father, please be prepared. It is not going to be a pretty sight. They all have sustained very grave injuries in the fire. I have given them shots of morphine to ease the pain," the physician said.

"It is fine, Doctor, I have seen injuries before."

They were horrifying burns, their faces were unrecognizable. Some of their underclothes had melted into the skin and could only be removed surgically. The smell of burning flesh was nauseating and overpowering.

Even though they had endured massive traumas they were still alive.

The Priest asked the Lord to take these four brave men into his kingdom and open the Pearly Gates.

Their eyes were open but they could not speak.

Holy water was sprayed on them, the priest blessed them and said prayers for absolution, penitence and reincarnation.

"They do not have much longer to live, Father," said the doctor.

"I will stay with them until the end, Doctor, if it is agreeable to you."

"You can stay as long as you want, Father, I will be in the other room if you need me."

Father Romeo took out his rosary and began a set of prayers for the three brave men and their chief. A few minutes later they died.

"We will keep them in the morgue overnight until all their families have been notified," said the doctor.

On his way to church, Father Romeo was morose. Four courageous firemen had lost their lives on duty and had suffered a terrible ordeal. They had saved and helped people, day and night. He thought that to be a firemen was not a job, it was a vocation, like a priest's in some way.

The emergency services were still deployed in full force and more bodies were scattered on the streets. On the late news they announced that The Lustre, the minimart and the petrol-station had been totalled, the emporium had suffered considerable damage, and the fire department was still battling the blaze at the pumps.

*

"Father, you must have been extremely busy during the catastrophe. How many people lost their lives?" asked the Colonel.

"Two hundred and fifty perished in the fire and three hundred were injured, some very seriously."

"The fire department lost their chief and three valiant men. The town must have been in mourning, not counting all the other victims of this tragedy," stated the Colonel.

Father Romeo smiled.

"Wait for the end of the story, Colonel."

*

*"General what a bunch of amazing stories, I was not able to interrupt you, not even once. The council really had a lot of experience in dealing with Satan, and by contrast, with angels and apparitions. They surely were very experienced ecclesiastics. You were lucky to have met them. I envy you."*

"Yes Sergeant, Sister Marie Catherine and Sister Yvonne brought back spirituality into my soul. In a way it was like a resurgence of beliefs that I had lost. In times of war, as a special forces officer, you do not experience kindness, compassion, or righteousness anymore. You lose all sense of other people's emotions, you focus on completing your mission, on the enemy, on how to survive; and very often that means 'to kill before being killed'. I did not pray to God, the angels, or Mary, any more. I just did not find the time.

"This stay at the Monastery cleansed me, it also helped me plan and succeed in my escape, I may have lost three good men during the mission, but subconsciously I had changed, it was like a rebirth. Deep feelings of goodness, my love for God and respect for the clergy had resurfaced."

*"I understand you, General, I felt the same way after my last experience in Africa. But please continue! Your stories are fascinating."*

*

*Father Romeo's story continues*

Father Romeo did not sleep well. In the morning he decided to walk around the downtown area to try to find out if he could be of any help to the rescue services.

One of the firemen pointed out to him three black plastic bags on the sidewalk.

"We found them inside "The Lustre". They were employees of the restaurant... Please, Father."

Father Romeo gave them absolution and said a prayer.

He kept moving down the centre of the town, where the devastation had been extreme.

Many fire stations from the suburbs and larger cities in the state of Iowa had come to the rescue. The police, ambulance and the emergency services were still hard at work, trying to put an end to the havoc. The street were wet and dirty, littered with broken glass, refuse, burnt cars and buses. The lingering smell of smoke was stinging and acid. It was a hellish sight.

"Father, Father, can you bless my son? He was at the emporium with my wife and they both survived."

The priest obliged.

Father Romeo proceeded to the large intersection between what was left of The Lustre and the emporium. He stood still, watching the rescue workers fight the remainder of the blaze.

Standing on the top of very high ladders, two firemen were spraying water onto the burning petrol-station. They waved hello to him and he reciprocated. Why did Father Romeo have a tingling sensation in his stomach? He had a hunch that somehow they knew each other but he could not recall where they had met before.

"Father, Father would you bless me, please?"

The fireman, his face blackened by soot, was holding a piece of cut-up hose in his hand, and was smiling at the priest. Father Romeo complied. Once again he found the man familiar. He had seen him before...

Further down the street, a fire-truck was parked near a water-main and a group of people were gathered together near a hydrant. Father Romeo approached the fire-truck and inquired about the water supply sufficiency for the town.

"No problem, Father," he was told. "We have a large water-main and several trucks have been sent us as back-up. All the fires have been put out, with the exception of the one at the petrol-station. It's a tough one but we are working on it!"

The Priest nodded, gave the men some words of encouragement, and moved on.

"Father! Father!" someone yelled.

He turned around and...

No, he could not believe his eyes, how could it be possible?

Wearing the helmet with the fire brigade number "11" and the fire chief's emblem, he was standing in front of him, smiling.

"Chief? Is that you?"

"Yes, Father, nice to see you again!"

"But you were dead!" exclaimed the priest.

"True, but God had other plans for us," said the chief.

"Please tell me, you all died and I gave you absolution in the morgue?"

"We were in terrible pain, we could not speak but we were still able to see you when you sent us away with the rites."

"What happened next?"

"As we floated above the operating-tables, God called our names and we met at the Pearly Gates; however Saint Peter did not open them.

"The Almighty addressed us in a very solemn tone of voice. He said that it was not our time and that we still had a lot of work to do. The four of us had to return and do what we do best, fight fires and save lives.

"Then Mary appeared. She was the most beautiful woman that I have ever seen, she kissed us on the forehead and hugged us very tightly. At that moment all the pain, the burns and scars, disappeared in no time at all."

"Astonishing, unbelievable!" exclaimed Father Romeo.

"Mary was softly-spoken, very gracious, she had a faint smile on her face, a radiant personality, and a sense of joy emanated from her.

"She congratulated us for the risks we had taken and the fact that we had saved lives in very precarious situations. She blessed us and we suddenly found ourselves in the middle of the action again. We were all dumbfounded, looking at each other, but we shrugged our shoulders and took up our posts.

"You see, Father, it is true that God works in mysterious ways. The most intriguing part of it all is that, since we have returned on duty, no one has questioned us, no one seems surprised at the fact that we had died and that we are back fighting fires as if nothing happened. God and Mary exist and perform miracles, we are a living proof, and you are our witness."

Father Romeo nodded silently, but he still was baffled. The firemen had told him that their resuscitation period was short but very peaceful, surrounded by brightness, and that there was a very serene ambience at the Pearly Gates. Beautiful music could be heard from the Garden of Eden with a background choir singing canticles. They never saw God but he talked to them through a blinding light. Mary was wearing a light brown dress with a golden cord around her waist, a pale blue headscarf and she was barefoot.

Father Romeo listened attentively, not saying a word.

He then thanked the chief and his men for the information they had given him, shook hands and left briskly.

He had witnessed a miracle performed by the Creator. For a priest, it was somehow a consecration.

His mind was now working in double-quick time and he was on his way to the hospital morgue. He had to make sure…

"Father, I am so glad to see you, something unprecedented has taken place, four bodies have disappeared from the morgue. The fire chief and three of his men who had died yesterday have gone missing."

"Did you notify the families?"

"Yes, I did, but they seemed confused, they were telling me that the victims were alive and well. It is impossible, Father! However, they could have been in denial. It happens with relatives, refusing to accept that their loved ones are dead."

"When did you call them, Doctor?"

"This morning around 8am and they insisted that all of the men were fighting fires downtown."

"Doctor, this is no lie. They are all alive and fighting fires downtown. I just spoke with the chief."

"Father? What are you saying? You gave them absolution, they were dead. I signed the death certificates myself."

"God has decided on another path for them. He wants them to continue saving lives, Mary has healed their burns and they are back at work, doing what they do best, fighting fires. It is true, Doctor, I just saw them."

The physician was looking Father Romeo in the eye, shaking his head and murmuring, "Good Lord, Good Lord". He was dazed and confused.

"Father, you are a priest, what do you call what has happened?"

"A miracle, Doctor. Nothing short of a miracle could have saved them and brought them back to life. It is the work of God, and when he decides on something, nothing or no one can stop it. It was not their time, let's stay the course and carry on with our work, Doctor. It is all over now."

"Father, can you bless me? I am perturbed."

The priest obliged and left the morgue.

Back at the church, he knelt at a pew. He prayed hard and thanked the Lord for allowing him to witness a resurrection. He was crying…

*

Father Romeo received a standing ovation from the council and the Colonel shook his hand vehemently.

Sister Marie Catherine said, "We have all met Satan, the Lord, and Mary in person, at one point or the other. But what is more interesting is that we have been involved in miracles and exorcisms, watched people on the road to perdition and others saved by their guardian angels or the Almighty.

"Colonel, please take advantage of the wealth of specialized knowledge that our council has accumulated over the years."

"I will, and I am all ears, Sister."

"Our next speaker is Father Hervé who is also an expert exorcist sponsored by the Vatican, but who, like all of us, has met success and faced failures over the years.

"The floor is yours, Father."

*

*Father Hervé tells his story*

Father Hervé still recalled the sinister event that had taken place while he was a young priest in Boston, USA. He was sent by order of the local bishop to a suburban home to evaluate the strange occurrences tormenting a fourteen-year-old girl. The mother was a widow of Italian descent and extremely religious. She knew that something was wrong with her daughter and had even mentioned the word "Devil" over the telephone.

Father Hervé was not yet suitably qualified to perform an exorcism, but he was fascinated with the subject and had attended many lectures offered by the pontifical biblical institute in Rome, related to the powers of Satan. When he went to visit the teenager, he was ready for any eventuality, but he was not scared. God was on his side, and he felt that somehow good would triumph in the end.

It was a modest house, located in an area where the residents came mainly from two large ethnic groups – Italians and Portuguese – with a small French community. They were all Roman Catholics and got along well with one another.

Father Hervé rang the bell and a frail, pale woman opened the door. Her name was Angelina and her daughter had not been the same for the past seven months.

She had always been a straight-A student with a warm and friendly disposition, keen on swimming, and very much liked around the neighbourhood. She had a strong faith and attended catechism regularly. But it had all changed abruptly for no apparent reason. At first, her mother thought that it was just a phase that her daughter was experiencing, like all teenagers did, lower grades, missing church and team practice, listening to loud music, not cleaning her room and more… but as the months went by, it had become a very serious and obvious problem, Maria was out of control. She became dirty, slept late, missed school altogether and often came home inebriated.

When her mother got angry and wanted to reason with her, Maria hurled insults as her, spat at her and hit her constantly. Angelina knew that she had lost her daughter. Maria now swore like a trooper and abused her mother regularly.

Angelina was scared and had to find a quick solution to the matter. The family physician could not see anything wrong with Maria, but ordered a psychological evaluation. It came back negative. Maria was in perfect health.

Then Angelina asked the local priest to visit Maria at home.

When the priest left Maria's room, he was in a daze and Angelina saw that the father's eyes were filled with terror from the experience.

He curtly said to her, "Please call this phone number," handed her a note, and left without another word.

Father Hervé was told that Maria did not eat properly anymore, that she locked her room all the time and that a bad smell emanated from it.

It was time to meet her face to face.

He could hear loud music upstairs. He knocked on her door, but got no reply. He knocked again, harder, repeatedly. Then she was standing there…

She wore a black dress with short sleeves, she was barefoot, dishevelled, and her body odour was quite unpleasant.

"May I come in?" asked Father Hervé.

Her place was a total mess, it was in fact indescribable, the smell was horrible and even though the weather outside was warm, her room was frigid. She looked at Father Hervé with glacial eyes and did not even offer him a seat.

She must have been a very pretty girl but now she was haggard, unkempt and did not care about her appearance anymore. She was a shadow of her former self.

"What do you want, why are you here?" she asked in a raucous voice.

"Your mother in deeply concerned about your behaviour and she offered me the opportunity to talk to you."

"My mother does not know anything, she cannot understand me and I do not think that she even cares. Frankly speaking, I believe that she wishes me to leave home and I will do so very soon…"

"That is where you are wrong. Your mother loves you very much. If she did not, why would she have asked me to come and meet you?"

"Because the poor woman always asks God to solve problems. She goes to church and prays because she cannot handle anything herself; she is pathetic."

"Do you really believe that? She raised you by herself and went through a lot of hardship to give you a good education and all that you needed. I think that your mother is strong, but she worries about you. What is wrong, Maria?"

Suddenly the look in her eyes became as cold as ice; Father Hervé noticed her expression of disgust. She pointed her right index finger at him and yelled, "Get out my room, leave this house at once, never to return!"

She had foam at her mouth and her tone of voice was rough and gruff.

Father Hervé complied and went back downstairs. Maria went berserk and flew into an uncontrollable fury, shouting abuse and profanities at him. Angelina was sitting on the sofa with her head in her hands, sobbing profusely.

The Father approached her but… he felt a presence in the living-room. The house had turned chilly and plunged into darkness.

He turned around and in the corner near the cuckoo-clock

stood a dark spectre. He could not describe it in any other way. Its gender was indiscernible, the nails on both hands were long and pointed, the face had sunken eyes and was unusually pale. It was dressed all in black, and wearing a large hat.

It looked at Maria and snapped, "Let's go!"

Maria promptly obeyed, and as they were leaving, the spectre told Angelina, "Stop crying, you are finally free; she belongs to us now, she is no longer your concern."

Father Hervé interjected abruptly and asked, "Who are you? Why are you taking her and where?"

The ghost turned around and came face to face with him. "Priest, don't push your luck. You know very well who I am. I have been working on her for a long time and she is now joining my team in the abyss. You cannot do anything about it, so go back to your parish. But first you should console Angelina, she seems to be in need of 'tender loving care'.

The Devil laughed sardonically and he and Maria both walked out of the house.

Angelina was totally devastated and kept repeating, "The Devil took her, the Devil took her and I will never see her again."

The Priest felt deep hopelessness in his heart and never forgot the sinister encounter with Satan.

The bishop listened attentively and silently while the priest narrated the shocking details. He lowered his head when Father Hervé mentioned the smell of sulphur on the spectre's breath and the red, fiery, eyes looking through him.

The bishop then started to speak. "Do not blame yourself, Father, I wanted you to help a possessed individual, but unfortunately the devil was on site. There was nothing you could do to save her. It was already too late. I believe that this tragic occurrence will strengthen your desire to direct your attention towards performing exorcisms. The Catholic Church needs experts such as yourself. God will support you in your endeavour, my son."

*

The council fell silent, they understood the pain, the anguish, and his admission of defeat in that particular case.

However, Father Hervé knew that the greatest glory was not in never falling but in rising every time we fall.

He addressed the members of the council, saying, "The bishop was right, I knew that it was my destiny to become an exorcist. I wanted to fight Satan head-on. I moved to Rome. I studied hard and was commissioned as a fully-fledged exorcist by the Vatican two years later."

"Did you fail again, Father?" asked the Colonel.

"Of course I did, but I learnt how to deal with it, time after time. An exorcism can take only a few hours or perhaps a full year to succeed and on some occasions it is a complete failure. I was fighting Lucifer day after day, week after week and very often in horrible conditions. I trained on the job which is undoubtedly the best way to learn."

"What have you brought with you to this monastery, Father?"

"Humility, Colonel. Maybe at first I thought that I could conquer Satan without difficulty, but he taught me otherwise. I was younger, cocky, presumptuous, but now it is all in the past. Sister Marie Catherine has cut me down to size a few times."

The members of the council laughed, nodding and clapping at the same time.

Sister Maire Catherine addressed the Colonel, "Father Hervé is a renowned exorcist but he is a priest above all and his next story is definitely more joyful and inspiring."

*

*Father Hervé tells another story*

Father Hervé narrated the story of what took place in Provence in the small town of Forcalquier.

A member of his congregation had lost his twelve-year-old daughter in a tragic accident. She was an excellent swimmer and had gone to the rescue of three people in a small boat who had been stuck in a reef adjacent to a mole.

She had to bring them back one by one and the weather was bad with waves five to six metres high. Their little sailboat was being engulfed by water and sinking. She saved the first person and went back to help the others. They were hanging on to the dinghy but time was of the essence. She calmed them down, talked to them and swam through the waves bravely. The second person was brought ashore. Many people were watching this heroic display of courage and cheered her on in admiration.

The little boat had sunk and the third person was panicking. The little girl grabbed her firmly and commanded her to relax and stay calm. She was exhausted but managed to help the person to safety. The crowd was ecstatic.

When she came out of the water, climbing the reefs, she began to wobble, started to shake, and fell backwards into the sea.

The gendarme and coastguard scuba-teams searched for her relentlessly, battling bad weather, deep depth, high waves and strong currents.

When her dead body was recovered, France had lost a heroine.

The autopsy concluded that she had died of a heart attack, caused by extreme exhaustion.

She received posthumously the highest honours of courage and bravery from the French president, but her death had rendered her father inconsolable. He just sat at home, looking through the kitchen window, grieving and crying, all day and all night long. People around him became concerned that he was now suicidal, always talking to himself and wishing to join his daughter in paradise.

One night as he was praying to the Virgin Mary, he unmistakably recognized his daughter's calling him.

"Papa we need to talk, I will be waiting for you at the Garden of Heaven. I am fine, I love you."

Mary's words resounded loud and clear, "The time for grieving has passed, pull yourself together and talk to your daughter."

The man sat in his bed dumbfounded. Was he dreaming? Where did these voices come from? How could he meet his daughter in the Garden of Heaven?

All of a sudden he received a strong jolt of heat through his body and passed out.

He saw himself floating in a very bright tunnel surrounded by blinding light. It was all very peaceful and he felt no fear at this extraordinary occurrence.

The tunnel bent sharply and he landed in very pleasant and beautiful surroundings.

It was the Garden of Heaven, the harp, the flute and the 'cello could be heard playing in the background – lovely pieces that gave the entire area a magical and serene atmosphere.

"Papa, it is you at last!"

She was standing in front of him, dressed in a white gown, her blond curly hair loose over her shoulders.

She hugged her father tightly and he kissed her on the cheeks.

"She seems so happy," he thought.

He started crying as he drew her into his arms.

"Come on, Father, none of that!" she told him.

They walked around, hand in hand, and talked for long time. She was happy and healthy, and kept busy at doing the things she enjoyed the most, like reading, drawing, painting and playing the piano.

She told her father that Jesus and Mary had visited the garden and that she had met them face to face. Finally, she emphasized that her death was not a misfortune but fate. The Lord had other plans for her and they would materialize only when she was ready. She gave her father reassurance and said, "Please, Father, promise not to worry about me anymore, you must start living your life again. I will visit you every once in a while to see how you are doing."

At that moment, a handsome young man came over and said, "Sir, it is time for you to leave now. I am Angel Lionel, please do not be concerned, as you can see that your daughter is in good hands with us. She is a great girl and will become an angel when she is ready. Please follow me..."

Father and daughter kissed and he followed the angel...

When they reached the gate at the garden entrance, he felt as if someone pushed him with extreme force. He was falling and going very fast into a very steep and bottomless precipice. He could not stop, then he blacked out.

When he opened his eyes, he was lying down on his bed and wondering, "Did I dream it all? It was such a nice feeling to be with my child again. But it can't be true. How can someone go to paradise and back? It was a beautiful illusion, anyway."

He got up and went to the kitchen to make a cup of coffee. He saw a small envelope on the counter. He opened it. Inside there was a small card that read, "Papa, it was great to see you again. As a single dad you raised me all by yourself and did such a fantastic job. Remember your promise, no more tears, you are a great professor and your students need you. Please focus energy on your career.

"I am fine and I love you,

"Your Cathie"

*

"It was an amazing story, Father; very inspirational. In fact I find it motivating because we should not be afraid of death. When the time comes, we should embrace it, plain and simple. Sister Marie Catherine explained her reasoning about the end of life when we toured the cemetery; she was right and your narrative confirms it," the Colonel said.

The council gave Father Hervé a standing ovation.

Sister Maire Catherine then addressed the members, "To close our meeting, I will ask Sister Yvonne to tell us about a very special event that took place when she worked in Paris. It is completely unlike her frightening ordeals with Satan. It is a story that is very close to her heart, from what I can gather.

"Sister Yvonne, the floor is yours."

"Thank you, Sister."

*

*Sister Yvonne tells another story*

When I worked at the American hospital in Paris, I became fond of a ten-year-old boy who was a patient in my ward. He was dying of brain cancer. However, his spirit, sense of humour and inner strength were absolutely unshakeable. He was going through a battery of tests, X-rays, MRIs day after day. But he always found time to talk to me, he was ten but going on forty. He had amazing powers of deduction. His elocution and wide vocabulary were surprising for a boy of that age.

One day he asked me, "Are you a nun?"

"No, why do you ask me that question?"

"Because you act and look like one."

"Maybe I will become a nun one day, you never know."

"You should. In fact I know that the Virgin Mary is waiting for you, so don't take too long."

"What did you say?"

"Yes, I talked to her and she mentioned your name in the conversation. She has high expectations for you. Please do not disappoint her."

"You talked to Mary?"

"Yes, quite often. She takes care of the sick, the homeless, and old people. She knows my situation and that I am dying. I am ready, Yvonne; I am not afraid. And if Mary takes care of me after I pass away, it is fine. She is a very kind lady. You and she will make a good team."

I was totally taken aback and left the room.

Ben (this was his name) had a very large tumour at the back of his brain. It was inoperable. The surgical team had told his parents that any attempt to remove it could cause paralysis and/or loss of other bodily functions. They did not give any time-frame for his death and they were quite surprised that he was still alert, energetic, and in such good spirits.

"My boy is a fighter, he will pull through," his mother had claimed.

Because the parents were very rich, the world's top specialists had come to Paris to look at his test results, diagnostic examinations, and various assessments, and to meet the patient face to face.

After all this, they concluded that the American hospital in Paris was perfectly correct, there was no hope. Ben was going to die, but no one knew exactly when.

The tumour had grown to the size of a plum. The number of tests had been curtailed and the chemotherapy sessions cancelled.

The boy was still gregarious and was often seen chatting

with other patients and comforting them on occasion. The physicians were at a loss. He had not yet been prescribed morphine because he was not suffering from any pain.

"Le Grand Patron" asked Yvonne to speak with him in an informal and friendly way.

*

"Did you talk to him, Sister?"

"Yes, Colonel, I did. He was a great kid with a lot of courage and determination. He had the will to survive.

'He had the premonition of imminent death but he felt that he was going to return to be with us. He wanted to become a doctor and save lives.'

"Same as you, Yvonne."

"We had the same goals, Colonel."

*

He told me that Mary was going to help him achieve his objectives and that she was mentoring him. His mother visited him and she thanked me profusely for taking good care of him in these difficult moments, but she said something that has stayed with me to this day.

"You know, Yvonne, Ben will not die. He is a child of the light and he is blessed. Please help him through his return; you have the know-how."

She kissed me on the forehead, turned around, and left. That night I talked to Madame Labelle.

The following day Ben was in a great frame of mind and we talked about our families. He told me that his grandmother had been his role model at an early age. She had taught him many skills, including how to read people's character. He admired her and said that she was the first person he wanted to meet in Paradise.

Later in the afternoon, the chief surgeon notified Ben and

his family that the brain surgery, scheduled on the following day, had been cancelled. The tumour had now doubled in size, posing too many risks to operate.

Ben looked at me, shrugged his shoulders, smiling, and went for a walk in the garden with an orderly.

In the evening after my rounds, I went to visit Ben. He was calm and jovial.

"I wish you a good night's sleep and I'll visit you tomorrow."

"You know, Yvonne, I will not die. The doctors diagnosed that I have terminal cancer of the brain and they do not feel that an operation would serve any purpose. But Mary is going to intervene."

"Why do you say that, Ben?"

"Because she told me so, and I have an inkling that she is going to save me."

I kissed him on the forehead and turned off the light. Did he really communicate with the Virgin Mary? I was inclined to think so. However I never discussed it with anyone including his family, became I knew from personal experience that these private moments were not to be divulged.

Ben was a brilliant little fellow who had been struck by an incurable illness that was slowly taking his life away.

Mary had the power to cure him through divine intervention.

I went to have some shut-eye.

"Brrrr! Brrrr! Brrrr!"

It was five o'clock in the morning. This damn little beeper was going to be the end of me...

I was summoned immediately to Ben's room and I rushed there, expecting the worst.

Had Ben died?

But no, he was sitting on his bed smiling, with Le Grand Patron by his side.

"Good morning, Yvonne, I feel much better today," he said.

I was totally confused and looked at Le Grand Patron for an explanation.

"Take a peek at the night-table and tell me what you think happened, I do not know what to make of it."

It was the strangest thing that I have ever witnessed as a hospital nurse.

A bloody scalpel and trowel were placed on a small plate beside a stainless steel bowl which was holding human brain fragments with a large malignant tumour in the centre.

"Monsieur, what… what has happened here?"

"That is what I am asking you, because you are the spiritual influence around here and something very, very unusual has occurred in this hospital room, would you agree?"

"Yes, Monsieur but… who knows about this?"

"Only you and me, Yvonne. Ben called me and I came over right away. Then I beeped you."

"Ben, please tell us everything. We need to know how you got better. Can you do that?" asked Yvonne.

"Of course. After you left, I went to sleep. Around one o'clock in the morning, Mary woke me up and told me to stay still on my bed because she was going to cure me of my illness. I had to keep my eyes closed during the procedure. She carried the tools that you see there, a large straw bag and a few towels. It did not hurt at all, I did not feel any pain. I heard some scraping sounds, she was rubbing towels on my face and we talked through it all."

"Talked? About what?"

"You, Yvonne! Mary likes you a lot. She told me that one day you will become an angel and help her with her tasks. I told her that you are the best nurse in this hospital and she agreed. She has plans for you, but I cannot say what they are. I promised her, it's our secret."

"I see, tell me the rest."

"Well, after it was all over, Mary told me to rest, kissed me on the forehead and wished me good luck. I asked her if the cancer was gone forever, because sometimes it can resurface. She confirmed that it will never come back again. She waved goodbye and walked through the door. She left the mass of cells for the doctors to see."

"Thank you, Ben, you have been very helpful," Le Grand Patron said.

*

"What happened to Ben, Sister?" asked the Colonel.

"Well, we analysed the fragments and the tumour several times to be sure. We did not to tell the family that Ben had been cured, until we were certain that he was.

"We asked him not to say anything about Mary's intervention. Le Grand Patron had prepared a battery of tests to show the doctors present and the family that he was cured.

*

The kid was remarkable and handled it very well. The international delegation of physicians was recalled to perform more examinations to confirm that the brain was now intact and conclude that the cancer had gone. All the results were negative. Ben was now a very energetic and physically fit little boy. There were no scars, no complications, not even a sign that surgery had taken place.

The medical world was baffled by this happening. This unorthodox surgical procedure was little short of a miracle, and we all know that scientists have little understanding of abstract principles, in this case a divine intervention.

Le Grand Patron was going to undertake further research to obtain data to be sent to the medical representatives who had worked on the case.

"Yvonne, please come to my office," said the little monster beeper.

I could see that Le Grand Patron was annoyed.

"Is it about Ben, Monsieur?"

"Of course, Yvonne. The tumour was the size of an orange and the Virgin Mary performed the most difficult type of surgery in a hospital room with a scalpel and trowel! There were no scars, no side effects and no blood anywhere. I witnessed a miracle at the American hospital in Paris! It would make great news for the media, don't you think?"

"Please, Monsieur, do not be angry. In this situation it is important to maintain clear channels of communication. I will help you as much as I can. I will handle the spiritual side of the event and you will deal with the medical and administrative matters, agreed?"

"Agreed," replied Le Grand Patron.

"For now, Monsieur, I am going to give you my version of the occurrence night."

"I am all ears, Yvonne..."

*

"Did he accept your explanation with an open mind?" asked the Colonel.

"He did. You know that to face a miracle can give a shock to your system, but in this case the facts were undeniable and there was also Ben's recollection of events."

"How did it end, Sister?" inquired the Colonel.

"Very well, much better than I expected. The hospital staff were very professional and discreet; the media were never notified."

*

Le Grand Patron received the final test results – they were all negative –and they were forwarded to the delegation of physicians, as promised. A meeting was held with the team members who had worked on Ben's case and they were told the truth.

Everyone rejoiced over the results. Le Grand Patron stated that the cancer had been in remission for a while, and had finally dissolved. He used the words "miracle" and "God's help", for which he received a thunderous applause.

Ben was invited to say a few words and was given a standing ovation.

He spoke calmly, thanking profusely the American hospital for his healing, full recovery, and the kind attention of the staff.

His attention was to become a doctor and jokingly he asked Le Grand Patron if he could give him an intern position when the time was right. Everyone laughed at his good sense of humour.

He had met the Virgin Mary once before and explained how he was helped through prayers and dialogue between the two of them.

"Miracles happen and many people are cured every day because of divine intervention," he said.

His speech drew enthusiastic applause,

Yvonne was next to talk from the floor and discussed spirituality, faith, and courage, within the nursing profession. She touched on the importance of Divinity, because a case like Ben's proved that the Almighty makes the final decision on our fate after all. He was never going to die, Mary protected him. The meeting was a brilliant success.

Le Grand Patron thanked Yvonne for her participation in the meeting.

"The staff like you and respect you, you did well."

"Merci, Monsieur."

"Could you please draft three letters, one for the staff, one for the foreign delegation, and the last one for Ben's family."

"You want some spirituality in a light tone, am I right?"

"Yes please. I need them quickly so that I can put this supernatural occurrence behind us."

"I will give them to you tomorrow, for sure."

"Yvonne?"

"Monsieur"

"Why a trowel?" he grimaced.

"I do not know, Monsieur. Perhaps Mary found it more practical to scrape the cranium with. They work in mysterious ways, you must have heard that before!"

Le Grand Patron placed his head in his hands and let out a sigh of exasperation. "I am so tired, Yvonne" he said. "Please do not forget the letters."

"Non, Monsieur," and she closed the door.

At night Mme Labelle helped her to draft the copies and she was astonished at the speed with which she worked.

"Thank you, Madame Labelle. Writing letters was never my forte."

"But you have many other qualities and a heart in the right place." They both laughed.

"Great job, Yvonne!" Le Grand Patron said the next day. "You have a way with words. I know that their recipients will relate clearly to your explanations. Thank you again."

"My guardian angel helped me, Monsieur."

Le Grand Patron looked at Yvonne perplexedly, and shook his head. She knew that he did not believe her.

She went to Ben's room. It was full of balloons, toys, stuffed animals, and books, it had been transformed into an entertainment venue and Ben was beaming in the centre of it.

Nurses, doctors and other patients came to say goodbye.

He was an inspiration, a legend; he had demonstrated courage and resilience and restored the faith of everyone he met.

The hospital's chaplain gave him communion privately in the chapel and they talked at great length about the circumstances of his full recovery.

His parents were on the way and Yvonne was instructed to speak with them about Mary's surgery. They deserved the entire truth, with Ben present at the meeting.

He was placed under observation to undergo tests twice a year. Fifty percent of patients suffered a relapse within a year. He understood the importance of this procedure.

The parents were thrilled, joyful and baffled, all at the same time. They wanted to know the story in detail.

Yvonne, Ben and his parents sat in the boardroom. Le Grand Patron had already shown them all the pertinent test results in his office.

His mother did not seem very surprised. Nevertheless, she was very eager to meet Yvonne, because Ben had praised her numerous times for being the major focus of his recovery.

Ben calmly and clearly described all the details of that particular night.

"Is that what really happened Ben?" his father asked.

"Yes, Father, this is the truth."

"Proof of that miraculous surgery was left on the night table," said Yvonne.

"I knew that my son was going to recover. He has extraordinary inner powers, he is a child of the light. Mary has helped him all the way because she has great plans for him, down the road," the boy's mother said.

"I agree with you. I have spent enough time with him to say that he is a special person. That is why Mary has chosen him to assist her later in life. He will become a doctor – that is his dream – but he will also be a servant of God; and that is his calling."

Everyone hugged each other tightly and said goodbye.

Then Ben's mother approached Yvonne closely and whispered in her ear, "You also are a child of the light and you will be Mary's favourite angel. I saw you in my dreams." She smiled and nodded.

As they drove away, Yvonne felt a surge of emotion, Ben had a second chance at life and he was such a great kid!

*

"Did you ever see him again?" asked the Colonel.

"Yes and the cancer never returned."

"Did he do well at school, Sister?"

"Oh yes, he went to college at Harvard in order to get into medical school. He was a brilliant student with a great future ahead."

The council stood up and cheered Sister Yvonne in unison.

## CHAPTER NINETEEN

## ON THE ROAD AGAIN

Sister Marie Catherine announced, "Colonel, it is now time to part company, you must resume your mission and we will pray for your success".

The members of the council stood up and Father Benedetti said a few words. Father Hervé blessed him and the two farmers. Sister Yvonne hugged them tightly. It was a deeply moving time.

The colonel addressed the council. "I will never forget your hospitality, your words of wisdom, and inspirational stories. Satan's demonic trickery is no match for you. I thank you with all my heart."

"Now you are ready to face the Devil on his own ground. Good luck, stay safe and God be with you!" said Sister Marie Catherine.

Dr Henri was asked to notify Rose, the village leader, of the fact that the two men were going to suffer an appalling fate at the hands of Lucifer. Nonetheless, they were to escort the Colonel to the boat-house as planned.

When he walked out of the monastery the Colonel was wearing clean black pyjamas and he immediately went to check on Jason. He was nowhere in sight. A nauseating smell was floating across the bushes and blood was splashed everywhere. He had obviously been at work killing VC patrols coming across his path. The Colonel called him a few times, but in vain.

They were late for their rendez-vous at the boat-house and needed to make up for lost time. They took a small sinuous trail across the forest. One farmer walked the point, the other stayed in the middle, ten metres behind, and the colonel remained at the back.

He carried an Ithaca 37 pump-action shotgun used by Navy Seals, an M21 sniper weapon-system, designated Marksman rifle (DMR) used by the US Army and a Browning High Power handgun with a silencer. They stayed absolutely quiet and moved along briskly. Then the point man raised his fist and they crouched down.

One of the farmers climbed a tall tree and looked over at the horizon. As he climbed down, he said that if they crossed a steep rocky gorge they could save at least five hours. It was worth trying but there would be hardship.

They climbed rocks, hills, cliffs and more rocks. Then, at the top of a peak, the farmer pointed across the valley at a blue shining streak scintillating under the sun, the River Hăn! We had finally approached our destination. It would not be long before we reached the boat-house and the team waiting for us.

The Colonel was wondering if the others had made it. Were they all alive? How long had they been waiting? They were almost four days behind time and they might have decided to leave without them.

In combat, delays often occur, but they were escapees, not members of a regular military operation organized by headquarters. Even so, they were very late and had to speed up. The colonel was an optimist and trusted these men who were seasoned and well-trained soldiers. "They will be at the boat-house," he muttered to himself.

Descending from the top was difficult, the terrain was fragile. Slabs of rocks were breaking up and falling off all over the place. Because of this, they had to move slowly on very narrow ledges, keeping their bodies very close to the cliff. They advanced very cautiously, centimetre by centimetre, holding to the surface area by their fingertips.

Suddenly they stopped. The path had been completely cut off by an avalanche and it had created what is commonly called a "chimney". They could not jump to the other side and would have to abseil. Fortunately, they had brought ropes. The Colonel wanted to be the last man down. The point-man was first and managed well, considering that he was not an experienced climber. The second farmer was nervous and slower, and went down, a metre at a time.

"SNAP! ZEEP! CLACK!"

Unexpectedly, the rope broke. The farmer went head first, his screams of terror piercing the mountain's silence. The colonel watched in horror as the incident unfolded in front of his eyes. The body bounced a few times on the rocks below and then landed on a large chunk of stone. The farmer's friend was crying and screaming, falling to his knees, making the sign of the cross.

The Colonel froze, looking at the horrible scene. He could not comprehend what had happened.

"How could the rope break after we checked our equipment so many times. It is impossible!" he thought.

Out of nowhere, dozens of furry monsters surged, moving hastily, making slurping and gurgling sounds. They were looking at the second farmer with their yellow, drooping, eyes, but did not attack him. They were eating at the dead body with fury, laughing hysterically, cutting the flesh, breaking the bones and licking the blood. They beheaded the corpse and removed the limbs. Some were gnawing voraciously at the internal organs, ripping them out in frenzy. There was blood everywhere. It was a dreadful scene to watch. It was too much for the colonel to bear. He went down to the bottom of the cliff. Once there, he was immediately surrounded by the monsters. He raised his weapon.

"Don't be a fool, Colonel! Why die needlessly?" a loud voice spoke resoundingly. "Both farmers must die and they will.

Do you remember? Look around you, they can eat you alive in a second, so lower your shotgun. My loyal servants will not harm you, but the other farmer will perish sooner or later." Satan laughed raucously.

The Colonel was furious; he proceeded down the trail with the farmer without saying a word.

"I will be waiting for you at the River Hăn, have a good swim, Colonel," mocked Lucifer.

They kept silent and advanced rapidly. The narrow trail ended near a landing zone (LZ) used by the US cavalry regiment to park their helicopters. They took a short break. The punishing heat was almost unbearable.

The Colonel talked one-on-one with the farmer and tried to boost his spirits. The man knew that death was imminent. Father Benedetti had discussed it with him at great length during confession, and he was at peace with himself, ready to face his fate because he had received communion, and the body of Christ was going to protect him.

The Colonel admired him for his courage and devotion to God. They shared some food and were on the road again. The Colonel pondered what the farmer had just said. Sister Yvonne and Father Benedetti had sought solace in religion. He believed that we all do this from time to time.

They heard voices and laughter from a distance, a patrol was coming, they could be VC or NVA. They both jumped into the bush and waited, totally silent, guns at the ready. The group consisted of six men wearing their uniform black pyjamas; some were barefoot. They were smoking, laughing, and joking, and they all carried automatic rifles with back-packs. The Colonel made gestures to the farmer to stay put. There were too many of them; a confrontation was not advisable. The group passed by and the Colonel and farmer waited twenty minutes before returning to the trail.

"If it had been Jason, he would have killed them all," he thought. "Where is Jason?" What has become of him?" – Probably still alive, but a rogue warrior.

Patrols were on the prowl. Prudence was paramount when they were so close to their objective. The farmer left the trail and plunged into the bush; he knew a short-cut. They proceeded through very thick vegetation. The heat was intolerable. Mosquitoes buzzed incessantly. Coming out of the bush, they arrived at a grassy patch. The area was small and the edge of a dense forest was defined by a narrow trail. The farmer explained that the path led to the boat-house. The colonel was anxious to meet his team and hoped that they were still alive. He walked the point in total silence, keeping a sharp eye out and his ears open for any eventuality.

The trail wound, twisted and turned; and then, down a corner, they saw a small brick house. It looked empty from afar. The Colonel raised his fist, and they crouched down. They observed the area for a while, but nothing moved. It seemed abandoned, but they would have to search it because the VC often used old houses for caches. The farmer would take the back and the colonel the front. The farmer ran around the corner and the colonel kicked the front door open…

...she was on her knees and raised the crossbow. "TCHOUC, TCHOUC".

She went down on her face, two bullets in the head.

He had used his Browning high-power handgun with a silencer; the shotgun would have been too noisy. He turned her body around with his foot and fired two bullets into her heart. "Just to make sure," he thought.

She cannot have been older than fifteen or sixteen, a VC mercenary. She wore her hair in a pony-tail, the uniform black pyjamas, and was barefoot. On the floor was a sniper rifle (SVD Dragunov), two hand-guns and a case of ammunition. It seemed that the crossbow was her favourite weapon. With a box of one hundred plus arrows by her side, she was a redoubtable enemy.

But where was the farmer? The Colonel called his name but there was no answer. He looked outside. OH NO! The farmer was lying dead on his back, an arrow through his right eye. She had shot him at a distance from the window. Her marksmanship had been extraordinary and lethal.

The colonel knelt down, made the sign of the cross, and recited a prayer. He felt a flitting presence across the grass. He lifted his head and saw that the furry monsters had formed a circle around him. Their odour was putrid, their yellow, drooping, eyes were creepy, their claws terrifying. It was strange that he had not heard them coming. He scrutinized the group and wondered if it was the end of his escape.

"No, Colonel, they will not touch you, they are waiting for you to leave so that they can have their lunch. If I had wanted you dead, they would have eaten you already. These two farmers have suffered the fate they deserved. Now, move on, the fisherman and your team are waiting impatiently. Remember that you will lose one more man and that you have a fourteen kilometre swim ahead. It is going to be tough. But you enjoy challenges, don't you?" Satan gloated.

"Where is Jason, my Lord?" inquired the Colonel.

"Doing a fantastic job for the US Army, killing gooks, as you call them. Did you know that he keeps count of his victims in a black book?" Satan asked.

"No, I did not," replied the Colonel.

"He has accumulated two hundred and eighty-eight kills. It is a staggering number and the war is still young. He has his country at heart and has become a small army within. He will win a few medals on the way," stated Lucifer,

"The US Army will consider him an MIA (Missing in Action), AWOL (Absent without Leave), or even a deserter," my Lord.

"None of that rubbish, Colonel. You will help him and he must be valued for his heroic actions. I count on you for that. I want him to be treated with honour and respect, particularly when he is doing such great service for his country. Are we clear on this one, Colonel? You know that I can change any fact, any decision; and I can influence what anyone thinks if I want to, but I will let you deal with Jason's situation for now," said Satan.

"I would like to talk to him again, my Lord."

"I will arrange it, Colonel, very soon."

"Yes, my Lord, I will do my best."

"Now get back on the dirt road and enjoy your swim!" the resonant voice commanded. Lucifer was laughing hysterically.

"On the road again," grumbled the Colonel.

He was now alone but knew the way to his destination. He had to keep clear of VC patrols, avoid villages where traitors could be hidden and NVA soldiers. He climbed a tall tree to look for the River Hăn. It was glimmering under the sun; and he felt very hopeful of reaching it by the next morning, provided no drastic interferences took place. He needed a rest; he hoped to walk at night when it was not so hot. A power snooze (as he called it) was the best choice and since there was a serpentine stream running close by, he would refresh himself a little. The cold water felt very nice and he plunged into a deep sleep in the safe hideout that he had hastily fabricated.

## CHAPTER TWENTY

## THE MONTAGNARDS

"HONK! HONK!" SCREAMS! SHOUTS!

"Bring them here, all of them, place them on their knees!"

The Colonel was still naked and looked through the foliage, wondering what the noise was all about. He had to stay put and very quiet so as not to attract attention. A military truck and a car arrived, it was the NVA army, and officers exited from the vehicles.

But … was it possible? A woman came out of the car, she was wearing a pony-tail, shiny boots, leather gloves, and carried a whip. It was Anh herself, Colonel Anh from the General Department of Military Intelligence and a monster, Lucifer's favourite.

He slipped into his black pyjamas quickly and put on his sandals without attracting anyone's attention. He counted his enemies, one by one. There were three high-ranking officers, Anh herself and three VC mercenaries, totally seven.

He very quickly pulled his Marksman's rifle out of its sheath, checked the magazine and the dum-dum bullets to make as much damage as possible in the course of the kills. He crawled into a good position and waited…with Anh in charge, gruesome and horrible acts were going to take place.

He was perhaps fifty to seventy-five metres away and would not miss his targets; however he could not neutralize them all at once. After the first shots they would run away, scatter all over, or hide. They would immediately begin to search for him. He would have to kill them at close range Thinking this, he placed the silencer on the handgun.

An entire family had been arrested on suspicion of being traitors to the state and helping Americans. They implored her to spare their lives; they denied the charges and explained that they were just farmers. She whipped and beat them mercilessly. The members of her team were laughing ecstatically.

A little infant was crying in his mother's arms.

"Shut that baby up at once!" Anh yelled.

"He is hungry, he needs to be fed," the mother replied.

"I do not care, you are all going to die, you hear!" she shouted.

Anh's men were beating up the prisoners at random. The farmers were crying and begging for their lives. Anh struck them with brute force, using her whip. She kicked and punched them, flying into a rage for no apparent reason. She used profanities and insults. The Colonel wanted to intervene but it was not the right time, and he decided to observe the scene a little longer. It was a large family and they were all kneeling, with their heads down, execution style, waiting for the end. A VC pulled out his handgun to shoot a man behind the ear.

"NO!" screamed Anh.

"Do not waste our bullets on those dirty pigs; use your bayonets, blades and axes. We need to save our ammunition for our mortal enemy, the USA."

The baby started crying again and the mother opened her dress to feed him.

Anh approached her and yelled, "What the hell are you doing?"

"Feeding him, what do you think I am doing?" she retorted.

Anh slapped her with full force across the face, "Don't take that tone of voice with me, you bitch. I told you not to feed that little bastard in my presence, is that clear?" she growled.

The woman got really angry; she spat in Anh's face and

shouted, "Don't you call my son a bastard, you whore. You sleep with the brass and come here to execute us farmers without reason, because you cannot do anything better with your miserable and pathetic life. You are a crap officer and a murderer. Fine, kill me, it will not change the fact that you have disgraced yourself, behaving this way!"

The VC raised his handgun to her head but Anh made a sign with her hand and he placed it back into his holster.

"No, no, no, this is not good, not good at all," thought the colonel.

He had understood most of the verbal exchange and knew that Anh was going to act violently. That is why he had to move quickly to make his kill. He moved position slowly to get the proper line of vision. He adjusted his range telescopic sight with precision and accuracy, verified that the magazine contained twenty explosive bullets, and began regulating his breathing. He wiped the sweat off his face and closed his eyes for a few seconds. He placed a bandana on his head. The target was between fifty and seventy-five metres away, the M21 sniper rifle was a formidable weapon and he was going to score a bull's-eye.

"I could squash you like a worm, but I want you to suffer before you die, you have insulted *me*, Colonel Anh from the General Department of Military Intelligence!"

The woman shrugged her shoulders and said, "Do what you have to do and I will do what I have to do."

Anh came close to her, looked straight into her eyes and nodded a few times, forcing a faint smile. The Colonel was alarmed. "No, no, no! What is that woman thinking? She is confronting the Devil; she will be executed, without any doubt. She has already signed her death warrant," he whispered to himself.

Anh gestured at the mercenaries and they took the baby

from his mother's arms and forced the women down on her knees. She was screaming profanities and spitting at Anh. The entire family were looking at her, crying, and shaking their heads. Her father was yelling, "STOP! STOP! You are making this worse for all of us!"

But the mother's hatred for the officer was intense, and she kept abusing her vociferously.

Anh asked the VC to put the child on the ground; then took a bayonet and pierced the little body twice.

There was complete silence on the terrain.

Then the mother became hysterical, screaming, "My baby, my baby! You have killed my baby!"

All the members of the family were weeping with emotion for the loss of the newborn. The scene was abominable.

"Now or never," muttered the Colonel. He quickly took position, took aim and fired.... The bullet hit her on the top of her head and blew off her skull. She was lifted up by the force of the impact and landed against the door of her limo. The second shot struck her under the left eye. "No more Anh!" The Colonel breathed out slowly and aimed again. A NVA commandant was gesticulating with a handgun in his hand barking orders at the VC mercenaries.

"POW! POW!"

Two shots, one in the mouth, the other in the right jaw. His face was no more.

From the corner of his eye the Colonel noticed that a VC was getting too close for comfort, hiding behind a Peugeot motorcycle.

"POW! POW!"

Two bullets into the petrol tank. There was a loud explosion and it erupted into flame. The mercenary was now a human torch, running all over the place, screaming in pain. He collapsed onto the ground and burnt to death.

The Colonel took a few seconds to assess the situation. There had been seven enemies. Four were left; they had scattered and gone into hiding. He had not been discovered because he had placed a silencer on his rifle. However it would not be long before they found his location. He decided to move, and crawled about fifty metres to his left. He paused and waited. He wiped sweat out of his eyes. "Where are they?" They must still be on the perimeter, hidden. The combat zone was large. He hadn't noticed anyone running into the bushes.

He scanned the area again slowly, with the telescopic sight, millimeter by millimeter, searching for any signs of life or unusual movements. He did not move. It was terribly hot but he did not drink. He had gone undetected because he had used dark and green foliage for camouflage. Special Forces and particularly snipers were experts in the area of guerilla warfare.

Using the silencer was also essential not to attract attention. Undoubtedly more NVA and VC were operating in the vicinity and Anh must have told them where she was taking the prisoners.

"Where did the family go?" the colonel asked himself.

They had been terrified and had gone into hiding in the bush.

"I am happy and proud to have killed this beast," the colonel said to himself. "She deserved to die."

Rose, the village leader, had narrated the shocking details of her vicious acts of violence towards American soldiers and peasants. Anh enjoyed torturing people. She had been known to keep an individual in a room continuously for three days, inflicting the most unbearable and unbelievable painful abuse one can imagine. She thrived on hurting human beings.

Jason had recalled the day when a man was dumped outside

the gates of his unit. He had had his eyes gouged out and been castrated. – They found the genital organs in his pocket. – He died before the medics could save him. Anh had used her pocket-knife!

Dr Henri had recalled when a farmer was skinned alive by Anh herself. "She had peeled him like and orange. He died in my arms, I could not save him. What a horrible way to die!" he had exclaimed.

She was in the habit of cutting the index fingers of her victims with secateurs – particularly in the case of US Army soldiers – so that they would not be able to shoot again. The dead bodies were found with their severed finger between their teeth.

The Colonel started to focus his mind again on the four deadly guerilla fighters who wanted to kill him; they were very dangerous men, now out for revenge. They could not be very far away. He scrutinized the perimeter...nothing! But what about the vehicles? There was a truck that had carried the prisoners, a jeep, Anh's limousine and a motorcycle that had already been destroyed. They had to be hiding inside. But their time would now be short-lived.

He smiled and checked his weapon once more. The sniper's motto was, "One kill, one bullet." The Colonel understood the reasoning behind this, but he always shot his victims twice. "Just to be sure" was his rule of thumb. He now had fourteen explosive cartridges left in his rifle, one full spare box of the same, plus additional regular bullets in his backpack. It was sufficient to foil an NVA attack, or to annihilate any VC patrol that might be snooping around searching for Anh.

They could well be doing that and might even send for reinforcements. The Colonel would then be in very big danger! He wanted to terminate the four men hiding in the vehicles and then leave the area quickly. He had a hunch that very soon this place would be crawling with VC. He checked from right to left and vice versa, and then he repeated these actions. "Somehow they will move or show their faces," he thought.

He stayed calm and collected, wiping sweat off his face and hands, not drinking any water to reduce urination. The colonel had accumulated more than one hundred and ten kills during three tours of Vietnam, but to have eliminated Anh was going to be the highlight of his career in the Special Forces.

"Well, I am a wanted man as an escapee, but now I will be the number one criminal who shot Anh, a sadistic officer who took pleasure in torturing soldiers and civilians," he thought.

He wiped away some tears of joy; it was retribution for all the murders she had committed. He felt a resurgence of enthusiasm in his heart; he needed some motivation under this stressful condition.

"CLICK, CLACK!" He heard a very light noise.

One of the VC who was slowly exiting from the cabin of the truck had left the door open.

"Come on, boy, show your face to Papa," he mumbled. The mercenary was crouching and moving with caution. His head peeped out of the rear of the lorry, the Colonel waited, waited and waited until the man moved forward. Half of his body was now visible. "POW! POW!" One in the head, one in the heart! And he went down.

"Three more," whispered the Colonel. From under the jeep the VC was crawling towards the limo, he was slow. Then all of the sudden he stood up and ran to the car.

"Gotcha," he murmured. He fired one shot into the knee, to stop him and one at the temple. A deathly silence followed…

"Two left!" smiled the officer.

"They are still in the vehicles, they must come out at some point," he pondered.

He observed some activity within the limousine. It was a Hotchkiss, French made, a 1953 black cabriolet Adenauer right-hand drive, a beautiful automobile. It was spacious and two men could easily hide in it. From a distance he heard crackling sounds, voices and short beeps, then he realized that reinforcements were on the way. They were using the radio of Anh's car to call for backup.

"I must finish the job and do it right now!" he realized.

He got out of his hiding spot, moved further right and was now facing the limo's windshield. Both VC were sitting on the front seat. It was now or never. They lifted up their hands. That was the last thing they did. Two shots, two dead men. He opened the door and shot them again in the right eye. "Just to be sure," he said aloud.

He went back to his original spot, wiped the sweat off his face and hands, breathed a sigh of relief after a job well done, checked his rifle and refilled the magazine with explosive bullets. He cleaned the silencer, placed more foliage and branches on top of the hideout and waited, waited, and waited…

They roared in with a deafening noise. Three military trucks carrying approximately seventy-five men. They were NVA officers and soldiers, and a large group of VC, and mercenaries.

"It is going to be very difficult to get out of this predicament," he said to himself. However, he knew that, despite being outnumbered, he would fight back bravely.

They all jumped out of the truck, rifles in their hands. The officers stood by Anh's corpse, saluted and went to check the other bodies. They barked orders, they were angry, and now they gathered together while the officer in charge gave them the plan of action.

"If they split up into six or seven groups, I will not be able to kill them, I will become the 'hunted', he thought.

"WISHHHH! WHISHHHH! TCHAK! TCHAK!"

A rain of arrows and spears fell onto the enemy. It came out of nowhere and caught them by surprise. They did not have time to react and died on the spot and immediately. A few seconds later, waves of the same came down, soldiers lay dead on the field. The Colonel was confused and wondered who had helped him and why? A small number of VC and NVA officers were running around, agitated, shouting, trying to escape. They wanted to hide in the bush. The Colonel aimed… eight bullets, two shots each, four dead.

"Just to make sure," he smiled. The forest was eerily silent. He left his hiding place, handgun at the ready and walked to the vehicles. He checked them all and went over to the dead bodies. He shot at close range anything that moved. When it was all over, he was going to go to the boat-house. He was leaving the field when he heard someone call him aloud:

"Colonel, Colonel!"

He turned around and stood transfixed in shock and disbelief.

"Bonyo, is that you, my friend?"

They hugged each other tightly.

Bono was the leader of the *montagnards* and they had done some operations together in the past. The Degar – also known as the *montagnards* ("people of the mountain" in English) – were the most loyal allies of the Americans in Vietnam. They were located in and around the central highlands. These indigenous people were a carry-over from the French Colonial period in Vietnam. Special Forces recruited them because of their quiet resolve and skills in tracking. Combat experiences formed a close bond between them. Bonyo's warriors had just saved his life. They were silent, lethal, invisible and used bows and arrows. They were redoubtable fighters.

"Thank you, Bonyo. You arrived just on time, they were too many to deal with all at once.

"We saw that you needed a hand, that's all."

They walked together around the field and stopped in front of Anh's body.

"You have killed a monster, Colonel. She was evil, devious, self-centred, and arrogant, with an iron heart."

Bonyo was perfectly correct. Little did he know that Anh was Satan's favourite soldier.

"I cried when I killed her, Bonyo, but they were tears of joy, she was a real psychopath and deserved to die. It was retribution for all the people that she had tortured and murdered needlessly."

The *montagnard* looked at the Colonel and nodded. "Even the VC hated her, Colonel. You have rendered great service to our country, we are sincerely grateful to you for avenging the victims and families afflicted by Anh's cruelty."

The Colonel pulled the bayonet out of the infant's body. He cradled the motionless little body in his arms and wrapped him up in a blanket. He kissed him on the forehead and asked Bonyo, "should we bury him?"

"No, Colonel, we should ask the family what they want to do"

"Where are they?"

"In the forest nearby, hiding. let me call them."

He then instructed his men to bring them back to the field. After a few minutes, the family reappeared and gathered together. The mother dropped to her knees sobbing uncontrollably with the baby in her arms. She was torn apart by her baby's horrific death. Everyone was standing in tears, silent, motionless. Then Bonyo discussed the burial with the family. They were Catholics and requested to go to his village to celebrate a mass prior to cremating the child. Before moving on, members of the family approached Anh's corpse and spat on it. The baby's mother told the Colonel that the entire family was immensely grateful to him for killing Anh. They were going to spread the news around the region and give him the recognition he deserved. He was a hero for all Vietnamese people.

"I hope that the US Army gives you a medal for your action. You deserve it," she said.

"I agree, at least a silver star," said Bonyo.

The Colonel explained that what was most important right now was to reconvene with his team at the boat-house and complete his escape successfully. The entire NVA Army and the VC were looking for them; to stay alive was a challenge.

Bonyo said, "I will take you safely to the boat-house, I know the short-cuts and the fisherman is my friend. He hates the VCs. Do not worry, I will keep you safe. Let's go to my camp, we need to talk and bury the infant. We must give the grieving family peace of mind."

After a long march they reached the *montagnards*' village. They were very hospitable people and took great care of the distraught family. They also prepared the ceremony for the baby's funeral. It was very moving. Bonyo who was a Catholic had called upon a friend who was a priest and had brought a bible with him. The Colonel said a few words and so did Bonyo. After the cremation, the ashes were spread across the camp because it emanated good vibes and the girl's soul was to rest, free and at peace, in the vicinity of the village. The child's mother also took some of the ashes with her in a small urn. Bonyo asked some of his men to escort the family back to their village and to protect them against VC patrols.

"Thank you again for eliminating Anh. You have freed us all from the devil. Your name will be famous all over Vietnam, I promise," the mother told him.

They all hugged warmly and then they were on their way. Then Bonyo invited the Colonel into his hut.

"You have to get something off your chest, Colonel, but first I must give you something…"

The *montagnard* leader took out a bracelet from a pouch and handed it to the Colonel.

"This is a *montagnard* bracelet, made especially for you, Colonel, it is long overdue, but we were both busy fighting a war. Please accept it with all the symbolism and friendship that it represents."

"Thank you, Bonyo, it means a lot to me to receive this gift. I will wear it always with pride and honour and respect," he replied. (The *montagnard* bracelet, a prestigious symbol of friendship and respect was given to US Army Special Forces Soldiers, "Green Berets", and others during the Vietnam War. The bracelets were made of brass taken from the casing of used bullets.)

An old lady came into the hut and brought food and drinks.

"Now please tell me everything from the start Colonel, we are friends, remember, do not hold anything back," said Bonyo. He wanted to know all the details of the escape and what had ensued. The Colonel satisfied his curiosity. Bonyo listened attentively, never interrupted, and on occasions pulled a face. He was genuinely interested and undoubtedly was going to give the colonel some advice. The old lady brought some french bread, cheeses, and cold cuts, and offered coffee.

"Coffee, Bonyo? You have VIP treatment in your camps?"

"Why not, Colonel? You only live once, don't you!" laughed the leader. He then began to talk.

"You know, Colonel, you have had some difficult times during your escape, but it could have been worse. The VC did not catch you and you avoided the NVA. The six of you were enemy number one in North Vietnam, now you are the only one left.

We do not know yet what has happened to the other team, but I sincerely hope that they all made it. Do not be concerned about your delay, it always occurs in such situations. It was an escape, not an official mission. They may have been delayed also, and may not even be at the boat-house yet. If they are, they will be waiting for you. The fisherman will take good care of them.

Yes, you are four days late at your rendez-vous, but due to the circumstances that have taken place during your escape, it is not unusual. Your team of seasoned professionals will understand.

Your plan can be carried out but it will be very, very hard for all of you. The Hăn and Cam rivers stretch for fourteen kilometres before they enter the Gulf of Tonkin. You must be picked up before that, otherwise nobody will notice you in the Gulf and you will drown. You will all be cold, exhausted and perhaps injured. Crocodiles, alligators and snakes will be all over the place, not to mention the boats manned by pirates. They will shoot you on sight. They are trading illicitly between Vietnam and Korea carrying opium, heroin, cocaine, prostitutes, and arms. I want to add that they hate Americans. Finally, there are two or three waterfalls on the way, up to sixty metres high. Avoid them at all costs, because of the rocks at the bottom. Just take knives with you, any arms or other equipment will be far too cumbersome and will get wet."

"Thank you, Bonyo, this is good advice."

"During your escape, you met many leaders. I know them all; they are honest and upright citizens, friendly with Americans and trustworthy. It was your good fortune."

"Yes, Bonyo, they were there for me when I needed them most."

"You seem to have an excellent rapport with the Dark Lord. Are you going to tell them about it?"

"No, I will not. Before an operation, the officer in charge always makes sure that his men have a clear mind, no money or car problems, no family, wife, or girlfriend issues, nothing to preoccupy them, so that they can entirely focus on the task at hand. In addition they would find my story quite unbelievable, don't you agree? No, I will not discuss this episode. God will be my rudder."

"I understand, Colonel, and I agree with you."

"Bonyo, what is your thought about Jason?"

"I believe that he still fights for the US Army. Somewhere in the bush, he keeps killing VCs and increases his body-count. I have no doubt that he is still loyal to you and that if you were in trouble, he would help you in a second."

"Why do you say that, Bonyo?"

"Because Jason is a soldier's soldier. You trained him, he respects authority. The Dark Lord cannot erase that."

"I hope that you are right, Bonyo."

"What did Sister Marie Catherine tell you about him?"

"Sister Marie Catherine told me that Jason is lost for now, but can still get his seat in Paradise. Satan is not invincible. Jason must ask God for forgiveness and be willing to receive God; if not, hell will be his home. If God allows it, a person can go to Paradise. If you live in harmony with God, it's harder for evil to take you."

"Well, it is his decision to talk to God, Colonel. He has to make the move; nobody else can do it for him."

"Yes, Bonyo, it is in his hands now."

"Have you seen him recently, Colonel?"

"No I have not, but he must be in the bush killing VCs at an alarming rate, as you say"

"What do you think will really happen on the swim?"

"The best scenario is that we shall be four at first, but Lucifer will decide at some point to take one of my men. The three of us remaining will have a good chance to be picked up by the Air CAV (Cavalry) patrolling the waterside areas. Otherwise the Prince of Darkness can play dirty tricks on us and we shall die. Remember, Bonyo, that I killed his best servant, Anh; she was his protégée and he will make me pay for it."

"I know that, Colonel. I would not want to be in your boots! What are you going to say to your superiors about Jason?"

"Probably that he is MIA (Missing in action). He should get a chance to return to his unit if he wants to. But his frame of mind has totally changed and I do not believe that he can function in a normal environment."

"Can he ever become himself again?"

"No, Bonyo, unless God cures him. He has received the Devil's blood into his veins; nevertheless, he may occasionally experience a resurgence of sanity or normal behaviour. Right now he is a deadly killing-machine, who is luckily on our side."

"We should all pray for him."

"I agree, and the power of prayer is limitless."

"The mission has given you strength and resolution to deal with Satan, hasn't it?"

"Yes, Bonyo, the council made me realize that Satan is not invincible, that God is stronger, and that Satan lives with constant delusions of grandeur. He is a deceiver, a liar, an egotistical creature, very dangerous because he retains the intelligence of an angel. He was a favourite archangel before turning against God, who banned him from heaven. Lucifer is a fierce adversary, but I am not afraid; and I will fight him to the end. I will protect my team, and he knows it."

"Why do you think that Beelzebub appeared to you as a

tiger?"

"Sister Marie Catherine and her council told me that he can look for prey anywhere at any time. He had chosen Jason and wanted to exhibit his power. The Vietnamese tiger being fierce, strong and terrifying, was a perfect way of doing this.

"Usually some people are more prone to meet Satan than others. Like those who have lost faith, who are superstitious, or practice black magic and Satanism. That is not my case. I have led a good, clean, and honest life. I cannot become his victim, but only a challenge, or, if I may say so, a pain in the neck! Jason is a brave soldier, but he had a past stained with bad memories. They still haunted him to this day. Lucifer always looks for weak, troubled and unstable people to join his stable in Hell. They become his servants."

"What a great explanation, Colonel!"

"Thank Sister Marie Catherine for it, Bonyo!"

They both laughed.

"We should be moving on, I want to reach the boat-house as soon as possible"

"No problem. Let me get my men ready and we'll be on the way."

Bonyo had assembled six men to escort the Colonel to the boat-house. They were some of his best warriors, carrying longbows and arrows, crossbows, blowguns with poisoned darts, and homemade knives. They walked barefoot and only wore loincloths.

"I want to pray before we leave," noted the Colonel.

They all stood in silence talking to the Almighty. It was getting dark and they observed total silence. The VC patrolled at night and the team wanted to avoid facing any violent confrontation. Bonyo walked the point; *montagnards* were excellent trackers and knew the region like the back of their hands.

It was a full moon and they advanced through dense foliage so as not to be detected. Bonyo raised his right hand and they all crouched down. Voices in the dark announced that a patrol was coming.

A few metres away from their position, a very narrow pathway led to a hamlet called Săn Niam. It was known to be a VC hideout, seldom searched by US Troops. They had to traverse this area to go to the boat-house, their final destination, which was located at an intersection remotely situated on the banks of the River Hăn. It was late and these groups of mercenaries were unwinding after a long day, smoking, talking loudly, and joking. There were ten of them, carrying automatic weapons. They were closing in…

Bonyo and his men took their positions on both sides of the trail, the Colonel screwed the silencer on his gun on tight, and they waited, communicating only by signs. When the mercenaries were five metres away, the colonel sprang from the bush in front of them. The effect of surprise was astonishing and he placed two head shots at the VC in front of him. Arrows and darts rained on the rest of the group. They had no time to react and died immediately. The Colonel placed two more shots in the right eyes of his victims. "Just to be sure," he said with a nod of approval. Bonyo collected a full bag of US Dollars and some food.

"Where they are going, they won't need it," he said.

VC mercenaries often carried large sums of money, preferably in US currency to purchase arms, medicine, drugs, and alcohol, and meet their expenses while on the road.

The Colonel complimented the fighters for their remarkable accuracy with the blowpipes. They were made of hollow sugar canes about one metre long and deadly poisonous arrows were launched by the force of their breath.

"They train from a young age, Colonel. By the time they are ten or twelve years old, they are marksmen in their own right. The same applies to the bows and arrows. They are our traditional weapons."

"It certainly shows, Bonyo. I am glad you were there."

When they reached Săn Niam, they hid behind thick bushes and decided not to cross the hamlet but rather circumvent it. because it was crowded with VC and civilians. They observed the action for a while. There was a lot of commotion, mainly created by the VCs doing business on a large scale. The hamlet consisted of a few huts, two low-level buildings, and a line of military tents. There were a couple of food vendors with their stands outside in the open air. Two military trucks arrived and stopped in front of the buildings. An officer barked some orders and the soldiers started loading. Crate after crate was transferred to the vehicles.

"Arms," said Bonyo.

"Where from?"

"North Korea, South Vietnam, USA."

The Colonel looked at him inquisitively.

"Because there is a war going on, there is big money to be made. Asian gangsters are selling to North Vietnam left, right and centre and I want to tell you that C.I.A operatives deal on all fronts and make a killing. What you are witnessing is a very, very small, part of a large and complex web of activities. You could not count how many VC villages are being used as caches for illegal goods."

"Drugs make big money."

"Our soldiers are dying because of this poison."

"Unscrupulous people say that money has no colour, no odour, no soul. It is only money."

"War brings out the worst in people."

"The supplies are moved around the country. The pirates are strong collaborators and navigate through rivers and estuaries way down to the coast. They are ruthless and often kill their prisoners on board. They brag that they feed the alligators better than the zoo-keepers."

Loud screams could be heard in one of the buildings. About twenty girls appeared, followed by VCs.

"Prostitutes," said Bonyo.

Two of the girls started arguing with the guards. The men hit them hard across the face and they fell down. The men kicked the girls savagely, grabbed them by the hair and threw them into the trucks.

"They are sold for a high price," quoted Bonyo.

"Where do they come from?"

"The countryside, small villages and farms, usually the VCs kidnap them and if the parents argue they get shot on the spot. These girls are lost forever."

Once completely loaded, the lorries drove off, followed by NVA soldiers on motorcycles. After the vehicles had gone, the traffic did not seem to diminish. Scooters, bicycles and military vehicles circulated continually in and out of the locale. Mercenaries were patrolling the downtown area, their guns at the ready, as the trucks were being loaded.

"Where are these people coming from?" asked the Colonel.

"Tunnels. There are probably five to six of them in this village," answered Bonyo.

Tunnels gave power to the North Vietnamese Army, particularly the VCs; they were a silent military giant. They were used as the way in and out of battlefields. But there was also a complete life-system underground, consisting of hospitals, surgical-wards, schools, training centres, obstacle courses for soldiers, shooting ranges, meeting-rooms, dining-halls, bedrooms, kitchens and more…

Nobody could imagine the astonishing intricacies and the wide range of organizations situated in the North Vietnamese army tunnels. It was a phenomenal system which the US Army could never penetrate and rarely discovered. The infantry team – called "tunnel rats", made up of small-sized men – had minimal success in their searches to find arms, ammunition and plans of attack. Many lost their lives because of the deadly traps left behind by the VC.

"I've heard that the tunnels have reached the perimeters of Dan Nang and that the VCs are listening from down below to the US soldiers talking among themselves," observed the Colonel.

"Yes, Colonel, special forces told me that story."

As they started to move on, Bonyo exclaimed, "Look, Colonel! Look at the tent on the left, American prisoners!"

Two men wearing black hoods over their heads, hands tied behind their backs, their feet in shackles, were led towards a military truck. Their clothes were covered in blood from a very bad beating. When one of them fell down on his knees, a VC guard hit him with the butt of his rifle. They were pushed roughly into the vehicle and taken away out of the hamlet. The colonel clenched his fists; his knuckles were white and he was muttering insults, totally devastated that he could not help the servicemen.

"Calm down, Colonel, there is absolutely nothing that you or any of us could have done. To interfere would have meant to sign our own death warrant, and you know it!"

These men were taken up to North Vietnam into camps, where rats were bigger than dogs; and sadistic, barbaric officers bore a deep hatred for Americans. Later they would be transferred to work camps or gulags, either in North Korea or

Russia, and die in appalling conditions. These mysterious displacements were tabulated as Missing in Action by the US Army, but no one could really explain the reason why American prisoners were sent to these countries in the first place.

Thousands were unaccounted for and were never found or returned to the USA. The Colonel had witnessed secret movements when, being held prisoner, servicemen were exchanged for merchandise, some taken away and others brought in, very often in terrible physical condition, and now and then with North Korean or Russian officers supervising the transactions by themselves, without reference to superior authority. The Central Intelligence Agency did not get involved and more men continued to disappear.

"Let's go," the Colonel said angrily.

For about three hours, they walked briskly through swamps, foliage, and forests, sometimes ankle-deep in streams of water; then…

"Look down on your right," Bonyo said.

"Thank you, you are the best, we made it!"

There it was – a blue two-storey building – the boat-house! They cautiously moved closer, silently, on the alert just in case the enemy was on site.

"Welcome to my modest home!" said a deep, booming voice.

The fisherman was a man of medium height, with grey hair, and a muscular body. He was barefoot, wearing navy-blue pants and a grey shirt. He spoke English very well and had a gracious personality. Bonyo had known him for a long time and they hugged and laughed cheerfully.

"Your men arrived yesterday morning. They were delayed and so were you. It seems they are waiting for you."

That was excellent news.

## CHAPTER TWENTY ONE

## THE BOAT-HOUSE

The men were ecstatic that their leader had rejoined the team, they cheered, hugged, and slapped the colonel on the back. Of course they all wanted to exchange stories. The fisherman's wife prepared strong coffee and cooked a copious breakfast. The fisherman was determined to show everyone the boat-house; it was his pride and joy. The facilities were clean, spacious, and well appointed, with a lot of fishing equipment on hand. The second floor provided storage for nets, hooks, fishing-rods and spare engines for boats. A long table in the centre could be used for meetings or a dinner. It was spartan but functional. The master-bedroom adjoined a smaller room with four bunk beds. There was also a full bathroom and shower.

"You have a great installation," commented the colonel.

"It took five years' hard work but it was worth it."

"Do you have serious problems with the VC?"

"Not really, they check my place on a weekly basis but they never find anything." He smiled happily.

The lower floor consisted of a dining-room, a small living-room, a large kitchen, and a spare bedroom with two bunk beds and a shower.

"How many boats do you have?"

"Two, a sampan with a powerful engine and a medium-sized junk with a sail and a small engine. I will use the sampan to drop you into the river, you can hide below deck on the way, and it is safer. The boats are docked outside, but now let's eat and talk. Colonel, my wife wants to hug you tightly for killing Anh. You have rendered a precious service to Vietnam;

we can never repay you for what you did. Even the VC despised her, she was a vile human being, even the 'two-step snake' is less dangerous than she. You are now a hero, you deserve it, the event has been given full and wide media coverage, thank you."

The lady gave the colonel a kiss on the cheek and thanked him profusely, the team applauded the colonel, and shook his hand.

The colonel said, "We were public enemy Number One for escaping a camp. The NVA and VC have been looking for us ever since. But now, after killing Anh, our status has risen dramatically. We are the famous four!"

They all cheered and applauded. The food was delicious, the coffee hot and strong. Stories, anecdotes, opinions, and advice were exchanged. The fisherman and Banyo were locals and knew the area and the dangers that could occur during the planned swim.

They Colonel and the others needed to leave quickly to avoid getting caught. The fisherman had helped many servicemen escape by the rivers; but a large number had died doing it. It was a perilous journey.

"The locals call this body of water a stream but it is the size of a river, with strong currents and turbulence, it is also very cold at times. The Cam is larger and deeper, with extremely strong currents and some high waterfalls. Please avoid them at all costs because you may drown or break your bones on the rocks at the bottom."

"Are you all good swimmers?" asked the fisherman.

They all nodded.

Bonyo added, "Two of my men did that swim once and reached the end of the Càm, but swore never to do it again!"

"What is your chance of being extracted from the river?" Bonyo asked.

"Good, the Air Cav, Riverine and Seabees boats patrol up and down the river frequently."

"The water is very filthy, many objects and dead bodies are always floating in it, and alligators feed on them. I will give you gourds to carry drinking water," said the fisherman.

The conversation somehow shifted towards Captain Henderson's death and Jason's disappearance. Sister Marie Catherine and the council were also discussed. These topics made the colonel feel uncomfortable; he did not want to bring up the Prince of Darkness and the episode with Jason's possession by an evil spirit. Mike, a master sergeant with the Special Forces "green berets", was particularly inquisitive and felt that the colonel's story was full of holes. The colonel had not thoroughly answered some of the questions posed by his men.

Mike said, "I know Jason well. He is not a deserter, he is a great soldier. He would never have left you in the lurch. Why did you spend so much time at the mission after burying Henderson? We are a team, we may die in the river. Colonel, let's not have any secrets between us!"

The room went quiet. Bonyo said, "The colonel did not want to worry anybody unnecessarily. A leader must make sure that anxieties do not cloud minds before a mission. He told me the full story, it is mystifying!"

Inquisitive looks were exchanged. The colonel decided to break his silence about the Dark Lord. He cleared his throat and began. "I am sorry, I should have been more truthful, but the events were too bizarre and seem highly improbable. Please keep an open mind."

He gave a full account of the escape. Some nodded in approval; others were intrigued by the events, while the fisherman's wife had a look of consternation on her face and was holding her husband's hand firmly. The colonel's account of the transformation of Satan into a tiger, the disturbing stories of the council, and Jason's possession by Lucifer had a striking effect on the group. The colonel finished his story.

"Now you can form your own opinion," he said.

Everyone was looking at the colonel in silence, perplexed.

Mike spoke. "It is quite a story; we understand your hesitation to give information."

"Satan's decision is to take one of you as his servant, like he took Jason, and he will follow through as promised."

The three men looked at each other, shrugged their shoulders, smiled and said, "Better talk to the Devil than be tortured and killed by the V.C!"

"I understand your predicament. but there is nothing I can do."

"We are ready, Colonel," said Mike.

"Let's all pray before leaving," said the colonel.

"Agreed," they said in unison.

They all formed a circle and asked the Almighty for courage, help, and the good fortune not to get hurt. It was time to go.

*"General, I have not interrupted you for a long time because the story is mesmerizing. Last time we talked, it was about Sister Yvonne. Did she ever become Mary's angel?"*

"Yes, she did, but it took a few years. She was an emissary for the mission; she helped Sister Marie Catherine and the council, and assisted Dr Henri and Benedetti with medical cases and difficult operations. What an extraordinary person!"

*"The council's stories were dark, scary, and at times sordid; but they were all true, am I correct?"*

"Yes Sergeant, Satan is unscrupulous but also powerful."

*"You dealt with him very well, didn't you?"*

"I would not say that, but I was not afraid of him. I blocked his tricks as they came along, one by one."

*"What about Jason, General, did you ever see him again?"*

"Yes I did. He saved us all on the swim and later received top honours from the First Infantry Regiment, the "Big Red One". I was happy to have listed him as "M.I.A." because he resurfaced, joined his unit for a little while and later left the army. He was entitled to full military benefits and I am sure that he appreciated it. It was well deserved. Later, I met him again in a café in New York City. He had not aged a bit. His demeanor was the same."

*"What did he do in the Big Apple?"*

The General lowered his head in embarrassment. "I will tell you later, Sergeant. He could no longer handle military life; particularly its rules and regulations but he had been awarded two silver stars and two medals of valour. He was shortlisted for a medal of honour, but his heroic actions had not been standard military procedures or assigned missions. He was a great soldier and had shown bravery under enemy fire."

*"Did he recognize you in New York?"*

"Surprisingly, yes, and we had a good conversation."

*"How many kills did Jason have at the time he left the army?"*

"Officially registered by his regiment and on record, three hundred and forty-two (342)."

*"Amazing! He should have received the medal of honour just for that count General."*

"Agreed, but he claimed four hundred and forty-four kills, all listed on his little black book, with times, dates, and locations carefully noted. He was very organized. But because he had been a rogue warrior, the US Army did not accept his figures. However, he still was the best and most famous sniper in the US Forces."

*"Did the council's stories about the Dark Lord disturb you*

*General?"*

"Not at all, Satan and I played a game of cat and mouse waiting for a chance to trap each other. The stories only clarified my opinion about him."

*"Who did he take on your team during the swim?"*

"You must wait to find out, Sergeant. He clouds the hearts and minds of his victims, but he cannot always control them. Some have resisted to the end, like Sister Yvonne! The council was composed of very seasoned experts; they all had faced Lucifer off and on and gave me invaluable advice, which saved my life. I will never forget them Sergeant!"

*"He killed the two farmers and showed no pity."*

"Yes, he did. However, they knew that he would keep his promise, they expected death and that is why Father Benedetti blessed them before their final trip. I could not stop it in any way. The Prince of Darkness was extremely angry with them, so he retaliated by killing them both, a true act of the Devil."

*"Now your story enters a critical phase, the swim! How did it go, General? Was it as hard as you expected it to be?"*

The General chuckled softly. "Wait, Sergeant, wait! The boat-house was the last comfort-zone for us, we knew what was coming would be hell, nightmarish, even deadly. The place was homely and clean. The fisherman and his wife were kind people. I felt relaxed and safe in that environment.

Bonyo and his men left and I thanked them profusely.

We hugged and he said, "I have full confidence that you'll make it and return to base safe and sound. Once again, thank you for killing Ahn; you are a hero in Vietnam!"

The fisherman's wife said, "Take good care, colonel, you are our saviour, you shot Ahn, a demon. She was not invincible after all. Be careful, the rivers are wild and treacherous, we shall pray for you!"

We only carried gourds of potable water and our combat knives, did not have any underwear and wore no shoes. We went below deck on the sampan. The fisherman was the pilot on that risky mission.

# CHAPTER TWENTY TWO

## THE HAN

We had been labeled enemies of the state for killing the guards and making the NVA and the VC lose face. I was definitely the main focus, the infamous one who had committed sacrilege by bumping off Anh, a high-ranking NVA officer, a barbarian, a murderer, and a sadist. Mike, a Master Sergeant Green Beret, Watson a Navy Captain pilot and Gomez, a Sergeant Major of the illustrious 173rd Airborne Brigade, formed the team. They were solid, reliable, men with considerable military experience. We wore black pyjamas with a bandana that we had been given at camp #1. The Air and Riverine patrols could spot us quickly if we were sporting dark colours.

The engine was puffing down the river very slowly. There was total silence. It was daylight and we were waiting for the fisherman to give us the "go ahead". It was unbelievably hot and stuffy below deck.

"Now," he said.

The boat slowed down and we slid into the water silently.

"Honk ! Honk ! Honk!"

We could hear a horn in the distance. We quickly swam to the edge of the river and hid from sight in the thick, dark-green, foliage. We wanted to avoid pirates like the plague! A small boat passed in front of us without incident, probably just a fisherman going home. The currents were strong and we stayed close to each other, looking out for deadly reptiles. Gomez pointed to a large uprooted tree floating towards us, we grabbed the chance and hung on to it tightly. It would help us move faster and prevent us drifting apart. The sun was burning and insects were buzzing around us. The dirty water stank like sewage. We checked on each other continually, but kept silent unless it was absolutely necessary.

The Colonel turned and saw on the top of a branch of our tree, very close to Watson's head, a ruby-eyed, green, pit viper, a trimeresurus snake, one of the most venomous in Vietnam. It was dozing, rolled up, its body enlarged, probably with prey inside it. He gave Watson a sign with his eyes, the pilot glanced at it and nodded. They left it alone because it did not present a serious danger at the time.

Carcasses of dead animals, corpses, and faeces were carried along by the strong currents. Rats and reptiles moved frenziedly among them.

We had not yet been subject to any attack and progressed through the Hăn up to speed. We constantly scrutinized the sky for choppers, but in vain. We had not seen any Riverine or Seabees patrols either. It was the calm before the storm.

"Honk! Honk! Honk! Tuut! Tuut! Tuut!"

A boat was on the way. We hid in the bamboo on the right side of the river and watched for what would happen. A large sampan, painted red, with powerful engines and a huge sail flopping down the mast, was slowing down. It hummed in the water, motor idling, just waiting… We could not distinguish all the activities taking place, but we heard the captain barking orders at his crew, and preparations being made at the bow and aft of the vessel.

"Pirates delivering goods," whispered Mike.

"Vroom! Vroom! Vroom!"

A medium-sized speedboat came close to the side of the mother-ship ready to load. A team of pirates carried long metallic boxes and large wooden crates to the speedboat, while others watched the river and the sky for enemy interference.

"Arms dealers," said Gomez quietly.

Once the delivery was completed, the speedboat left promptly, moving up the river with a full shipment, but the red sampan did not depart...it was still waiting.... After a few minutes, a long black barge converged on the vessel and ladders were thrown starboard. Laughter and chirpy voices could be heard on deck.

"Prostitutes," said Mike softly.

The girls were very young, wearing flashy dresses. They moved swiftly over the barge under the watchful eye of the pirates. Suddenly, a fight erupted on the sampan. We could not see the action from our position, but an argument had started between two girls and a pirate. We could hear shouting, swearing, and screaming.

"POW! POW!"

Two gunshots resonated loudly, and then, total silence...the two bodies were thrown overboard.

"Nice guy," murmured Watson.

The barge left rapidly while the girls were chatting away.

The alligators tore the dead girls' bodies apart and the river was red with their blood, dozens of seagulls were picking up pieces of flesh.

*"What a horrible way to end your life!" the colonel said.*

The red sampan was still waiting, motors idling... We looked at each other, puzzled...

"More dealings," whispered Gomez

"Hush money, large amounts," said Mike quietly.

A green military speed boat, its engines roaring, moved up close to the mother-ship. Large bundles, covered with silver or grey paper, and wrapped with string, were thrown into the speedboat. Some pirates used ladders to carry them down.

"Drugs," said Mike quietly.

"The poison that kills our troops," replied the colonel.

The delivery represented massive amounts of illegal substances that would destroy thousands of US servicemen.

"These men are North Korean," said Watson.

We all knew that extensive trafficking was taking place between North Korea and Russia and corrupt US politicians and high-ranking army officials. It was a disgrace! The speedboat was a "ghost vessel"; it did not bear any identification or regimental logo. It was used strictly for contraband and shabby operations. VC mercenaries were watching it all, guns at the ready. The captain had placed one pirate at the top of the mast to alert the gang in case there was any incoming military presence. Bundle after bundle was loaded onto the speedboat, millions of US dollars changed hands in the transaction.

Once it was all over, the "Phantom vessel" sped hurriedly up the river. But the notorious red boat was still waiting, not moving…

"What else?" asked the Colonel

"More dealings," replied Gomez.

Three medium-sized junks came and moored alongside the sampan. Men climbed on board and friendly verbal exchange took place.

"Money talks, Colonel," said Mike.

Big square crates and long carton boxes were distributed equally among the junks. There were hundreds of them, carefully placed one on top of the other. A huge amount of manpower had been assigned for the job.

"Liquor and cigarettes," whispered Watson.

Once all filled up, the junks moved slowly down-stream.

"These pirates are doing a thriving business," murmured the Colonel.

"All because of the war," replied Mike.

The red mother-ship honked its horn three times and left, up the Hăn. Yes, the pirates made a small fortune that day, but the largest share went to the corrupt officials, both foreign and US.

The colonel was angry with this state of affairs.

"Do not get all worked up, this is a dirty war and you cannot change a darn thing about it!" said Gomez.

We were being carried by strong currents, still hanging onto our tree. Watson pulled out his combat knife to cut off the branch holding the viper. The deadly snake dropped into the water and swam away furtively.

"Good riddance," observed the colonel.

Crows were cawing and feasting on a pig's entrails, rats were gnawing at a floating corpse and alligators were tearing up the remains of a wild boar. It was a dreadful sight!

The currents became stronger and stronger, they were picking up speed. Within minutes, a deafening noise alerted us of imminent danger.

A cliff shrouded in thick mist was on the horizon. The rumble continued, increased, louder and louder. It was hard to see anything because of the heavy haze that enveloped the river.

"Waterfalls on the way! Let's swim to the opposite bank!" the colonel commanded.

They were at the very centre of the river, when they got caught by the wild turbulence.

"Push, guys! Push harder!" yelled the colonel. The foursome were in deep trouble. "Do not let go of the tree, hang on to it!" he shouted.

They tried as one to push it to the left side. They were strong swimmers but the force of the currents overpowered them, the falls was only a few metres away and closing on them uncontrollably.

"Let's wait for each other, try to find the tree again! Good luck!" were the colonel's instructions. One by one they were plunged off the cliff and disappeared into the foamy water; a steep drop of about twenty metres. At the bottom was a deep basin that flowed into the Hăn. The colonel resurfaced and called their names. In vain! The water was calm and clear. He performed a few dives but he found no one under the water.

"Colonel, here!" he heard.

The team were gathered together, holding on to the same uprooted tree at the mouth of the basin. They had made it safely without any broken bones and had recovered the tree-trunk.

"It was just floating there, waiting for us, Colonel!" Gomez said, laughing.

He nodded, smiling, and said, "Let's move on, boys, it's still light and with some luck we may get picked up".

Away from the falls the Hăn looked much calmer and we were now back in control of the swim. A loud engine-noise was approaching speedily in the opposite direction; we quickly hid behind the branches of our uprooted tree, on the lookout for an adverse presence, but it was a US coastguard carrying a Navy Seal team for a classified mission.

They were a legend in Vietnam but very few people even knew that they existed. They specialized in covert operations and put the fear of God into the VC mercenaries. Their enemies called them, "the little green men", because of the paint they used on their faces while in combat. They were the "number one" US élite force in Vietnam.

We were hoping to be picked up before dark but it did not happen. We moved closer to the right bank of the river and crashed for the night on a small sandy area protected by thick bamboo canes. I prayed that the alligators and poisonous snakes would take a long nap as well!

"BOOM! BOOM! POW! POW!"

Sounds of battle. From the deck of a small junk, VCs were returning US Riverine personnel gunfire. There were only four sailors on the Seebees and twelve mercenaries on the substitute fishing boat.

"They won't make it, Colonel," said Mike.

"Yes, they are in deep trouble," replied Watson.

"They are overwhelmed, they do not have a chance," stated Gomez, shaking his head.

But out of nowhere an unmarked military speedboat rushed to the rescue and stopped its engines close to the battle area. Four men, clad in black, their faces painted green, jumped onto the junk, handguns at the ready. It was quick, effective, and over, in the space of one minute. All the dead V.Cs were thrown overboard. The alligators enjoyed their lunch that day! Another Navy Seals team on the way to a covert operation had given a hand to the Riverine patrol.

"Great timing!" said Watson.

"All in a day's work!" replied the Colonel.

They swam for more than two hours, hiding behind their uprooted tree, they passed boat-houses along the way and dingy homes raised high above water by wooden stilts, some with pontoons for mooring junks or barges. They were VC-friendly and not to be approached under any circumstance. Fishing was a cover for smuggling merchandise, fuel, and even girls for prostitution, to the enemy. They watched fishermen throw their nets into the water.

"How can you eat that fish? The river is so polluted, it's pure poison," stated Gomez.

"The VC eat them raw," said the Colonel.

"They must be immune from bacteria," Mike joked.

They heard the sound of choppers and looked at the sky, ready to give them a sign; unfortunately the choppers flew past them in diagonal formation and at high altitude, not noticing them.

"Next time," said the Colonel.

They were still hopeful to be retrieved from the river, one way or another, either by choppers or a Seabees' patrol; it was only a matter of time. Unexpectedly, alligators were circling around too close for comfort, requiring immediate action. Out of the corner of his eye, Gomez noticed a wild boar carcass and pushed it towards the reptiles. They tore it up in no time at all. Mike went for the bodies of two dead VCs, which were floating down the current, carried them over, and soon the beasts were feeding on the corpses. There was blood everywhere, you could hear the bones cracking, the gnawing of the teeth, the slurping. It was a dreadful scene to watch.

"Let's go," commanded the Colonel, shaking his head.

Soon the team was holding onto the uprooted trunk again, hoping for imminent rescue. After a couple of hours, the river formed into a large bend. They could just about discern, on the horizon, a village located on the left bank of the Hăn. They approached it with extreme caution.

"VC hangout," said the Colonel.

"Death trap," said Watson.

Junks and a sampan were moored outside and fishermen had thrown their nets from rowing-boats. The surroundings projected a calm atmosphere, but the team knew it was just a façade. They swam silently, not to attract attention, scrutinizing the periphery so as not to fall into VC hands by surprise.

Then, coming smoothly out of the water, a long cobra slithered along their tree, it was five to six metres long, dark brown in colour, with yellow rings around its body. By the time the team noticed it, it was too late. Watson was on the receiving end. He did not react fast enough when the serpent stuck its deadly fangs into his neck.

The Colonel grabbed the reptile and cut off its head, but in vain!

It was a dramatic development, Watson was going to die. A naja's bite is always fatal. Death usually occurs within the first thirty minutes. Cobra venom is highly toxic and can kill tigers, horses, giraffes, and even elephants. Bespectacled (or water) cobras are common in Vietnam. One of these was what had bitten Watson. His face turned blue almost immediately. He was foaming at the mouth and rambling incoherently. The bite on his neck was clearly visible. He was vomiting green bile and sweating profusely.

"Our only chance is to get him to the village to a doctor," said the Colonel.

"This is VC territory," Mike retorted.

"I know, but if we don't try, he'll die on the water!"

They all nodded in agreement. There was a large stilt house ahead on the left bank of the river. They climbed the ladder; Gomez carried Watson on his back. The fishermen looked at them with a puzzled frown. They laid Watson on a bed. He was immobile.

"Is he dead?" asked Gomez.

"Not yet, but it is imminent," answered the Colonel.

The fisherman sent his daughter to fetch the doctor from the local clinic. He arrived within minutes and examined Watson's snake-bite and vital signs. He gave him two large doses of antidote to fight the poison in his bloodstream and combat the mortal reaction to the reptile's bite. (The serum is made of cobra venom itself.) The doctor looked at the team and shook his head. The expression on his face said it all. The squadron leader was dying; it was too late to save him. – A naja bite is irrevocably unforgiving. The serum could extend his life for maybe two hours at the most. – The doctor asked them to make the patient as comfortable as possible and left the room.

"What an irony, to be a fighter pilot in NAM and get killed by a snake during a daring escape! Can you comprehend it?" asked Mike.

No one responded. The serum had very little effect on Watson's condition, but seemed to relax him and he had fallen asleep. He was not sweating anymore, the vomiting had ceased and his face was only slightly swollen. He was talking incomprehensibly in his sleep and breathed heavily.

"He looks better," stated Gomez.

"Will he survive, Colonel?" asked Mike.

"No he won't, the doctor has sedated him for two hours at the very most; he will die afterwards. The poison has spread out into his system," he replied.

"At least he does not seem to be in too much pain," said Gomez.

"True, let's hope that he dies peacefully in his sleep," said the Colonel.

"He will not die!" a voice snapped.

They all turned around. A very handsome man was standing at the door. He was in his mid-thirties. wearing his black hair long, a smart blue shirt, a pair of faded blue jeans and leather boots. He sported expensive jewelry around his neck and on his fingers.

"I am happy to see you again, Colonel," said the Dark Lord loudly.

"My Lord is that you"? the Colonel asked.

"Affirmative," replied the Prince of Darkness.

"Are you going to save Watson?"

"Of course, he belongs to me now; because I bit him, I will cure him. You should all leave now; he is no longer your concern."

Mike and Gomez had puzzled frowns but stayed silent. Satan was showing himself in his original form, a very good-looking man with long black hair, casually dressed, with an ostentatious display of wealth.

"You know, Colonel, I like pilots. They are usually highly-educated with a sound knowledge of mathematics and are always in top physical condition. Unfortunately, Henderson was not my choice, but Watson fits the bill. Pilots always make excellent recruits for my kingdom"

"Are you going to deal with Watson in the same way you did with Jason?"

"Exactly," nodded the Dark Lord.

"So you were the cobra!" stated Mike.

"Yes, I am the Great Serpent, one of the deadliest snakes on earth and I have chosen Watson."

"Have you seen Jason, my Lord?" inquired the Colonel.

"He is doing a great job and will be the most famous sniper with a phenomenal body-count by the time he leaves Vietnam. He respects you and he will always be true to his country. He is a great warrior. Please make sure he receives the promotion, decoration, and military pension that he deserves. He can actually still save your life before the end of your escape. Your misery is far from over yet. You are in for some surprises, you'll see…"

"What about Watson?" Gomez asked.

"He stays with me, I take care of him from now on. Please leave, go back to the Hăn," the Dark Lord replied.

"Special forces never leave their men behind," retorted Mike.

Beelzebub slowly walked towards him and hissed, "Look deep into my eyes soldier!"

He obeyed and was immediately transfixed in shock and disbelief. After a few seconds he dropped to his knees and started crying.

"What has happened, Colonel?" inquired Gomez.

"Satan has taught him a lesson and he has tasted the fury of hell."

Lucifer announced, "I am glad to have met you but you must be on your way. Watson is in good hands. It may be some consolation to know that he will not die. Good luck with your rescue, Colonel!"

They left silently and were soon swimming in the water, holding onto their uprooted tree. No one spoke; Watson was on their minds, now in the hands of the Devil. The Dark Lord had kept his promise. They were aware of the malefactor hovering above them, waiting at the first opportunity to foil their escape.

The Colonel kept a watchful eye on Mike, who was not the same after his brief encounter with Lucifer. He was holding on to the uprooted tree, silent, with his eyes fixed on the horizon.

They were going at a good speed, carried by the strong current and were not far from branching off into the Cam. They had not seen any Seebees or choppers for a long time, probably because they were needed for other missions. However the team was not in dire straits and kept going with great courage. Then they heard a distant rumble. A thick haze was forming above the river.

"Waterfall," said the Colonel.

"Are we going to survive it?" Gomez asked.

"What do you think, Mike?" he repeated.

Mike shrugged his shoulders without saying a word.

"Let's do it!" the Colonel ordered.

As they approached the cliff, powerful currents, combined with wild air movements, swept them uncontrollably towards the edge. The noise was deafening and the thick haze blinded them. The force of the water was unimaginable.

"Waterfall!" yelled the Colonel

It was a tumultuous landing but at the bottom at the periphery of the pond, the water was calm, fresh, and clear. The Colonel dived, looking for his team. He shouted their names, but there was no reply. Gomez finally appeared.

"We were lucky that there were no rocks at the base of the waterfall and that this creek is very deep," Gomez said. "Most people could not survive such a plunge."

"Affirmative," said the Colonel.

"Where is Mike?" asked Gomez.

"I could not find him under the water and he is not around, I am worried about him. His encounter with Satan has affected him and he has changed. It is essential to stay focused if we are to succeed in our escape. The two men called Mike's name in unison, but in vain.

Mike had not drowned, he was a strong swimmer and the Colonel had checked the entire body of water thoroughly. He was not there. They searched the river banks, went through dark foliage, large bamboo patches and thick bushes...no trace of Special Force master sergeant Mike.

Suddenly out of nowhere they were encircled by VC mercenaries, guns at the ready. They were ordered to kneel down; the VC shouted obscenities, spat at them and urinated in their faces. They were laughing, yelling profanities, making rude gestures and mocking the two soldiers. Their leader barked orders and they were beaten mercilessly.

"Colonel, look!" whispered Gomez.

Mike was brought before the two prisoners with a knife at his throat.

"They are going to kill us all, say your prayers!" the colonel said.

They began to talk to the Lord.

"POW! POW! POW!"

Three shots were fired with a silencer and three VCs went down. A tall man rammed his way out of the bushes and confronted the enemy. He broke the neck of the first man facing him, cut the throat of the second and stabbed the last one in the right eye. He did it with professional ease and without hesitation.

The colonel and Gomez gazed at their rescuer in awe.

"Hello, Colonel, I thought you could use a hand in the precarious situation you were in."

"Jason, how did you know?"

"The Dark Lord asked me to keep an eye on you, so here I am. By the way, Watson has become one of us but will return to his unit until further notice. The River Cam is very close, I will escort you to its confluence."

On the way, the Colonel told Jason that he would help him as Lucifer had requested, but it could only be done if he rejoined his unit. Jason agreed.

## CHAPTER TWENTY-THREE

## THE CAM

They had swum the Hăn – a length of seven kilometres – and now they reached the Cam, which emptied into the Gulf of Tonkin, seven kilometres further downstream. Here they would face the same adversities: reptiles, VCs, mercenaries, bad water and ruthless pirates.

The Hăn entered the Cam through a forked convergence and a small estuary.

They thanked Jason profusely and entered the water. It was a river of a larger size and they needed to find a new uprooted tree or similar floating device. The currents were very strong and they had difficulty staying together.

Gomez shouted, "Here, this long tree! Let's swim over and grab it, it will do perfectly!"

It was very bushy and they cleaned it with their Ka Bar knives. Mike was still very quiet, following the team but not communicating like before. He had seen the devil's eyes. Being taken hostage by the VC had certainly not helped the situation. He had been traumatized and needed professional help. But first they had to be rescued and it was now or never before they reached the Gulf of Tonkin.

No Seabees or choppers were in sight. The prognosis was gloomy but the Colonel did his best to keep cheering his men up to try to give them hope.

"They are here. They have to fly at high altitude to avoid rockets, but somehow they will see us."

A few navy speedboats were zooming down the river at top speed, taking Seal teams to perform their missions, but they could not stop to rescue them.

Although larger, the Cam was very similar to the Hăn: putrid yellow in colour, with roaming alligators, garbage, faeces, floating corpses and a nauseating smell in the air. Clouds of insects were buzzing around over the river.

“TUUUT! TUUUT! TUUUT!”

A large sampan, painted green, was approaching at slow speed. The team moved to the right bank of the river to hide on a small sandy area. The boat slowed down and anchored off the left river bank.

“Pirates again,” said Gomez.

VC mercenaries were moved around the bridge of the sampan. One man climbed to the top of the turret to take position with a sniper rifle. This was followed by shouting, loud voices, and the barked orders of the Captain.

The VCs were hired by the pirates to guard the vessel during transactions and to maintain security. The pirates wore civilian clothes and red bandanas with white stripes. It was their trademark. A large flag with similar colours adorned the ship. They were cocky, audacious, and very cruel. They had gained a monopoly over the waters during the Vietnam War and had facilitated many shabby deals between Russia and North Korea, worth millions of US dollars. They had carte blanche to operate across the entire country (both North and South) which gave them complete freedom to navigate with impunity. Now the boat hummed in the water, engines idling, ready to unload its illicit shipment. The team was watching it all…

A man, blindfolded, his hands tied behind his back, stood on the side of the deck. He was shot in the head and thrown overboard. Alligators swarmed around his body in a frenzy. A second man took his place. The mercenary in the turret shot him with his long sight rifle. His compatriots applauded in unison.

"If you double-cross pirates that is where you end," said the Colonel.

Another man was brought on deck but refused to stand on the side. He yelled, kicked, and went berserk. A pirate grabbed him by the hair and cut his throat. The body was thrown overboard. Several young prostitutes were placed in a line-up, their hands tied behind their backs. They were shot, one by one, falling overboard, where alligators tore them apart, taking their bodies below the surface, making the water red with blood. Crows and seagulls were making shrieking sounds, picking up pieces of flesh along the surface of the river and around the sampan.

Then those on the boat brought a rope with a noose and attached it to a large boom.

"They are going to hang someone," said the Colonel.

"Why not shoot him like the others?" asked Gomez.

"They want to make an example of him," the Colonel replied.

Two military officers were brought on deck. They were wearing full uniform with decorations.

"Look closely, Gomez! One is Russian; the other, North Korean".

"That is incredible, what did they do?"

"They cheated the pirates. Probably huge amounts of dollars were involved. They must now pay for their stupidity."

The two officers were standing on deck, waiting for their sentence to be carried out. The sound of engines could be heard. Two unmarked military speedboats moored alongside the mother-ship. Two five-star generals came on board. One was Russian, the other North Korean. Two huge crates were set on deck. The high-ranking officers carried whips. The culprits were beaten to a pulp and bled profusely. One of the generals ordered the two men to undress. Their uniforms were thrown into the river; the noose was placed around the Russian's neck. They pushed the boom above the water; he was soon hanging dead like a sausage. His body was served to the alligators, they ate it quickly. The North Korean officer pleaded for his life. It was a mistake. He received another whipping and the noose around his neck. Death came quickly and the stark-naked body was served to the large group of reptiles around the sampan. Justice, "pirate style," had been served.

The generals opened the crates, the captain checked them thoroughly. It was repayment for the money stolen by the two officers. They all shook hands, the slate was clean, everyone was back in business. The generals left, motors roaring.

"You see, Gomez; these people know how to do business effectively. They put the fear of God into their partners and cannot be cheated. They never sign contracts, only use a handshake the old-fashioned way."

"How much do you think was in those crates?" inquired Gomez.

"Looking at the size, maybe thirty to forty million. They probably contained arms, drugs, liquor, cigarettes and prostitution money. The Generals had to repay quickly because the profits are channeled into various cartels and everyone must get their share, including the pirates. If you con them, they know only one punishment, death!"

Two junks painted with bright colours arrived slowly and aligned themselves along the side of the sampan. Laughter, screams, and high-pitched voices filled the air.

"Prostitutes," said Gomez.

The pirates were notorious for slavery and human trafficking. The young hookers were transported from Vietnam to the four corners of Asia, including North Korea and Russia, in the most appalling conditions. They were lost souls who often encountered violent and tragic deaths.

Once on deck they were counted and separated. The captain wanted to keep one of them for himself. She refused. He talked to her but she shook her head violently. She was then attached to the main mast and stripped naked. The captain took a horsewhip with long leather straps and small lead balls at the end. Everyone was on deck, watching the punishment.

The Captain shouted, "No one disobeys my orders on board. She had the chance to become my mistress and she arrogantly refused. This is my boat, your fate is in my hands. I decide if you live or die, I am the ultimate master after God, do you hear me?"

No one replied. He yelled at the top of his lungs:

"Do you hear me, morons?"

"Yes Captain, we hear you," they all shouted in unison.

The girl was fidgeting and sweating profusely.

"You whore, I am going to teach you respect," hissed the Captain.

"Go ahead, I am not afraid. I may be a whore but I will never be your lover, never! You are a waste of life and a dirty swine!" she screamed aloud.

The Captain slapped her face with all his might and she spat at him. Her death was indeed imminent…

"Count the strokes," he ordered a VC.

He began whipping her again, and again, and again…the powerful blows resonated through the deep silence of the jungle. Her back was torn to shreds and she was bleeding excessively. Pieces of skin had separated from her body and fallen onto the deck, feeding crows and seagulls; dogs were licking the blood avidly. It was repulsive. The lashes continued incessantly. Mercenaries and pirates stood motionless, watching the flogging. The prostitutes were crying, covering their faces with their hands.

"Fifty, Sixty, Seventy, Eighty," the man keeping count said aloud.

"Colonel, this is something from medieval times," observed Gomez.

"No one will disobey him again," replied the Colonel.

"Nobody can survive such a beating," said Gomez.

"She is already dead," stated the Colonel.

"Ninety, one hundred," counted the VC.

The Captain stopped; he was sweating like a pig and motioned a pirate to get rid of the body. The girl's corpse was thrown overboard.

The whistle blew as the green sampan prepared to leave.

"They are all the Devil's henchmen," whispered Mike.

The Colonel and Gomez looked at each other, baffled. It was the first time Mike had spoken in a while.

"What did you say?" asked the Colonel.

"Lucifer ordered the captain to kill that girl. Pirates are evil souls and sampans are chariots of misery. Nothing good can come out of these rivers. They are paths to perdition. We must get extracted as soon as possible!"

"We'll make it, Mike, I promise!"

Mike had finally broken his silence and it was a good sign. The team would have to rely on him if things got tough, but at the present time he was definitely shaky. They needed to find a way out of the Cam. They were keeping all their options open and were prepared for any eventuality.

*

*"Well, General, things were hard on the rivers, as I can see."*

"Yes, Sergeant. There were only three of us now and the Cam was definitely hostile territory."

*"Watson had become Lucifer's servant; but did he eventually return to his squadron?"*

"He did. He was picked up in the bush by an infantry LURPS (Long Range Patrol Units) team. He was fine and had not been injured.

*"Could he fly again?"*

"Yes, but he had difficulties readjusting to military life, like Jason. You see, once you have been touched by Lucifer, you become predestined to a lifestyle change and it is usually diabolical.

"Neither of them could follow orders anymore. They had picked up bad habits. They had lost all decorum and their personal hygiene left a great deal to be desired.

"They had to resign their commissions. I helped them with proper recommendation letters, and a testimony of the escape. I submitted statements for promotion and citations and they received full military pension. I did all I could for them."

*"It was a great gesture of support, General."*

"They deserved it. They were great soldiers. Jason received two silver stars and two medals of valour. He was called a hero on television and in many magazines. He saved our lives on the Hăn."

*"What does he do now?"*

The general lowered his head and muttered, "He has become an enforcer for the Mafia in New York."

*"An enforcer for the underworld?"*

"Yes, he admitted it when we met in New York. He beats up people who do not pay their debts, he assassinates prominent figures, terrorizes members of juries not to testify, and works as a bodyguard for the head of his family. He lives a life of crime. He is doing a great job, enjoys it immensely, and is extremely well paid in consequence.

*"What about Watson?"*

"It's a very similar situation, He couldn't join a commercial airline, as many former fighter pilots aspire to do, but became the commandant aboard the private jet of a Columbian drug baron. In addition he transports illicit merchandise on large aircraft owned by the cartel's companies.

*"Did you see Watson again, General?"*

"Once, when I was in Florida. We met in my hotel. He was happy in his job and told me that he'd never made so much money in his life. Neither of these boys seemed to understand that their duties would be ephemeral because people like their bosses never live a long life."

*"I agree, General. But both were doomed to failure. Satan had taken hold of their future. It is better to forget about them."*

"We had been very close and they were great soldiers. It was distressing to see that these men have gradually faded into oblivion. Once again, Lucifer had played his demonic tricks on war heroes. I hated him for it."

*"How did you get rescued? Was Watson a burden throughout the remainder of the escape?"*

"All in all, he was fine. He stayed calm and never gave us any trouble. He talked to himself a lot, but we didn't pay much attention to this. We kept him busy looking out for Seabees and choppers. We were eventually extricated from the Cam before we reached the Gulf of Tonkin and that was what we were aiming to do."

*"Please, General, tell me the end of the story. I am dying for details of the rescue."*

*

Fate turned in our favour at the end.

The trio had progressed quickly, hiding behind the bushy tree and keeping a sharp eye on the river, still infested by reptiles and rodents. Helicopters flew over them, unnoticed in the overcast morning.

"I hope the clouds dissipate soon. We need a clear sky to be rescued," said the Colonel.

A red junk, a golden dragon adorning the bow, was slowly moving towards them, they could hear the puff-puff of an old steam-engine.

They were hiding behind their tree, not attracting attention. But as they passed the vessel...

"POW! POW! POW!"

Two VC mercenaries, standing on the deck, shot at them, yelling insults and racial slurs.

"Dive!" shouted the Colonel.

Bullets zipped past them over the water. They came back up to the surface for some air and plunged down again. No one was hurt. The VCs were shooting at random, and couldn't see them. The team swam for shelter into some dense bamboo to get more air into their lungs.

"POW!POW!POW!"

More shots were fired. They plunged and reconvened under the hull of the ship. The situation was dire and dangerous. It was clear that the VCs were shooting to kill.

The soldiers could not return fire. They were trapped in the water at the mercy of the VCs.

Suddenly a powerful engine could be heard coming their way. A medium-sized US military speedboat carrying Navy Seals rushed to their aid.

Shouting-match! Gunshots! Then total silence. They had been saved at the last moment.

The master chief in charge of the operation told the colonel that they had been spotted in the river, forty-eight hours prior to the rescue. But the Air Cav helicopter in question couldn't pick them up at that time, due to enemy fire.

The Seals immediately radioed for a chopper to take them back to base. They stayed with them until the rescue arrived and then moved on to carry out another operation. They were remarkable warriors trained for guerrilla warfare.

At the Air Cav base, the team was questioned by the central intelligence agency and officers of the military security bureau. Once everything was cleared, they returned to active duty. The colonel was highly praised for his leadership, courage, and the fact that he had killed Ahn, enemy number one of the US Army in Vietnam. Jason and Watson were recorded as "M.I.A.s" but later were found in the jungle and sent back to their respective units. During his interview the Colonel had cited their bravery and determination in combat and under duress.

The escape had ended successfully, but they had been six and now they were three. It had been as bad and hard as expected. Back in barracks the colonel went to see the chaplain, they talked and prayed. The officer cried in the priest's lap.

## CHAPTER TWENTY-FOUR

## EYES OF FIRE

*"Well, General, you made it safe and sound."*

"True, Sergeant, but not everyone did."

*"It was not your fault. You took care of your team to the best of your ability. But Lucifer set traps on the way. You showed bravery, resilience and fought him to the hilt. You are a true hero."*

"Thank you, Sergeant."

*"Why did you stay in the Army?"*

"It was the only life I knew and also I wanted to help soldiers stay alive in combat. I felt that my expertise in guerrilla warfare and from five tours of duty could do that. I was promoted to general and went to teach at various Special Forces regiments until I received a full professorship at West Point and eventually tenure. I remained there until retirement."

*"You can be proud of yourself. You had a great military career, your conduct has been exemplary and I am convinced that many young cadets have learnt a great deal from you."*

"Yes, Sergeant, teaching is very rewarding. I enjoyed it tremendously."

*"General, I am really blessed to have met you. What an incredible escape! Your memory of events is absolutely astonishing. You described all the details to a T. I was right there with you all the way!"*

"Now it is your turn, Sergeant. You told me that you met Satan in Africa during a very difficult operation. What happened? I am all ears!"

*

French Forces are always called to Africa to subdue revolutions and coup-d'états, to intervene in civil wars, and to fight rebel groups whenever necessary. South Sudan and the Congo are particularly volatile areas and regularly request participation from French Special Forces.

On the day in question, we received orders from the top brass that a dangerous group of rebels had overrun a town in the north of Congo, massacred entire families, and killed a large number of foreign government employees. Many were deserters from the regular Congolese Army, who had joined these makeshift troops of brutal, undisciplined, and poorly trained revolutionaries. They had taken over the small airport and two hotels, and were holding people hostage.

French commandos of the reconnaissance units, the French Foreign Legion and the Gendarmes had already been parachuted into enemy territory, but the resistance was fierce and it looked as if the battle could be prolonged indefinitely. The rebels fought drunk, high on drugs; and used knives, machetes, spears, bows-and-arrows and stolen weapons. They had already killed and mutilated men, women, and children.

We left rapidly as a first-line combat unit. We landed amid gunfire, yelling, mortar attacks and the usual commotion of battle. Additional reinforcements had been sent from France to retake all the strategic locations, including the airport, which was essential for the success of the operation. Bodies were scattered around in grotesque positions. Many had been dismembered, beheaded, or horribly mutilated.

We fought hard, sometimes man to man. We pursued the rebels deep into the jungle and our orders were not to take any prisoners.

The cruelty and brutality carried out by these monsters was beyond imagination. Hundreds of locals and foreigners had been slaughtered on the first two days. No one had been spared. Pregnant women had their babies removed from their wombs and were left bleeding to death. Others had their breasts cut so they could not feed their children. Many men had been impaled and left to rot away on spiked wooden poles. Babies had been thrown into fires while still alive, and young girls had been gang-raped in front of their mothers. Bloated bodies, open wounds full of maggots, and severed limbs were strewn throughout the hills.

Many of our enemies had been killed and we were asked to return to base to guard the airport, consulates, and embassies. Flights had been arranged to evacuate foreigners back home. We were still under red-alert and in imminent danger. A resurgence of rebel attacks could re-ignite at any time.

"Meeting at hangar number two, on the double!" we were told.

The colonel in charge of the entire operation informed us that Capitaine de Vinassac, head of the DST (Département de la Securité de Territoire, the French Security Department) had been kidnapped by a group of former officers of the Congolese Army. They were insurgents – outlaws who would stop at nothing to get what they wanted. They ordered the French Army to leave the Congo at once.

We had no doubt that they would execute the captain. Probably he had been tortured by his captors and was close to death. The Colonel asked for volunteers to take part in an extraction to save Vinassac from his captors' hands. It was a very risky mission of mercy, with strong possibilities of no return.

Amongst others, I raised my hand and went through a short interview as part of the selection process. Within the hour I was informed that I had been chosen to lead a team to bring back the captain. I recruited three of my best men for the operation and we left immediately. Time was of the essence.

The reconnaissance unit had identified the location where the captain was being kept prisoner. The choppers dropped us close to a small dilapidated house which was part of a farm. We approached silently, cautiously, guns at the ready. We couldn't hear a sound.

After checking the perimeter, we climbed the stairs. We used sign-language only, moving one step at a time. On the third floor we heard loud voices and laughter. We knelt down by the door and listened attentively.

"You pig! dirty dog!" a man shouted inside the room. "How much will they pay for your release?" Three or four of them were hitting the prisoner with full force and laughing at the same time. He was screaming with pain and they were rejoicing at his suffering.

We were ready to storm in at the count of three. I was the closest to the door with my left knee on the floor. My team was standing in a fan position with handguns drawn.

"One, two..."

The door suddenly flung open with full force. A man pressed the barrel of his revolver against my forehead. He was not african but middle-eastern in origin. I froze on the spot. I looked into his eyes and saw rage, hatred, and evil. Red and yellow flames filled the pupils of his eyes.

He pressed the trigger four or five times.

"CLICK! CLICK!"

Nothing. The handgun had jammed. He was mad, and swore at me in Arabic.

"POW! POW!"

Blood and brain matter splashed onto my face. My team had shot him dead. We went in and killed all the rebels.

There was an Arab mercenary and three dead officers of the

Congolese Army who had deserted and joined a mutiny, lying down on the floor. They needed money to finance their coup d'état and wanted France to pay a ransom for Vinassac's release. Fortunately they did not succeed. We had stopped it.

The Captain was alive, but in bad shape. They had pulled out all the nails from his right hand, broken many of his teeth with a hammer and screwdriver, and carved the word, "Traitor," on his chest with a razor-blade. He had been beaten up with a wooden sock full of wet sand and his face was grossly swollen. – This mode of torture does not draw blood but the blows are very heavy and cause substantial internal damage. – He had a broken nose, black eyes and an open fractured cheek. He was unconscious. We called a chopper to take him to the military hospital without delay.

He survived. He was tough and fully recuperated after a few short months. We had performed a successful mission, but I was not out of the woods yet.

*

*"Why didn't you shoot the mercenary when you had the chance?" asked the intelligence officer.*

"Because I had the barrel of his gun pressed on my forehead and I froze on the spot."

*

A review board had been appointed with all my superiors and my team members as witnesses. I had to face the brass because I had hesitated under fire and almost died in the operation. I really could not figure out why I was the one on the hot seat. Perhaps they wanted to kick me out of the Special Forces or terminate my commission altogether.

I had seen Satan holding a gun at my head, saw the flames of hell in his eyes! Providentially, his gun had misfired and I was still alive. However I couldn't mention Lucifer when subject to a military review.

*

*"Are you sure, Sergeant, that it was Satan holding the gun?"*

"Who else could it have been, General? I had seen the eyes of fire!"

"True. But it was merely a messenger of hell, unleashing his dominance. Lucifer wanted to scare you and the gun jammed because of his doing. He could have killed you on the spot. He is unorthodox, a deceiver, a cunning creature. He got you into trouble with your superiors, while laughing about it. But please continue. Tell me the rest."

*

"Many people spoke in my defence. Following the eyewitness testimonies, there were deliberations. My performance during the extraction was judged adequate. It should have ended there, but I asked to speak to the panel."

*

*"Sergeant, in the Army this is a no-no, don't tell me you gave them hell. Is this what you did?"*

"I made a mistake, General. But I have never regretted it. Even so, it ended my military career. After that there was no reason to stay in the Forces."

*"What did you tell them, Sergeant?"*

"Only the truth."

*

I stated the fact that the operation had been a success, one hundred percent. Captain Vinassac had been saved. We deserved praise for our bravery. We were heroes. Citations, medals and full military honours should have been in order, not inquiries and irrelevant questions. I questioned the logic for me to face the panel. I was firm, but polite. There was total silence in the room.

All the officers were looking at each other.

"Thank you, Sergeant, that's all," they replied.

*

*"You blew it! Your frankness did not work in your favour!"*

"True, General but I never apologized for the position I took regarding that inquiry."

*He smiled and said, "I like your style. You are brave and a man of integrity. Please never change."*

## CHAPTER TWENTY-FIVE

## GOODBYE, GENERAL

"General, yours was an amazing adventure, thrilling and mind-boggling. It was a cruel war, but you painted it into a gripping story. You fought Satan with resilience and relentlessness, and you came out the winner at the end. Yes, you lost men in that escape, but Lucifer was solely responsible for their fate. You are a true hero."

"Thank you, Sergeant. Coming from you, that is praise indeed!"

He was now ready to go, we shook hands and hugged tightly. Telling me the details of that audacious escape had had a soul-cleansing effect on him,. I suggested that he return to see the places in Vietnam where he fought, and revisit the mission. If he did, it would be a spiritual journey of great value to him.

We said goodbye and this larger-than-life hero left me with mixed feelings about the Vietnam War. Many good men had died. He survived, because very courageous and loyal allies of the USA had helped him. Sister Marie Catherine at the mission had been a turning-point in his escape and had left a mark on his soul. Bonyo's team of *montagnards* had saved his life. Satan had tried to defeat him, but the general was a tough cookie. In the end Lucifer let him be.

He never met Lucifer again. But he had killed Ahn, one of Satan's protégées. Could the demon forget and forgive? Fat chance!

Life goes on. The general was enjoying his retirement, reminiscing about his amazing exploits as a Special Forces officer. Sharing stories had been a once-in-a-lifetime experience.

## CHARACTERS IN THE STORY

The Colonel: a retired General from the Special Forces
The Sergeant: listens and discusses army escape and military operations
Captain Willy Anderson: US Air force pilot
Gomez: Sergeant major 173 Airborne Brigade
Watson: US Navy Pilot
Mike: master sergeant green beret
Jason: first LT Big Red One infantry regiment
The village leader: helps the team escape
ANH: Colonel in the special bureau of the general department of military intelligence
Rose: a nurse, teacher, and village leader
Dr Henri: physician, surgeon for the village; owns his own clinic
Two farmers who help the team in the escape
Sister Marie Catherine: head of the Mission in Vietnam
Father Benedetti: chief medical officer at the mission
"The Council": Sister Marie Catherine, Father Benedetti, Father Lucien, Father Romero, Sister Yvonne, Father Herve, Sister Angele
Sister Yvonne: a nurse, a teacher, a devoted member of the council
Mme Labelle: the guardian angel for Sister Yvonne
Father Guillaume: the priest at Chartres Cathedral, France
Le Patron: Chief of surgery General Hospital in Montpellier, France
The Chaplain: priest at the General Hospital
Monsignor Dominique: Bishop of Paris France
Le Grand Patron: Chief of surgery at the American Hospital in Paris

The chaplain at the American Hospital in Paris, priest of the hospital
Father Edmond: priest at Aix en Provence
Father DATRIA: exorcist of the Diocese of Rome
Sebastian, Adrian, Lionel: Angels
Germain: young boy possessed by Satan
VC: the Viet Cong during the Vietnam War
NVA: the North Vietnamese Army during the Vietnam War
Ben: a brain cancer patient at the American hospital in Paris
Bonyo: leader of the montagnards who helped the US special forces in Vietnam
The fisherman: owner of the boathouse

**FICTION IN ENGLISH**
**PUBLISHED BY PROVERSE HONG KONG**

## NOVELS

A Misted Mirror by Gillian Jones.
A Painted Moment by Jennifer Ching.
Adam's Franchise by Lawrence Gray.
An Imitation of Life by Laura Solomon.
Article 109 by Peter Gregoire.
As Leaves Blow by Philip Chatting.
Bao Bao's Odyssey: From Mao's Shanghai to Capitalist Hong Kong by Paul Ting.
Black Tortoise Winter by Jan Pearson.
Bright Lights and White Lights by Andrew Carter.
Cemetery miss you by Jason S Polley.
Cop Show Heaven by Lawrence Gray.
Cry of the Flying Rhino by Ivy Ngeow.
Curveball: Life Never Comes At You Straight by Gustav Preller.
Death Has A Thousand Doors by Patricia W. Grey.
Enoch's Muse by Sergio Monteiro.
Hilary and David by Laura Solomon.
HK Hollow by Dragoş Ilca.
Instant Messages by Laura Solomon.
Man's Last Song by James Tam.
Mishpacha – Family by Rebecca Tomasis.
Paranoia by Caleb Kavon.
Professor Everywhere by Nicholas Binge.
Red Bird Summer by Jan Pearson.
Refrain by Jason S Polley
Revenge from Beyond by Dennis Wong.
The Day They Came by Gerard Breissan.

The Devil You Know by Peter Gregoire.
The Handover Murders by Damon Rose.
The Monkey in Me by Caleb Kavon.
The Perilous Passage of Princess Petunia Peasant by Victor Edward Apps.
The Reluctant Terrorist by Caleb Kavon.
The Village in the Mountains by David Diskin.
Three Wishes in Bardo by Feng Chi-shun.
Tiger Autumn by Jan Pearson.
Tightrope! A Bohemian Tale by Olga Walló.
University Days by Laura Solomon.
Vera Magpie by Laura Solomon. (Novella.)

## SHORT STORIES

Beyond Brightness by Sanja Särman.
Odds and Sods by Lawrence Gray.
The Shingle Bar Sea Monster and Other Stories by Laura Solomon.
The Snow Bridge And Other Stories by Philip Chatting.
Under the shade of the Feijoa trees and other stories by Hayley Ann Solomon.

## FIND OUT MORE ABOUT PROVERSE AUTHORS, BOOKS, INTERNATIONAL PRIZES, AND EVENTS

Visit our website: http://www.proversepublishing.com
Visit our distributor's website: www.cup.cuhk.edu.hk

Follow us on Twitter
Follow news and conversation: <twitter.com/Proversebooks>
OR
Copy and paste the following to your browser window and follow the instructions: https://twitter.com/#!/ProverseBooks

"Like" us on www.facebook.com/ProversePress
Request our free E-Newsletter
Send your request to info@proversepublishing.com.

**Availability**

Most books are available in Hong Kong and world-wide
from our Hong Kong based Distributor,
The Chinese University Press of Hong Kong,
The Chinese University of Hong Kong, Shatin, NT,
Hong Kong SAR, China.
Email: cup-bus@cuhk.edu.hk
Website: www.chineseupress.com
All titles are available from Proverse Hong Kong
http://www.proversepublishing.com
and the Proverse Hong Kong UK-based Distributor.
We have stock-holding retailers in Hong Kong,
Canada (Elizabeth Campbell Books),
Andorra (Llibreria La Puça, La Llibreria).
Orders can be made from bookshops in the UK and elsewhere.
**Ebooks:** Most Proverse titles are available also as Ebooks.